Chestnut Springs

Chestnut Springs

Carol J. Bova

Random Tangent Press

http://www.randomtangentpress.com

First Edition: September 2017

Library of Congress Cataloging-in-Publication Data
Names: Bova, Carol J., author.
Title: Chestnut Springs / Carol J. Bova.
Description: Santa Monica, CA : Random Tangent Press, 2017.
Identifiers: LCCN 2017954038 | ISBN 978-0-9907415-1-0 (pbk.) | ISBN 978-1-9479578-2-4 (large print) | ISBN 978-0-9907415-4-1 (ebook)
Subjects: LCSH: Life change events--Fiction. | Baby boom generation--Fiction. | Self-actualization (Psychology) in women--Fiction. | Man-woman relationships--Fiction. | Country life--Fiction. | West Virginia--Fiction. | BISAC: FICTION / Small Town & Rural. | FICTION / Women.
Classification: LCC PS3602.O8952 C54 2017 (print) | LCC PS3602.O8952 (ebook) | DDC 813/.6--dc23.

Dedication

To my son, John Doppler,

who introduced me to the internet in 1995

and opened a world of possibilities for me.

Chapter 1

Brenda Maxwell sang along with the radio, planning how to spend her sales bonus, until a car swerved in front of her during L.A.'s usual morning combination of creep and stop. She hit the horn and the brakes at the same instant and missed the intruder by an inch, but the van in back plowed into her car. The low-speed impact jolted the middle-aged woman, and she swore between clenched teeth. Turning to point to the curb before she edged out of the lane of traffic, she parked and slammed the door of her Porsche hybrid SUV. While she checked the damage, the van's driver emerged, screaming at Brenda while he tore open his front passenger door.

A breath away from screaming back, Brenda settled for a furious glare and an icy tone, shaking her head so that her salt and pepper hair moved side-to-side. "You're the one who ran into me." Her anger shifted to concern when the man lifted a crying toddler from the floor of the van.

"Is he okay? Why wasn't he in a car seat?"

The man thrust the child toward her. "Hold him while I look at the bumpers."

Startled, Brenda patted the little boy's back. It was hard to tell if there had been any more damage to the van's dented and rusty bumper, but cracks and scrapes now marred the otherwise pristine surface of the silver Cayenne S.

The man snatched the boy from Brenda and shoved his insurance card at her. She reached into her car and pulled her card out of her wallet. While they copied each other's information, the man grumbled under his breath. He turned and pushed the child up onto the van's passenger seat. Still muttering, he looked over his shoulder at Brenda before he climbed into the van and pulled out into traffic.

Brenda shook her head. "Some people don't realize how precious kids are."

The incident left her on edge all day. At 2:30, she jumped when the direct line in her office rang. After a few words from the nursing home administrator in Florida, she got up and locked her door before returning to the call.

"When did it happen?"

"Just a little while ago. Your father had a little soup at dinner and said he wanted to take a nap afterwards. When the aide came to check on him, she found he'd just slipped away."

"I'm glad he didn't suffer. The last ten years have been hard enough."

"It's hard for everyone involved when the stroke damage takes their memories. I know how it felt when it happened with my mother, so I understand it's been difficult for you, with your father unable to recognize you."

"Sometimes, I used to wish he could remember me, just for a minute." Brenda's voice cracked. She swallowed hard. "Do you have all the paperwork for the mortuary and the Navy Burial-at-Sea Coordinator?"

"Yes, the mortuary should arrive any time now. They have a lot of experience with the Navy program. Will you be having a memorial service here?"

"No. There's no one left but me. Dad hated wakes and church funerals. Before the strokes started, he told me just about every week that he wanted to be buried at sea." Brenda closed her eyes, her father's words echoing in her memory.

"Promise me, Bren. I want the Navy to take care of it. I wanted to stay in, you know? But your mother wouldn't have it. If I wanted to be with her, I had to leave the Navy. But I loved the sea. That's where I want to rest."

The administrator broke into Brenda's thoughts. "I'll see your father's personal items and photographs get packed and mailed to you with copies of all the paperwork. What would you like us to do with his furniture and clothing?"

"Can you arrange to donate everything to a charity?"

"Of course."

The administrator offered condolences and said something about Brenda's father, but Brenda couldn't make sense of the words. She thanked the woman and got off the phone as soon as she could.

Leaning forward, she rested her forehead against the heel of her palm with her eyes closed for almost half an hour. *What's wrong with me? I should feel more than numb relief that it's over. But the person in that nursing home wasn't really my father. That was just a living shell. My father faded away, bit by bit, years ago.*

Her self-reproach subsided to be replaced with harsh images of visits where he yelled at her to get out of his room or sat staring for hours without a word. Brenda sat back in her chair thinking about all the long weekends and vacations spent with her parents over the last 30 years. Surgeries, hospital vigils, holidays, one weekend each month after their health declined. They were her only family, and she was all they had in their last years.

The background sounds of phones and copiers died out as people left for the day. Someone tapped on the door. Brenda unlocked and opened it.

Her assistant Katie asked, "Need anything before I go?"

Brenda sat down again. "No, thanks. Katie, I'm going to take a couple days off. My dad passed away this afternoon."

"Oh Brenda, I'm sorry. Can I do anything for you?"

"No, all the arrangements were made a long time ago. He would have been 98 on his next birthday. There is one thing I need you to do. I'll leave these export docs here when I finish them. Would you run them down to shipping for me?"

"Of course, and if there's anything else, just let me know."

"I will, thanks."

After Katie left, Brenda rummaged through her desk drawer for an Irish Breakfast tea bag. Returning to the forms, Brenda filled in descriptions and codes on customs papers for the export of the large shipment of machine tools she'd sold that earned her the bonus. It took three more cups of strong tea before she finished and addressed the interoffice envelope to the shipping department. She ran out of tea bags before she answered all her emails and correspondence.

Fighting fatigue, she followed the steps for bereavement leave in the employee manual. She emailed a form to Human Resources to let them know she needed time off on Friday and Monday and left instructions for Katie. She attached a copy of the HR form to a brief email to her boss and said she'd see him on Tuesday. Close to midnight, the click of her sturdy high-heels echoed across the parking lot, the only other cars those of the security guard and cleaning crew.

The streets going home were almost as empty as the parking lot. Doesn't seem right. No one to share the news of Dad's passing with. All his friends are long gone. Fourteen-hour days were good for my bonus checks, but not for making friends.

Once inside her Century City condo, Brenda swapped her business suit for her favorite fleece pajamas. She moved along the floor-to-ceiling built-in bookcase searching until she found a worn family photo album. With each flipped page, she stepped further back in time. She stopped at an image of her father as a young man with jet-black hair and a ready smile. Her mother's pleasant face smiled back from the page, and a three-year-old Brenda, nestled in her mother's arms, grinned at the camera in front of a neighbor's Christmas tree.

Brenda closed her eyes remembering her mother's quiet voice and gentle touch and how it felt to be part of a family. She blinked away from the memory and looked around the room at the black and white photos that marked special times with her parents. She settled onto the couch with the album and took out a later photo of her father. The date on the back was 1986. She looked again at the stern face staring at the camera.

Oh, Dad. Mom was already gone in 1986. I came out for your birthday, and you were surprised I cooked your favorite dinner for you just the way you liked it. Roast chicken, mashed potatoes, green beans with bacon. Biscuits and cake from scratch. I think that night was the last time I saw you laugh with your friends. The last time you said something that made me feel good. The next morning, we watched the Challenger take off and then fall from the sky. We didn't talk. We never talked. Just sat there watching the TV reports all day long.

Brenda sighed and put the photo back in the album before she went to the kitchen and opened a bottle of Pinot Blanc. She brought the bottle, a glass and a plate of crackers and cheese to the living room. After she filled the glass, she clicked the remote and turned off the lights in the room. Wrapped in the darkness around her, she felt the nudge of other old memories and pushed them aside. Through the expanse of windows extending across the entire wall, high above the streets, she could see the horizon for miles. Lights flickered here and there along the Hollywood Hills. She tried to remember when she had changed from being the child who was the center of her father's world to a silent witness to his depression, sitting with him watching movies on TV. Standing next to him fishing. Never talking. Never sharing.

She poured another glass of wine, ate a few crackers and stared into the nighttime hills. She yawned and returned to the kitchen. She stopped in front of a photo of her father fishing off a pier. The old thoughts caught up with her, but this time, she answered them aloud.

"Daddy, you blamed me when Charlie left me. You thought he was such a great guy, the son you never had. I couldn't tell you why he left. You'd never have believed that he'd treat me like that, so it had to be my fault." Old hurt and anger boiled up. She threw the wine glass into the sink, where it shattered into tiny shards.

"Why did that guy have to push his kid at me today and remind me?" Her scream turned to a wailing cry, and she stumbled back to the couch and collapsed against the cushions. Curled up like a lost child, she cried out the pain and loss until she fell into exhausted sleep.

On Tuesday morning, the phone was ringing as Brenda walked into her office. She snatched up the receiver. "Good m...."

Her boss spit out a curt, "Get in here now."

"Bill, what's...," but before she could say another word, he slammed the phone down.

Brenda dropped her handbag in a drawer, her forehead furrowed, trying to figure what prompted the summons.

She had just closed Bill's door when he shouted, "Look at this. You put the wrong descriptions and used outdated codes on this order from Wednesday. It took you forever to close that sale and then you go and pull a stunt like this."

"Wait a minute. Nobody else was able to get to first base with this client, much less make that sale." She took the papers he waved at her and looked at the red marker notations on them.

"What good is that when we're going to have to jump through hoops over there and go through a full inspection to verify what's in the shipment. Do you have any idea of how much that'll cost us? I had to send duplicates of a couple of the key pieces by overnight air. The first shipment will be hung up in customs at least another five days."

Brenda shook her head, her hands shaking, feeling sick to her stomach. The mistakes were there, and she'd made them.

Bill's face was scarlet as he ran his hands through thinning hair and loosened his tie. "It's not bad enough we have to fight China and Taiwan for every piece of business. Now we have to deal with your screw ups too."

"I'm sorry, Bill. I must have been more upset about my father's death than I thought, but I can smooth it over."

Her boss snorted. "I'm sorry you lost your father, but if I'd had anything to do with it, they'd never have kept you on when we bought the company. This proves I was right." He looked at her, his jaw muscles tightening. "Be here tomorrow at 8:00 a.m. Here's your official disciplinary hearing notice. In the meantime, bring the entire file to me, and go home so you can't make any other mistakes." He threw his wire-framed glasses onto the pile of papers on his desk.

"Bill, let me take care of it. I can pull it out of the fire."

"No. I can't risk it. It's my job on the line now too. You know what, give me the files on all your accounts so I can audit them."

Brenda paled under his hard gaze. "But Bill..."

"I'm not interested in anything you have to say now. You'll get your chance tomorrow." He went to the door and flung it open, motioning for her to leave with a jerk of his head.

Not trusting her voice, she nodded. She tried to hold her head up on the way back to her desk through the gauntlet of curious eyes. Imagining the looks on the faces of her co-workers, tears stung her eyes after she closed the door to her office. A soft knock interrupted her as she began assembling orders and customs papers. She grabbed a tissue and swiped at her eyes, but the door opened before she could speak.

Katie stepped in, closed the door behind her and put a cup of tea on Brenda's desk. "I couldn't help overhearing. You okay?"

Brenda just shook her head and picked up the cup.

"Come on. Move over and let me get this stuff together for you. It's not going to be a total disaster. A minor one maybe, but we can pull it off."

"I don't understand how it happened. I'm the one who wrote the procedure for the updated codes."

"Hey, I know that. If you hadn't taught me the ins and outs of this game, I'd never have the job I do now. I'll never forget what you did for me when I first got here."

Brenda sipped the tea. "You just needed a break and some time to learn the ropes. Nobody ever bothered to do that for me, and I swore that if I ever got the chance, I'd be a different kind of boss."

"Well, you are. And trust me, I'll pass on the favor whenever I get the chance."

"That was the idea." Brenda smiled and reached for the stack of folders lined up on one side of the desk, putting notes inside each one. "These should be in pretty good shape. Let me check out today's emails for any updates before you take them to Bill."

Brenda started to log into her email, but a window opened saying, "Your account has been disabled. Please see your systems administrator." She pressed OK, thinking it was anything but okay, and dialed the tech support office.

"Hey, it's Brenda in Sales. I can't log on to get my email. Can you straighten it out?"

"Oh. I... uh... I had to shut down your account."

"What do you mean?"

"Geez, Bren, I'm not supposed to say anything."

"Spit it out. What's going on?"

"Look, you didn't hear it from me, okay? But I was ordered to lock you out of the system... and not tell you."

"Like I wouldn't notice? I get it. It's not your fault. I know exactly who gave the order. Sorry to put you in an awkward situation." She hung up the phone and sat back.

Katie stacked the folders in a file box. "Looks like everything is here."

"Make sure you get access to my emails and check for updates before anyone does anything on the accounts." Brenda continued checking one drawer after another. There wasn't much of her own there. Makeup, deodorant, a hairbrush. A package of pantyhose. A few old greeting cards. She opened her briefcase and put the items into it.

"What are you doing?"

"I'm taking my personal things home with me. I doubt I'll have much time after the hearing tomorrow. Even if we salvage the account, they're not going to take a chance on me making another mistake. When they sent Bill over from corporate, it wasn't to pat us on the back for what we did in the past."

"Oh, come on, they're not going to fire you over one mistake."

"In this economy? Only today, tomorrow and the bottom line count with them. People are disposable. Paying accounts aren't. It's Bill's division and his decision. He's never believed that I don't want his job. I'm not sure he knows I turned it down. I've known my customers for going on 20 years, and I like what I do. I didn't want the extra pay for the added aggravation."

"You really think they're going to let you go?"

"I'm afraid so. The hearing is a formality so I can't claim wrongful termination and sue them. I'm going to try to talk them out of it, but we all agreed our employment was at-will when we were hired. That means they don't need a reason, but they usually like to have one. Outright discrimination is the only reason they can't use to fire you. Anything else goes."

"I hope you're wrong." Katie hugged Brenda before she picked up the file box. "Take care of yourself."

"I don't have much choice. You'll be fine if you don't make waves and follow instructions from the main office to the letter, no matter how wrong they are—as long as you get it in writing."

They both laughed and hugged again, sniffing back tears.

Brenda left the door open and turned to the closet. A suit, still in the cleaner's bag. A jacket, a sweater, an extra pair of shoes. An umbrella and empty carryon garment bag. She packed the clothes into the bag and put it back in the closet. *Maybe it will work out. Won't hurt to wait and see.* She looked around once more before taking the side hallway to the security desk at the exit.

"Hi, would you please search my bag and briefcase so there's no question that what I'm taking home belongs to me, and I haven't taken any company materials."

The young security guard stared at her. "Why do you want me to do that?"

"Don't worry about the why. Just do it. And I want you to sign this note that says you've done it." She slapped a printed page on his desk. The guard picked it up and stared at it.

"I don't know. I have to call my supervisor."

"Fine. Call him." She stood at the counter tapping her foot until the supervisor arrived and made an inventory of her belongings.

Brenda arrived just before 8 on Wednesday morning. At 9:30, she again stood at the security desk, a stone-faced woman from H.R. standing to the side. Five minutes later, Brenda left with the garment bag, a receipt for her office keys, and a letter of termination of employment.

Two months later, after the latest dead-end job interview, Brenda stopped off in the mail lobby before going up to her condo. There was an envelope from the Navy. Brenda waited until she sat at the desk in her office nook off the kitchen to open it. She read the details of her father's burial at sea and looked up the coordinates on the internet to find a spot on the map, far from any land. "Daddy, I miss you," she whispered to the air. "Miss you too, Mom. Wish I could be with you now." Tears fell on the keyboard as she turned off the computer.

Early the next morning, she drove in the pre-dawn darkness to the L.A. flower mart downtown. During the day, it was a drab, empty place, but now, it was a lively swirl of people and vans and flowers everywhere. Brenda bought some hemp twine and a wreath frame made of grapevines. In another shop, she bought large bunches of burnt orange chrysanthemums, bright yellow carnations and daisies, and lavender alstroemeria. A few white roses and greens completed her selections.

At home, she threaded flowers between the vines, tied them with the hemp and trimmed the ends with a knife before she filled in the open spaces with lacy ferns and sturdy heather. An hour later, she took the floral wreath from the backseat and walked to the end of the empty pier in Santa Monica. The tide was beginning to go out, and she tossed the wreath onto the waves and watched until it was a speck bobbing in the distance.

"Good bye, Daddy. Fair winds and following seas..." Her heart was full, but there were no other words.

Back at the condo again, she curled into a big chair on the balcony and watched the distant waves through the space between two buildings to the west until she dozed off. Something woke her hours later. The shadow of a cloud. A plane passing by. She stretched and went inside to read the news online, searching for some inspiration on what to do next about a job, pretending not to notice today was her birthday.

Days stretched into weeks. Frustration and anxiety took turns torturing Brenda. When she read an article in the Times about coping with unemployment, she recognized the author as a psychologist with an office in her building. Hoping for some insight or advice, she booked an appointment, not convinced it would help.

A week later, Brenda felt a glimmer of hope the therapist would be able to show her ways to cope with being out of work. When the intercom buzzed near the end of Brenda's session, announcing the arrival of the next patient, the therapist glanced at the clock and told Brenda, "We still have a few minutes."

"I need to get my head together and find work before I run through my emergency fund. I put aside enough for six months' expenses several years ago, but it's not going to last that long at today's prices. It's not enough that I'm twice the age of most of the applicants I run into. I've got this cloud hanging over me from being fired for failing to perform up to expected standards, as they phrased it. And calling it terminated sounds worse."

"It's happening a lot these days, all over the country. Justified, unjustified, people who have never missed a day of work in their lives are unemployed now. You may have to get creative to find what's next for you, but you can do it."

"I'm not sure what I have left. I feel wrung out and used up."

The therapist opened her calendar. "Give yourself a chance to bounce back, and try those affirmations we discussed. We'll talk about it more next week. Same time Tuesday?"

Brenda stood up and pressed a few buttons on her phone. "Why it looks like I have that day open." She laughed, the beginning of tears in the corners of her eyes.

The therapist opened the door. "I'll be here if you need me. Just leave a message with my service. They'll know how to reach me, and I'll call you back. I know it's hard to see now, but it will work out."

"Thanks, I need one of us to believe that."

At home, Brenda sat down with her notebook and a cup of tea. She tried to remember some of the ideas the therapist gave her to use in a meditation script

I am 56.

I've survived many things in my life.

I'm a strong woman.

I'm intelligent and caring.

I can handle whatever comes up.

I am safe.

Thoughts cannot hurt me.

Brenda scratched out the last line and threw the pen on the table. She ripped the page out of the notebook and began tearing it into strips. A thought accompanied each strip, ripping her heart at the same time. You've got no family. No friends—too busy with work to make any. No children. No one to love you. No one. Scrunching the torn bits into a ball, she dropped it in the trash and moved to the computer to look at online job postings, refusing to let more tears fall.

Chapter 2

Two weeks passed with nothing back except automated emails acknowledging receipt of her online applications before Brenda got an interview for a job as an assistant to a regional sales manager.

At the office, the receptionist handed her a clipboard and told her to fill out an application and return it with a copy of her résumé. It was identical to the one Brenda had submitted online. *Did anyone even read the one I sent in?*

When Brenda came back to the counter, the young woman said, "Wait a minute until I check this." She took the clipboard and ran a long red fingernail down the pages. "I have to make sure everything is answered."

Brenda felt her cheeks burn waiting to have a girl less than half her age review the forms. Dismissed with a nod, she waited an uncomfortable hour amid curious looks from a room filled with women the receptionist's age or younger.

I was doing this level of work when I was younger than all of them. And yet, here I sit, hoping to take a job they want. There has to be something else for me. But what? And where?

She was saved from further inner assault by the red-taloned receptionist calling her name and directing her to an office.

"Please, have a seat." The interviewer flipped through Brenda's résumé and application. "Quite an impressive job history. So why did you leave your last job?"

Brenda shook her head. "I can't go into details. I signed a confidentiality agreement. But there were a lot of changes at the corporate level, and we came to a parting of the ways."

The interviewer looked over the forms again and took off his aviator glasses. "I'm sorry. I don't think your background's a good fit for the position that's available." He stood up and moved toward the door. "I wish you the best and hope you find something soon."

All Brenda could manage was a weak smile and a handshake. Brenda stopped to pick up the mail and tore open an unexpected envelope from her insurance company. "Your credit card transaction was declined. Unless the full amount due is received within five days of the date of this letter, your policy will be terminated at 12:01 a.m. on the 24th of March."

After a brief call to the insurance company, she dialed the bank.

"I have my insurance payment automatically charged to my credit card, and I got a notice today that the charge was declined. There's some mistake, and I need it fixed."

After several minutes of requests for name, account number, phone number, address, and answer to secret question, another agent got on the line and asked the same questions again. Brenda lost track of how many people she talked to before she reached a manager.

"The records show the charge was declined because it exceeded your credit limit."

"That's not possible. I have a $20,000 credit limit, and my balance is less than $5,000."

"That was true before your limit was lowered. We sent you a notice last month, and the charge came in after the change."

"What? I didn't get any notice."

"I'm sorry, but it went out three weeks ago."

"How can you do this when I have the account set up to pay recurring charges?"

"The terms of the account state that any time there is a change in your credit status, we can change the interest rate and credit limit. Based on a recent credit report, your limit was reduced to $4,500."

"But I've never been late paying. Cutting my limit will make my credit report worse."

"I'm sorry. There's nothing I can do about that."

She sat with her eyes closed tight, trying to keep from shouting. She hung up the phone without another word and dialed the insurance company to make a payment from her checking account over the phone. Her hands were shaking by the time she finished and realized that she had been driving the past three days with her coverage lapsed.

Over the next month, the financial snowball grew. Her equity line of credit on the condo was frozen. A credit card without a balance was cancelled. The interest rate on a third jumped to 24 percent. She called one of the credit reporting bureaus, but after 15 minutes of automated recordings, still couldn't get through to a human. She threw her pen across the room in frustration and went online to order a copy of her credit report. *Nothing I can do now except find a job.*

Chapter 3

After more than five months of searching online, in newspapers and professional journals, and sending résumés to a long list of headhunters, Brenda was running out of options. Another month passed before she got her next interview. When she arrived at the office, she paused with her hand on the doorknob and breathed a small prayer. "Please, help me get this job." She took a deep breath, squared her shoulders and stepped into the waiting room.

She was ushered into an office with an exchange of pleasantries. The middle-aged interviewer fell silent as he read through the papers in the folder in front of him.

"I'm sorry, Ms. Maxwell. We were very impressed with your background and your interviews. We'd love to work with you, but as we told you on your first interview, we're government contractors, and our employees are required to have security clearance. When you filled out your application with us, you also signed an authorization for a credit report and background check, and your credit report doesn't meet our standards. I suggest you get a copy and see if there are any errors that can be corrected."

Brenda didn't remember the drive home. One minute she was leaving the parking lot after her interview, the next, she was pulling into her parking space. She sat with the engine off, trying to sort out her thoughts, but gave up after a few minutes and went inside.

Her phone was ringing as she unlocked the door.

"Hey Brenda, I've got time to go over your investment account now."

"I just got in, but I have everything waiting. Hang on a minute until I get my headset on." Brenda sat down at her desk, stacks of investment and bank statements and bills lined up in front of her and turned on her laptop. "Okay, I guess I'm ready."

"So how can I help you?"

"I'm between jobs, and there are no immediate prospects. What can I liquidate to lower my expenses and bring my credit score up, and have something left for retirement?"

"That's kind of a tall order these days, especially with another big drop in the stock market this week. Who knows what happens next? Well, let's see what we can do."

An hour later, Brenda sighed and put all the papers back into folders in a file box. "So it looks like my only choice is to take the hit and sell the condo?"

"I'm afraid so. Otherwise, you'll completely wipe out your investments and savings, and if you don't get a solid job soon enough, you're still going to have to sell the condo."

"Isn't it a bad time to sell?"

"It's not that bad in your case. You're in a great location, very desirable, and if you price it well, you'll get a quick sale in spite of the overall real estate market. You'll be able to pay off the mortgage and your bills and cover your expenses for a while. Probably, you'd have enough for a modest down payment on a new place. If you want to take an early retirement, we can set it up to minimize the taxes and penalties until you reach 59 and a half. But if you do that, unless you develop another income source over the next few years, your social security benefits will be less than they would if you worked longer."

"It's moot if I can't, though."

"True. Maybe you could consider moving away from the L.A. metro area, at least until you get relocated with a new job. There are a lot of places with a lower cost of living where you could easily buy yourself a little place. As long as you've got internet, you've got access to jobs anywhere."

"I haven't thought that far ahead, but that sounds like a reasonable way to go. In the meantime, to cover expenses, sell off my stocks that didn't crash, but haven't grown much either. I'll put the condo on the market and then decide what to do next. "

"Do you need the name of a good real estate agent?"

"You know someone?"

"Max James. I'll send you his contact info. Anything else I can do for you?"

"Yeah, pray I get a job before things get any worse."

Brenda finished putting her papers away before she stood in front of the window wall in her bedroom and looked out toward Beverly Hills. From her quiet retreat high above the bustle of the streets below, she had views in three directions. She walked to the windows on the western side of the condo, where she could catch a glimpse of ocean beneath the sunset colors of the sky. To make the down payment on the condo, she'd worked three nights a week at a second job, and for years, put every penny she could into savings or investments. *And for what, to sell it now just so I can survive?* She shook her head and went to bed, but sleep was elusive.

Chapter 4

In the morning, Brenda moved things around in the refrigerator. "I'm out of eggs, coffee, milk..." She started making a shopping list, but stopped and went to the computer. *Need to cut back where I can.* She looked up the current ad for the grocery store and finished the list, taking advantage of the specials and printing out coupons to save more.

At the market entrance, Brenda looked at the colorful display of real estate advertising booklets and papers. She gathered one of each and dropped them on a table at the side of the coffee shop inside the store. She stood in line and ordered a plain coffee. *No more lattés and pastries for a while.* Small economies, but her unemployment benefits only covered her health, car and homeowner's insurance and her utility bills. Everything else she spent was a piece of her reserve slipping away.

Flipping through the real estate booklets while she sipped her coffee, Brenda looked first for condos similar to hers. Two others in her building were up for sale, but both were larger. She made notes on the prices of each unit, feeling sick to her stomach when she saw their asking price was almost what she paid for her smaller unit. She worked out the price per square foot and realized even if she got the full price on hers, after the mortgage, realtor commissions, and settlement costs, there should be enough to pay off the car loan, but there wouldn't be enough to buy much of a residence in Los Angeles. She set aside the ad books for Santa Monica, Century City, Beverly Hills and Brentwood and looked at the ones for surrounding areas. Entire neighborhoods seemed to be up for sale, but most of the prices were still out of her range.

She sighed and got a refill of her coffee and picked up more booklets for rentals. Those that weren't too expensive were in rabbit warrens, run-down neighborhoods, or both. She pushed the books into her purse and threw out the rest of her coffee.

She moved up and down the aisles, picking up only essential items, almost by rote. Her mind filled with images that blocked out everything around her. She could see through them, but couldn't turn them off. They settled from a swirl of remembered scenes at school, at work, at the nursing home on her last visit to her father. Sitting in his room in the assisted care facility while he stared into space. Speaking to him and getting no response. Seeing him slump over and the rush to the emergency room. The days in ICU. The return to the nursing home. She shook her head and turned to the checkout counter and pulled out a handful of coupons.

Once she got back and put the groceries away, Brenda took out the real estate booklets. Looking through the listings online, she realized she couldn't afford to pay cash for any she liked. Without a job, a mortgage wasn't in the cards. *I just need something small, hopefully, only for a few months.* On an impulse, she clicked on vacation homes and found an interactive program with like and dislike buttons for a series of photos of different styles of houses, city and rural views, mountains, oceans, busy streets, quiet roads. At first amused, then entranced by the options, she clicked through dozens, ending by clicking on the Show Results link. She laughed at the first few—all with multi-million dollar views and prices. Then properties with reasonable prices started to show up on the screen.

The locations were places with no particular attraction for her, but she looked at home after home. She eliminated some by state, some by construction. Some appealed to her, but were much too large. She stopped clicking on images and instead jotted down the keywords brought up by her selections. Ocean, beach, dock, farm, sunny, forest, hardwood, cozy, cottage, wooded, retreat, hills, trees, mountain, cabin. Brenda was unsettled by the results. *Hey, they're vacation places. Of course there's no city references.* But a nagging doubt wouldn't go away. The phone interrupted her thoughts.

"Hey, Brenda, what are you up to?"

Smiling at the perky voice of her former assistant, Brenda said, "Not much, Katie. Just playing on the computer looking at houses in the country."

"Don't tell me you're going all *Green Acres* on me?"

Brenda burst out laughing at the reference to the 60's sitcom. "No, no way you'll see me getting up at dawn to milk a cow or feed the pigs.

Cherry tomatoes and herbs in containers on the balcony are as rustic as I get."

"So why are you looking in the country?"

"I don't know. Maybe I'll buy a little place somewhere and stay there while I look for a job. Then when I do get one, I can find an apartment near the place I'll work. That way I'll have a place for weekends and for when I retire."

"That's not a bad idea."

"It's just a thought for now. So how are things going?"

"Well, they'll never admit it, but boy, do they miss you."

Brenda chuckled, "I'm not surprised."

"I feel funny asking, but I need help with something."

"For you, sure. What do you need?"

After a quick review of a former client's quirky demands, Brenda thought about all the acquired bits of information that were now useless to her. *What have I got to show for all those years?* The phone rang, interrupting her thoughts. "Hello?"

"Hey, Brenda. It's Max James. I hear you're interested in selling your condo."

By the time she finished talking to Max, Brenda was optimistic about getting a reasonable price for her unit. *I'd better start working on plans for where I can go.* She browsed through the internet real estate sites again. *Maybe a vacation place isn't such a bad idea.*

The first listing she came to was next to a national forest. *Beautiful mountain views, babbling brook, country bathroom.*

Country bathroom? What's that? She clicked on the listing to get the details. When she found a footnote explaining a country bathroom was also known as an outhouse, she went back to the listings and started over.

This time, Brenda smiled as she put 1 in the box for the minimum number of bathrooms. She put 1 for bedrooms too, to eliminate one-room cabins. *Might as well ask for energy saving to get some insulation. That log cabin I saw last night looked like the wind would come right through. Now, let's see what they come up with.*

A series of dots scrolled across the page as the system searched, and a new list appeared. *Three years old, attractive outside, two bathrooms. South Carolina, 45 minutes from Myrtle Beach.* She read through the listing details and looked at the pictures of the various rooms. *Myrtle Beach. Charlie and I went there. He loved that place.* She sat back thinking about the house they stayed in on the beachfront, its living areas on the second floor in case of flooding from hurricanes. *I don't want to worry about storms at the beach, especially if I don't live there full time. Although, some time at the beach would be nice. I haven't had a real vacation since Charlie.*

Besides her parents, no one had ever been close to Brenda—until Charlie. She was 25 when they'd met in a university extension class in literature, "Romance in the Middle Ages." The instructor was a small man with piercing eyes whose whole being transformed with vibrant intensity as he explained the intricacies of the works of Chrétien de Troyes and led the class through the story of Abelard and Heloise. Each session, the class took a quick snack break midway into the three-hour class since most of the students came straight from work.

Brenda had finished her apple and nibbled on cheese crackers from the vending machine while she read over her notes. She jumped as a man sat down and spoke to her.

"Hi, I'm Charlie Abbott. I sit behind you in class, but I don't think you've ever noticed me."

At a loss for words, Brenda could only extend her hand and say, "Hi, I'm Brenda," but Charlie took over as if there'd been no awkward gap of silence and launched into a disagreement with the instructor's last statements before the break. Brenda easily held up her argument for an opposite conclusion on the way back to class.

At the classroom doorway, Charlie said, "We can't leave this unsettled. Pass me your phone number inside so I can call you tomorrow to arrange to continue our conversation."

Brenda hurried to her seat without answering, but five minutes before the class ended, she scribbled her number on a notebook page and turned to put it on Charlie's desk. He grinned at her, and her face reddened before she turned back to recording the homework assignment.

Brenda tried to stop the memories to avoid going back to what was closed and done, but her last weeks with Charlie still came back in a rush.

"The new chef here is even better than the last one. Do you want dessert?" Charlie reached across the table and held Brenda's hand.

"Well, yes, but not what's on the menu," she said grinning.

"Then I'd better get the check so we can figure out what that is." He leaned forward to give her a quick kiss on the lips.

Outside, they put their arms around each other's waist, and Brenda leaned her head against the side of Charlie's chest as they walked down the street to their apartment. He opened the door one-handed, holding her close with the other. Once inside, he tossed the keys on the hall table, and she dropped her purse on a chair, both turning to meet in a hard kiss. He unzipped her dress while she unbuckled his belt and tugged his shirt loose and slid her hands up his back, nails grazing up either side of his spine and making tight circles around his shoulders. He pushed her away long enough for her dress to slip to the floor and for him to unhook her bra. Leaning down, he lifted and kissed her breasts in turn, while she wrapped her arms around his neck, eyes closed.

"Your turn," she whispered and unbuttoned his shirt. They kissed again, and he pulled her tight against his body, sighing at the touch of bare skin on bare skin. Brenda pulled away, kicking off her shoes and leaving her dress puddled on the floor. Hurrying to the bedroom, she turned on a small lamp and pulled down the covers. Charlie followed right behind her and finished undressing. Brenda stepped out of her panties and slid across the bed, arms open to him.

Arms and legs tangled, touching, moving up and down each other's bodies, hunger for closeness growing with every contact. Pressing her against the pillows, one arm behind her neck, holding her wrist up by her ear, he caressed her body with his free hand, moving downward.

Her first reaction was a mild struggle, but in moments, she relaxed, accepting the sensations of his touch upon her. He watched the mirror of her face, changing his touch from feather light to harder to an insistent flutter, until she gasped, held her breath a long moment, and let go with a shuddery breath. He covered her face with tiny kisses and she pulled him closer. He soon joined her in satisfied sleep.

Their lives had a comfortable rhythm. Work every day, class on Tuesday and Thursday. Dinner out on Saturday, a quiet Sunday together and grocery shopping Monday night.

One morning, Brenda buttoned up her favorite white blouse. Frowning, she looked in the mirror. *Maybe I'd better start having salad for lunch.* She shook her head and put on a looser top and hurried out the door to work.

That evening, she opened the door to the pungent odor of sauerkraut cooking, and her stomach flipped.

"Hey, Bren. How was your day?" Charlie asked, poking his head out of the kitchen. "I picked up some kosher hot dogs and sauerkraut for dinner tonight."

"Hon, I'm sorry. I must be coming down with a bug. I don't feel well at all."

"You were fine this afternoon. What happened?"

"I don't know, but I think I'm just going to go to bed and see if I can sleep it off."

He kissed her on the forehead. "Can I get you anything?"

"Some ginger ale?"

"You got it."

A week later, Brenda was at the kitchen counter when Charlie came in. "Hey, babe, how you feeling?" He stood behind her and hugged her.

"Still not right."

"What are you making?" he asked, looking over her shoulder.

"I'm slicing some ginger root to make tea. You just pour hot water over it and add some honey. It's good for an upset stomach."

He wrinkled his nose at it. "Boy, that's some bug you've got. You've been sick for almost a week."

"I know. I'm so tired of ginger tea, stirred ginger ale and dry toast, but it's all I can keep down. I do feel better today though, so maybe I'm almost over it."

"I sure hope so. See you tonight, I've gotta run." With a quick peck on the cheek and a squeeze, he hurried out.

Brenda got ready for work and tried to add a little color to her face with blush and lipstick. About an hour before her usual quitting time, Brenda's boss stopped at her office door.

"Bren, why don't you cut out early and check in with your doctor? I can't afford to have you off your game, and I don't want you sharing whatever you've got with the rest of the office. I'll plan for you to be out on Monday, so that'll give you three days to shake this."

"Thanks, I think I'll stop at the walk-in urgent care on the way home. I haven't had a bug like this in ages."

"I'll see you on Tuesday then. Feel better."

Brenda was numb on the way home, replaying the doctor's explanation. She opened the apartment door and looked to see if Charlie's keys were on the hall table. Relieved that he wasn't home yet, she went to the bedroom and took out panties and a fleece sweat suit before showering. With a towel wrapped around her wet hair, she settled into her favorite 1940's barrel chair, so big she could curl up in it. There was something comforting about its size and half-round shape. Carved wood on the front of the arms gave it a simple elegance, reminding her of an Art Deco theater. She tugged the small afghan from the arm and covered herself with it. *How am I going to explain this to Charlie? I don't know what to think myself.*

The door rattled and banged shut. Charlie flipped the light switch. "Hey, what are you doing in the dark?"

"Thinking." Brenda sat up, pulling the afghan around her. " I need to talk to you. Can you sit with me for a while?"

"Why so serious? You're scaring me. What's wrong?"

"I went to the walk-in clinic on the way home. And... I can't believe this is happening, but I'm pregnant."

"Wait a minute. You have an IUD. How is that possible?"

"I know, Charlie. That's what I said too. But they told me that 1 out of every 200 women still gets pregnant with an IUD, although most miscarry so early, they don't even know it."

"I didn't even know you were late."

"I missed a cycle. It didn't even occur to me to think anything of it."

"So what happens now, Brenda?"

"I have to go in on Monday for more tests, and probably have the IUD removed. And that's where it gets complicated."

"Why?"

"The egg has already implanted itself. That's why I've been feeling so sick. If I don't lose it when they remove the IUD, I have to decide whether to have a procedure to end the pregnancy."

"Well, what else would you do?"

"If I don't do anything, there's a 50 percent chance I'll lose it anyway, and if I don't miscarry, it might end up being stillborn. But there's a 50 percent chance that it will survive and be fine."

"Get the procedure done. We don't want kids anyway."

"It's not that simple!"

"Yes, it is." Charlie got up and paced back and forth. "Don't make this more difficult than it has to be. I don't want a kid. It's probably not going to happen anyway, so deal with it."

"I don't know if I can do that."

"So, you're telling me you lied to me, and you want kids?"

"No, that's not it. I'm so confused. I never planned this, but I can't pretend there isn't something there either. I can't believe the way you're acting."

"The way I'm acting? I'm not the one trying to mess up our lives. Everything's fine the way it is, and you want to risk screwing it up instead of facing facts. It was your idea to go off the pill and use the IUD."

"The risk of staying on the pill was too high. You could've had a vasectomy, and we wouldn't be in this situation."

"Oh, nice. Blame it all on me."

"Charlie..."

"You figure out what you're going to do, and let me know." He snatched up his keys and slammed the door behind him.

She sat frozen, staring at the door, afraid if she moved, she'd fall into little shards. *How could he act like that? Do I even know him at all?* Shivering in spite of the afghan, she went to her bed and slid under the covers, leaving the room lights off. In a waking dream, she let images form and fade. Holding a baby. Rocking it in a cradle. Buckling it into a car seat. And then icy fear brought a new vision. Sitting in front of a small white casket.

Little teardrops opened the way for wrenching sobs and a soul-deep anguish trapped inside. She cried until she was exhausted, then lay there until she slept.

Something woke her late in the night. A sense of unease, something not right. She reached out for Charlie. He wasn't there. And then a pain so sharp, so sudden, it took her breath away. She pushed back the covers and stood up, but a wave of dizziness made the room tilt. She grabbed for the edge of the dresser and clung to it until the room settled down. And then the pain hit again, white-hot at the edge of her shoulder and deep in her belly. She never knew the taste of terror before, but it pushed her to stagger through the hall to get to her purse and the doctor's card. She reached his exchange on the second attempt to dial and answered the operator's questions. She unlocked her front door as the woman instructed, before she slid to the floor, clutching the phone, pain and fear making it hard to think.

Sirens. Flashing lights. Pounding on the door and muffled voices on the other side. A man's reassuring voice, a strong hand gently taking the phone from hers. Sinking into the spinning darkness.

A week later, after surgery for an ectopic pregnancy destroyed any chance for another, she came home to find Charlie gone. She never heard from him again and never let anyone get that close again.

Brenda sighed, shaking her head. *Oh, Charlie. Why couldn't you be the man I needed? If only... Enough of that. Ocean areas are out.* She closed down the real estate site and checked on job-hunting websites before turning the computer off. Still nothing new.

The silence rang loud in her ears. Flipping through the television stations, she came across something with rolling green hills in the background and paused to see what it was. A man in his 50's was talking to a reporter.

"Yes, it's a different way of life, but my old life was killing me. Two heart attacks in one year gave me a wake-up call."

"So you packed up, moved here, and left city life behind?"

"Well, that's not exactly how it happened. Don't forget my wife had something to say about it." The man chuckled and turned and put his arm around his wife's shoulders.

Turning to her, the reporter asked, "Why did you agree to change your way of life?"

"I wasn't so excited about giving up my city luxuries," she said looking at her nails. "But when my best friend's husband died suddenly, it made me stop and think about what really mattered to me." She looked up at her husband and smiled. "Hair styles and nail salons, fancy coffee shops or theater don't mean much when you're without your partner."

The scene cut to a view of a home, built into the hillside.

"Tell me about your house. Isn't it hard living without electricity?"

The man laughed. "We have electricity. We just don't get it from a public utility. We generate our own. Granted, it's not an unlimited supply, and we have to pick and choose how to use it, but there's plenty for our basic needs and a few extras. Come on in. Let me show you."

Chapter 5

Brenda mulled over what the couple had said. Their electricity came from solar panels, and a wind turbine charged large batteries. The only modern convenience they seemed to do without was air conditioning, but they had lights, fans, a computer, a water pump, a refrigerator and a small freezer.

"Could never happen here in the city," she said aloud to herself. She turned the lights off and got ready for bed. But a thought kept echoing. *You don't have to live in the city.*

The next day, in between job searches online, Brenda searched for off-the-grid real estate. Picking a site at random, she found country property sales listings accompanied by photographs. Scrolling through, she skipped over the ones in Colorado, Washington, Oregon, Massachusetts. *Winters are too cold there.* She shook her head. *I used to like to ski, but I don't know about a whole winter snowbound.* The homes available in Arizona and New Mexico didn't appeal to her, and she kept looking. She saw one in California and clicked on it, but the million and a half dollar asking price sent her back to the search engine.

I never imagined there were so many businesses handling off-the-grid properties. She picked another website: Wisconsin, Vermont, New Hampshire, Maine. She sighed. *This isn't getting any better. Maybe it's not such a great idea.*

But curiosity kept her looking through three more sites, before she picked up a stack of papers and pulled out the brochure from the real estate company with the online system to select housing preferences. She started with mountain properties. Reading through the state links, she was startled by one labeled Florida Mountain Properties. She clicked it, and burst out laughing when it came up as none. *What's the matter with you? You know there aren't any mountains in Florida.* She laughed again and went back to the list. She clicked on West Virginia. *Wonder what it's like there. I don't know much about it.*

Some of the buildings were little more than shacks, but others were farmhouses, small ranches, and split-levels. Just about every one had a stunning view. *Seems like a beautiful place. Would be nice to have a vacation hideaway once I do get back to work. Wonder what they do for internet and phone connections?*

When May brought nothing new on the job horizon, Brenda fought off panic at the declining numbers on her bank statement. *Maybe I can sell some of my stuff. Heaven knows I've accumulated enough over the years I really don't need.*

She took down some art prints she picked up on a cruise with her parents years earlier and went online to see what they might bring. She remembered the sales pitch that assured her the prints would go up in value because they were limited editions of a famous artist's work. Soon she was looking at a twin of one of her pieces.

Not many like it on the market, but the selling prices were all within a hundred dollars of what she'd paid. Not exactly the thousands of profit she'd anticipated. *Still, it's something I don't need.* She registered for an art sales website and placed the two pieces in the For Sale category. A tight knot formed in her gut. Fear of running through her cash reserves was making it hard to think of what to do next and harder to do anything. Pushing back from the computer desk, she read through one of her calming meditations. It didn't seem to make anything better, but it did keep the fear from escalating.

What was that TV ad about selling jewelry? Brenda hurried to the bedroom and pulled out her lingerie drawer, took out several small jewelry boxes from the back and stacked them on the bed. A jewelry chest with a music box was next, and Brenda sat down to look through its contents.

Tangled chains that had broken or lost a clasp were her first choices for a pile she put to one side. A stainless steel bracelet with a spring clasp opening and her name on a heart caught her eye. She smiled and put it on her wrist. Her 12th birthday present from her father. One of the few things he'd ever picked out for her himself. *Made me feel so special. No one else had one like it, and everybody at school thought it was so cool.* She touched the heart, still smiling, and turned to the items in the bottom drawer. Earrings without mates, mostly gold, some silver. *Amazing what accumulates over the years.* She put all the odd earrings together with the unusable chains, then moved on to the next drawer. Each pair of earrings there was a gift from family or friends. She touched one and remembered an aunt long departed, and another from a friend lost at sea. She closed the drawer. The top drawer held a mixture of bracelets and rings. Some she added to the growing collection on the bed; others, she replaced before putting the jewelry box back on the dresser.

Going through the smaller boxes took longer, and Brenda felt uneasy because she couldn't remember where she got the necklaces inside. *Was this one I bought on a trip, or one I bought for my mother? Does it really matter now?* Nothing seemed familiar. There were no immediate connections like she had to the bracelet on her wrist. Brenda sighed and put a few pendants on the pile and put the rest away. Scooping up the jewelry on the bed into one of the empty necklace boxes, Brenda carried it to the kitchen.

It took a few minutes of going through shelves and drawers, but she found a kitchen scale to weigh all the gold items. In a moment, she had a wiki site open to a page that explained that gold is weighed in troy ounces that are heavier than the food scale avoirdupois ounces.

Avoirdupois... my best Scrabble play ever. She chuckled. *Oh, what was that score, I played all 7 letters with letters on the board, right across two triple score spots and picked up some words crossing... 150! That was it.* She laughed out loud remembering how much fun she'd had that night with Charlie and another couple. And then the joy vanished, and a sad ache took its place.

She pushed away the thoughts and went back to figuring out the weight of her gold jewelry. *Okay, now, let's see what they're paying for gold these days.*

Within an hour, she'd looked and compared rates between companies buying gold online, and rechecked the amount of 14 karat and 18 karat gold items, Brenda figured it would come to a little over two thousand dollars. *Plus the silver I didn't count. Hmm. Not bad for stuff I don't use and don't need.* She entered her information and printed out a prepaid shipping label and form from the company and packed everything into a heavy plastic sandwich bag before tucking it into a padded envelope.

In the morning, Brenda picked up the envelope with her purse and keys and walked out to the elevator. *Okay, so this will be a little cash coming in, but I still have to figure out what to do next.* She stabbed at the down button with her finger. *As if I haven't been trying.*

Going around the corner to the FedEx drop-off bin in the mailbox lobby, she slid her package into an envelope from the supply rack before sealing it and taping the label onto it. After tossing the package in, she continued out to the parking garage. Just before she pulled out, her cell phone rang.

"Hey, Brenda, it's Max from the real estate office. We've got an offer."

"Already? It's only been on the market a week and a half."

"You priced it right, and it's in great shape. No kid or pet damage or neglected maintenance. And it's a desirable location."

He paused, and Brenda spoke up. "Okay, there's a but coming. What is it?"

"It's not a full price offer, but we can make a counter offer."

Before Brenda could reply, Max continued. "There's something more."

Her hand tightened on the phone. "Which is?"

"The buyer's agent wants to know if you would consider selling the furnishings?"

Brenda laughed. "You're kidding?"

"No, and I can understand if you aren't interested..."

"No, you don't understand. I'd be delighted if I got a reasonable amount for everything. Only two pieces mean anything to me, a nightstand and a cedar chest that belonged to my parents. Everything else was either designed for the condo or chosen for it. I have no attachment to any of that, and I can get new things to fit wherever I move. But why do they want the furniture?"

"It's a multi-national outfit, and one of their execs is going to be here on a long term project. He may end up heading a new office here, and from what he's seen in the photos, he likes what you've done with the place."

"Well, fax me the details of their offer, and what you think I should do. Can I get back to you in an hour or two?"

"Sure. It's a good idea to let them wonder if they're going to get it or not. Don't worry, I already checked and yours is the only one immediately available that fits all their criteria. We'll go over everything when you call back. How's noon sound?"

"That's fine. How fast do you think this could happen? I haven't made any plans yet."

"Well, you better get going. We could close with a cash deal in less than a month if you're happy with the final offer."

"I never imagined it could go that fast. How about the condo board? They have to approve the deal."

"I'm ahead of you already. I know the president of the board. We play golf together, and I talked to him off the record. He's cool with it and will call a special meeting if necessary."

"Well, I've got homework to do. Thanks for everything, Max. Talk to you later."

She sat back and closed her eyes, trying to still the swirl of thoughts coming from all directions. *Two hours. Where do I start?* As if she'd hit an instant replay button, she heard her mother's voice. *When you don't know what to do, go shopping. It will come to you.* Brenda laughed out loud at the memory. Her mother rarely indulged in shopping trips, but when she did, she took Brenda along. They always came home laughing and chatting with full shopping bags dangling from both arms.

She went back upstairs long enough to print out the fax from the realtor and was at her favorite bookstore in a few minutes. She found a book that looked interesting with advice on buying a second home and picked up one in the next rack on homesteading. *No, no, no. I'm not going to need information on herbal medicine or trimming my llamas' toenails or breeding emus.* She slid that one back on the shelf, but she did pick up one about off-the-grid homes and another about traditional skills. *I can skip making sausage and milking a goat, but growing herbs and baking bread, that might be worth reading about.* At the checkout desk, she added a copy of a local paper.

She set her purchases on a corner table in the nearby coffee shop and ordered a latté and a scone to celebrate while she read through the details of the offer and proposed counter-offer on the condo. *Not so bad. Only $20,000 less than I'd hoped for. I can live with that.* She signed it and put the real estate papers in her purse. While she sipped her coffee, she made a list of the furniture in the condo and added notes from the paper of prices for used pieces similar to hers. *There. All done. I think I deserve another latté while I read one of my new books for a while.*

An hour later, she was back in the condo for the phone meeting with Max, and after going over the details with him, she faxed the signed counter-offer and addendum covering the furniture.

"So, Brenda, let me send that to the buyer's agent, and we can talk about your plans." Back to her in less than a minute, Max asked, "Have you decided where to go?"

"Not yet." She kicked off her shoes and stretched out on the sofa. "I got as far as ruling out California, Arizona and New Mexico, and most of the northern half of the country—and oceanside areas, too."

"That eliminates a lot of places," Max chuckled. "Still leaves a lot of others though. Is there anything else that can narrow it down some?"

"I did see some mountain properties in West Virginia with beautiful views, but I really haven't explored them. At this point, if it's a good investment for the long run as a second home, I'm open to ideas, but no reason not to start there."

"You know, we have a number of east coast offices. Want me to check if there's anyone I've worked with I trust to give you advice almost as good as mine?"

"Max, you're the best. Sure, I need to do something, and fast, if this goes through.

"Here you go. I've got a name for you, Janie Allen. She's sharp, and she'll get you what you want at the best price. Good thing your buyer didn't have her for an agent."

By the next morning, Brenda had a list of properties in Chestnut Springs, West Virginia, to check out online. Four of them seemed like good possibilities. *Let's see what the area's like.* Within a few minutes, she learned about the huge lake created when a dam was built and how it was now a popular summer vacation spot. An equally popular ski resort was an hour and a half away, and less than an hour to the south, was a river with white-water rafting. *Well, no shortage of fun, that's for sure, but what's the climate like?*

Elevation between 1,800 and 2,400 feet, average temperature above freezing in the winter, except for January and February when it dipped into the 20's. *That's not bad at all.* Summers mild, just barely above 80 in August, and a modest annual rainfall spread out across the year. *No wonder the views are so lush and green. Definitely an area to check.*

While Brenda was writing an email to Janie to let her know which listings she wanted to see, she was imagining them again and trying to see herself in the picture in front of each of them. She wrapped up the message by saying she'd be in touch as soon as she made reservations.

But before she checked airlines and schedules, Brenda went back to the listings, looking at the houses and the land around them one more time, trying to conjure the views from inside the rooms. *One of these might turn out to be a great vacation home.*

Brenda purchased her tickets for a flight leaving a week later that would arrive midafternoon in West Virginia. *Okay, six and a half hours. Not bad, even if it's through Chicago.* With the details confirmed, she forwarded them to Janie.

The phone rang a few minutes later.

"How would you like a guided tour of Chestnut Springs when you arrive?"

"Janie?"

Laughter confirmed her guess. "Yes, hello, Brenda. I'm going to visit family in the area next week, and while I don't usually go quite that far for my clients, my clients don't usually travel that far for me either."

"A guided tour would be fantastic. The more I read about the area, the more convinced I am this is a terrific location for a vacation property."

"It really is. There is so much to do, and even doing nothing, it's a lovely place to unwind. We'll have to go whitewater rafting once you get settled."

"Sure, sounds like fun. I've always wanted to try it."

"I'll email you info on a bed and breakfast in town that's clean, comfortable, with the best breakfast on the east coast."

"Thanks. What's the situation with internet access there?"

"I think all the properties I sent you have some form of connection. I know one is satellite, one is close enough to town to be on the cable hookup, but I'm not sure about the others. Probably a hotspot through a cell phone. I'll find out, and let you know. And the B&B is connected. You can book through their website. I called Fanny and Joe and let them know to expect to hear from you."

The conversation continued for another 25 minutes while Janie gathered information and ended with her promise to have a fair sampling of the area's attractions lined up.

After the call with Janie, Brenda went through her closet and pulled out clothes to pack for the trip and things to be shipped later. She took out a formal gown that she wore to a company event and held it up in front her. *Great dress, but it will be out of fashion before I have a chance to wear it again. May as well get something out of it from the consignment shop.* She set aside some of her other designer clothes with the gown to take to the consignment shop in West Hollywood, then turned to the task of sorting out her books.

Lunchtime came and went before she made a sandwich to eat while she sat at the computer to check job listings. Nothing new. Clicking on bookmark after bookmark, the same story at each site. There were even fewer jobs now than there had been over the past few weeks. *Hey, you're going to have a vacation, so be glad there isn't anything right now.* She smiled and thought about spending the summer getting settled in a new place and trying out everything it had to offer before looking for a job again. And with that thought in mind, she picked up the clothes she'd packed into garment bags and set out for the shop in West Hollywood.

Later in the day, Brenda pulled into her parking space and sat with the engine off. She sighed and rubbed her hand across the leather cover on the steering wheel. She loved her car. It was a joy to drive. *Only a year of payments left, but with no income, it's a drain, not even counting maintenance and insurance. It's a luxury I can't afford, but I still hate giving it up.* She dialed the dealer who maintained the car. His offer for it was fair, and she accepted it.

The next morning, she parked a bland rental car in her spot instead of the Porsche and went upstairs. After an hour at the computer, she looked at her checklist. Internet, electric and cable turnoff dates all set. Private mailbox to hold and forward mail arranged. Pod ordered, storage and mover scheduled.

Piece by piece, she disconnected her life from L. A., but she felt nothing. No regret, no sadness, but no joy either. Just flat acceptance as she erased her existence from the city. *The condo's ready for the movers, but am I ready for what's ahead?*

The movers rang the bell just after her last walk through each room. Quick, efficient and quiet, the four men wrapped and packed everything that was going into the small storage pod waiting at the curb outside. Brenda kept an eye on them, but stayed out of their way. With only two pieces of furniture involved, it took less than two hours for the men to pack and load the other contents of the condo. Brenda went down on the elevator with them for the last load. She put her own padlock on the unit and thanked each of the men with a generous tip.

She went back up and stepped out onto the balcony, looking out at the hills for several minutes. *There ought to be a ritual for leaving your home for the last time.* She picked up her carryon bag, blinking away tears, and pulled out the handle of her rolling suitcase and set out for the title company's office.

Max was waiting for her. "Come on in. Everything go okay with the movers?"

"No problem at all. Good people."

"Okay, everybody's here, so let's wrap this up."

An hour later, Brenda packed a stack of papers into her bag. She gave Max the name of the hotel near the airport where she was spending the night and the info from the B & B where she'd be staying in West Virginia. He walked with her to the parking lot.

"Good luck, kiddo. Hope you find the perfect place."

"Me too. Thanks for everything." Brenda hugged him. "I'll be in touch."

It was still dark the next morning when Brenda dropped off her rental car and climbed up into the shuttle bus to the airport. *Maybe I'll be back by the end of the year if I can make a connection and get a job.* She heard her father's voice from years back, "...and if a bullfrog had wings, he wouldn't bump his a..." She smiled, thinking of the warning glance her mother always threw her father at this point and his grin as he adjusted the rest of the saying, "...he wouldn't bump his rear so much."

The driver looked at Brenda in his mirror. At the red light, he turned to face her. "Well, that's a nice big smile you've got there for so early in the morning. Thinking about what you're gonna do on vacation?"

"No, I just thought of something my father used to say."

"Are you going to see him?"

"Wish I could, but he passed away this year. He had a long life, but I miss him."

The driver nodded and moved forward with the change of the light. "Yeah, I know what you mean. My mom passed last year. Still pick up the phone to call her every now and then."

"Took me a couple of years to stop doing that after my mom died. Gets a little easier with time."

"That's good to know. Okay, here we are." The driver pulled to the curb and took Brenda's rolling bag from the luggage rack. He stepped down and held out a hand to help her down the steep steps. Keep remembering the good stuff."

"Thank you. You, too." She handed him a tip and took the handle of the bag. Smiling, she entered the terminal.

Chapter 6

The flight arrived a few minutes early in Chicago, and Brenda stretched before walking down the terminal to the boarding gate for the next flight segment. Brenda was delighted to find the seats in the much smaller jet were more comfortable than those on larger jets. Boarding took only a few minutes. But when the plane taxied to take off, her heart skipped a beat, and she held her breath. *Feels like we're being flung in the air by a slingshot.* Her fear faded once the plane leveled into a smooth flight, and she watched the changing terrain below.

Rivers and towns, rolling green fields, woods and mountains, all so different from the view from her big city condo. *Am I really doing this? What else could I do? Is there something I'm not thinking of?*

Lost in thought, Brenda was startled by the landing preparation announcement. She saw a river and bridges, a stadium and then a gold-domed building before the plane swooped in for a quick landing.

Turning to leave the baggage claim with her checked bag, Brenda heard her name.

"Hey, Brenda! Over here."

She turned to see a tall blonde woman waving at her. "Janie?"

The woman hurried to her and took one of her bags. "That's me. Sorry I'm late. Gram decided she needed me to pick up some milk just as I was leaving to meet you."

"That's okay. I actually got in a few minutes early. Can't believe we left Chicago on time. Don't ask me the last time that happened."

"Sounds like a good omen for house-hunting. That's my white SUV right over there. I figure we can get you checked in at the bed and breakfast and give you an hour to unpack and relax before I pick you up for your first home-cooked Chestnut Springs dinner."

"Thank you for going out of your way like this."

She laughed and said, "I'm mixing business with pleasure. My grandmother and aunt live here. So I get to see them and eat some of my favorite home cooking. Helping you find a nice house is icing on the cake."

"The views coming in were stunning. Even more beautiful than I expected from the pictures online."

Janie opened the back and put Brenda's bags in. "Climb aboard. We'll see some dramatic scenery on the way to Chestnut Springs. We've got three different ways to go. The shortest is sixty-some miles and the longest is closer to ninety. All three take an hour and a half, but I'm going to take the interstate partway. We'll cross over more rivers and pass through some little towns to give you a little taste of the region."

Brenda was mesmerized by the mountain and river views. "Everything is so green. Quite a difference from Los Angeles."

Janie chuckled. "I'll bet it is."

"The only river there is the L.A. River, and it's in a concrete channel. That bridge over there looks so old and rickety. Is it still used?"

"No, that's one of the abandoned rail lines. With the decline in coal mining, there aren't many left. Some of the old lines have been turned into hiking trails, but there are still a few active ones. None of them stop at Chestnut Springs now, but there's an Amtrak station about forty miles away."

The women fell silent for a while until Janie turned off the interstate. "This won't have the same scenery, but there'll be a few river crossings. Do you think you'll be up to seeing a few local views from some of the properties in person tomorrow? Or do you want some time to rest up?"

"No, let's start looking tomorrow. I'm anxious to see what Chestnut Springs is like."

"Then that's what we'll do."

When they reached the outskirts of town, Janie warned Brenda, "This is a pretty rough area. It's not typical of the areas we're going to look at, but places like this are scattered all over the state. People have been out of work so long, they've given up trying."

Brenda watched as they drove past a dirt lot with dozens of new mobile homes. "Do people live here?"

"No, that's actually a dealer. Those over there are what's called double-wides. They'll be set up on someone's lot and finished off. A lot cheaper than a regular house, and they work out for someone who's been out of work and loses their home, or someone who had to take a lower-level job. Sometimes, someone who gets divorced and needs a place can get into one of these." She sighed. "Times are hard. Some folks turn to drugs. It's a massive problem, with no cure in sight. You won't see it in the center of town, but on the edges, there's just too much of it."

Within a few blocks, the view changed to wide manicured strips of lawn next to neat sidewalks. Old-fashioned black wrought iron poles topped with street lights stood in front of old, but well-kept brick stores and banks. They passed county offices and a courthouse with a lawn and benches lining the broad walkway.

"There's the school complex, and that's the local garage. They do good work, and you can trust them. The diner's over there, and that's the shopping center with the market. The post office is up the street here, and the best hardware store you'll ever see is right here."

Brenda just nodded, trying to absorb it all. She blinked at an odd sight. "That phone pole looks strange, kind of bent to one side. What happened there?"

"I'm not exactly sure. Maybe a big storm? Fanny and Joe from the bed and breakfast will probably know if you ask them."

Small and large homes showed up between businesses, and more trees lined the street. Side streets were on gentle hills, with nice lawns and more trees than on the main street. Janie turned up one side street and turned back toward the business area, then turned again on a residential street.

"I circled back, so this is only two short blocks from the market and diner, but a block behind them. And here we are at Fanny and Joe's."

As Janie pulled into the driveway, Brenda looked out at a handsome Victorian home whose wide porch was lined with rocking chairs and a glider. She had just stepped down from Janie's vehicle when the B&B owners, Joe and Fanny Price, came down from the porch to greet her and take her bags. Joe was a pleasant-looking man just under six-feet tall with thinning hair and a wiry frame.

Fanny, dark-haired and petite, treated Brenda like an old friend and made her feel welcome in an instant, then turned toward Janie and wrapped her in a hug. "Hey, it's been too long since we've seen you. How've you been?"

"Just fine, thank you. Wish I could get down here more often, but that pesky work stuff keeps getting in the way. I don't get to combine visits and work here too often, so showing Brenda around is going to be more fun than work for me."

Fanny shook her finger at Janie. "Well, you'd better save some time to do some catching up over dinner one night, okay?"

"I promise. I will. Pick you up in an hour for dinner, Brenda." Janie grinned and waved as she climbed in and pulled away.

Fanny took Brenda on a quick tour of the bed and breakfast and showed her to her room. "If you need anything at all, you just let me know."

Brenda thanked her and set about unpacking her bag.

When Janie dropped her off after dinner, Joe called out as Brenda walked up the steps, "Come and sit with us. How was dinner?"

"I'd forgotten how good fried chicken can be. Haven't had any that good since my mother passed away. The greens and cornbread were wonderful too, and I loved the blackberry cobbler."

"Grandma Charlene is one good cook, that's for sure. Would you like something to drink? I kind of doubt you're hungry now," Joe said with a grin.

"I don't think I'll be hungry again before this time tomorrow. But I do need to get to bed. I'm afraid if I sat down out here, I'd fall asleep in a minute."

"Well, we don't want that when you've got a nice big bed waiting upstairs for you. Is everything okay with your room?" Fanny sat forward waiting for the answer.

"Oh, yes. It's beautiful. I've always loved the idea of a four-poster bed, but I've never slept in one before."

"Then you go along now and try it out. We'll be in the kitchen at 7, but we'll have coffee and tea and a few other things out while we're cooking, so help yourself when you come down."

"Thank you. I'll see you in the morning."

"Sleep tight."

Brenda left her clothes in a heap and took a quick shower before slipping into bed. She sat up against the pillows. *Long time since I've been to a big family dinner. All the people here have been so friendly. So different from the city.* She yawned and slid down under a handmade quilt. *Feels good.* She was asleep before she could turn out the light.

A soft beeping woke her. It took a few moments before she realized it was the alarm on her cell phone and turned it off. *That was the best sleep I've had in years.* She stretched and dressed in slacks and comfortable walking shoes before going down to the dining room. She went straight to the coffee pot.

"Need a little waking up?" Fanny was carrying a tray of warm muffins, scones and coffee cake into the dining room.

"If I didn't have plans to meet Janie, I'd have slept in. That bed is so comfortable, but I think the scent of your baking would have drawn me down here anyway."

"Then sit down and help yourself. Now, how should I fix your eggs?"

An hour later, Fanny was sipping coffee on the screen porch next to the dining room. Brenda settled into the adjacent rocking chair. "Breakfast was delicious."

"Glad you enjoyed it."

"Am I hearing a bit of Boston in your accent?"

Fanny laughed. "Doubt I'll ever lose that."

"How did you happen to settle here?"

"We came down here every year to go white-water rafting when we were younger. A few years ago, Joe was offered a bonus to take early retirement so a younger worker wouldn't have to be laid off. So, we came up with the idea of starting the bed and breakfast. We've always loved having company and cooking for friends."

"Well, you've certainly made me feel at home." Brenda saw Janie pulling up. "I'll be back some time after dinner. I'm not sure exactly how long we'll be out."

"Don't rush back on my account. I'll be up late watching movies tonight."

Brenda climbed up into Janie's SUV.

"Good morning! Ready for house-hunting?"

"Very. What do you have planned for me to see?"

"I've pulled five listings with different features. They may not be exactly what you're looking for, but these will help me narrow down what you'd like."

"Fine by me. I'm not exactly sure myself. I've always lived in apartments or condos, so this will be a new experience."

"Why did you decide on this area?"

"I think it'll be a good investment. A lot of vacation places are limited to one or two seasons. Here, there's a variety of recreation through the whole year."

"You're right about the year-round activities. What kind do you enjoy?"

"I didn't have time for much besides work in L.A. and looking after my parents in Florida before they died. You know, I can't remember the last vacation I took just for fun. I don't know what I'd like to do with my free time now, but if this doesn't work out for me, and I decide to sell later, it's still a great location. Isn't that one of the prime rules in real estate—location?"

"That's definitely one thing, but there are other factors to consider too. Real estate taxes are low. You're not planning to find work here, so that's not an issue. There's a nice little library in town and an art gallery, medical facilities are pretty good, and there are shops for all the basics. Specialty things, you need to order online or drive a ways to get. So the actual building and property are going to be most important things for you to consider, I think."

"Well, Max told me you're a fine agent, and I trust his judgment, so I'm relying on you to help me make a good choice."

"I'll have to thank him once we find you a place. Okay, here's the turn-off for the first listing. There's not much information in the database on it, and the listing agent is away on vacation. The price is on the low end, so I don't know what we're going to find. If it's not right for you, we'll just head on to the next one. That okay?"

"Sounds reasonable to me. But I don't know about this road. It's pretty rough."

Janie jerked the wheel to one side to avoid a deep rut and slowed down before she replied. "I'm not getting a good feeling about this one. Maybe we should just skip it."

"We've come this far. Let's see it and then head back down."

A sharp turn brought them to an almost level spot near the top of the hill, and Janie pulled over. Brenda got out and looked around. "Oh, the view is incredible."

"I wish I could say the same of the house." She pointed up to a ramshackle building. "It's falling apart. This should have been listed as a hunting cabin. They tend to be more basic and often run-down.

Well, that accounts for the pricing. You're buying the land, not the building. Jump in. I'll go up a little where I can turn around, and we'll go to the next one. Okay?"

"That's what I'm here for. What's the next one supposed to be like?"

"Let's see. It's about half an hour from here, a little further down the mountain in a small community. It has wired electricity and solar panels on the roof. Three bedrooms, a family room and a small but modern kitchen. Here are some pictures of the various rooms."

Brenda turned the pages while Janie maneuvered the vehicle back down the road to the highway. "Well, it's certainly in better shape. But...I don't know...it's so...."

"Ordinary?" Janie grinned.

"Good word. If you don't mind, let's skip it...unless someone's expecting us."

"No, all the listings I chose today are unoccupied. I figured there'd be one or two you'd want to pass on and this way, no disappointed owners. Are you still open to off-the-grid properties?"

"I'm curious about them. I read some books, but I still have a lot of questions. I think I need to get a better idea of how they work."

"The next one has solar panels so you can see for yourself. I'll fill you in on the basics as we drive."

Half an hour later, they turned onto a private road that wound upward for another ten minutes before leveling out in front of a log building.

"This house is about ten years old. It has a heat pump, wood stove and two fireplaces. The electricity comes from the solar panels. It has triple-glazed windows. Log and cultured stone construction. Garage or workshop behind the main building. Five acres."

"Janie, I'm trying to keep an open mind, but...it looks like a barn."

"I'm guessing by the look on your face, a barn's not your idea of the perfect home?" Janie laughed while she unlocked the front door. "It's okay. Remember, today is to help me see what you like, and just as important is what you don't like."

Brenda nodded and followed her inside, wandering from room to room, looking at each from one direction, then another. "You know, there's so much space, but none of it really connects." She shook her head. "The proportions are awkward...and the color of the stone doesn't go with the wood stain. Wouldn't this be expensive to heat too?"

"That's where the heat pump comes in. It uses electricity, but it runs off the solar system. The batteries keep it going at night or on cloudy days, as well as a little refrigerator and a few lights too. This place also has a generator. As far as the rest of it goes, a lot of these log homes are custom built and designed to the owner's taste."

"How big is the house?"

"About 3500 square feet, three bedrooms, three baths."

"Definitely too big for just me."

"No family to join you on vacations?"

"No, I'm on my own."

"Maybe you don't need something this large then, but you should still get at least two bedrooms, for visitors and for future resale value."

"Makes sense. Well, I think I've seen enough here. What's next?"

"How about a little sightseeing on the way to get lunch? There's a great diner off the main highway. Fantastic cooking and a wonderful view of the mountains."

An hour later in the parking lot, Brenda looked at the mountains around the diner. "I am going to have to start some serious exercise to keep up with these meals. I've never had barbecue that good, and the rice pudding was the best I've had since my mom's."

"You could eat here every day for months before you tasted all their specials. I have my favorites, but I've never had a bad meal here."

Brenda stopped, looking at activity on the mountain across the road. "What's going on over there?"

Janie frowned. "Looks like the latest wind farm development. I thought there was an injunction suspending construction, but I guess not."

"Why would there be an injunction? Isn't wind power a good thing for the area?"

"There's a lot of opinions going both ways, but I'm not sure about the details. Fanny and Joe are very involved with it, so they'd be your best source of information."

"I'll have to ask them about it. Okay, where are we heading now?"

"This one's a little more isolated, about half an hour to the nearest neighbor. Fairly new house, two bedrooms, two baths, unfinished full basement, used as vacation home only. Oh, it's on 380 acres."

"That's a lot of land! I can't imagine owning that much."

"Not sure how much is wooded and how much is mountainside, but we'll see in a little while. Here's the printout of the various rooms and views."

"I'm trying to look past the dark colors, but they make it feel closed in, and with so much space around, it only accents that feeling."

"It'll be easier to scope out once you're actually in the rooms. They're probably better in person than in the pictures."

"The views are amazing. All these are on the property?"

"I believe so. We're almost there. Watch out for survey markers on the corners as we go up the mountain. The property extends down to the road we come in on. See that pipe with the orange plastic streamers? That's one corner. We'll go up through the gated access at the other corner so you can see how wide it is at the bottom. The shape of this parcel's irregular, but the house is about halfway up, so you can get some sense of the size."

"This must be a quarter mile wide. What would I do with so much land?"

"Enjoy it?" Her laugh was cut off when they hit a deep rut and the vehicle lurched to the side. "Whoops, I'd better slow down. Get spoiled driving on all that nice highway." Janie glanced over at Brenda's frozen expression. "Relax, I haven't bounced off a mountain yet."

"Guess that's a good thing. I don't know. This is beginning to feel overwhelming. I hadn't pictured a specific place, but I certainly didn't expect something like this."

"Just remember, today is for looking and getting a sense of what's available. No one is going to push you into something that's not a good fit for you."

"Yeah, this all came about so fast. Yesterday, I was in one of the biggest cities in the country where a house on an acre or two costs in the millions, and here we are, climbing up the side of a mountain that I could afford to buy if I wanted to. It's hard to open my mind to the possibility."

"It's an adjustment to go from city to country, but it can really be worth it."

"I'm only going to be here until I get another job. After that, maybe I'll come back for long weekends and vacations until I retire." Brenda stared out the window.

"Well, there's plenty of time for you to figure those things to out. Try to relax and enjoy the time off."

The road leveled out, and they pulled into a driveway in front of a house with a porch running around three sides of the second floor. Tall windows reflected the mountains, and a creek glistened to one side. Trees behind the house whispered in the stiff breeze as the two women climbed the stairs to the entrance. Inside, the hall opened into a large room with a vaulted ceiling and a massive fireplace between the two windows that filled the wall on either side of it.

Brenda moved around the room touching the built-in shelves and looking back to the large kitchen. "I'm sure it would be perfect for someone, but it's too isolated and way too big for me." She sighed, shaking her head.

"We're only beginning, so let's push on to the last one for today. Then we'll stop at the diner again for dinner on the way back, and I'll make some notes to use in picking out more houses to see."

The last place was a manufactured home that looked lonely and isolated on a bare lot.

"Janie, let's not go in. I really can't see myself living here."

"Okay, then let's go have a good meal. Maybe a glass of wine will perk you up a little."

As Brenda entered the diner, her phone rang. "Catch up with you in a minute," she said to Janie and stepped back out into the parking lot. The number wasn't familiar. She answered and the person calling asked her to hold the line for Mr. Brown.

Brown. Brown. Where do I know that name from?

A booming voice announced himself. "Brenda, Jack Brown from the D.C. office of Jones, James and Whittier. I know it's short notice, but are you available for an interview on Thursday afternoon?"

"I'm in West Virginia at the moment, but I can check flights from the airport here and confirm with you tomorrow, if that's okay. What time did you have in mind?"

"Any time after noon will work. Let me know tomorrow when to expect you."

"Thank you. I'll talk to you then."

When Brenda slid into the booth, Janie said, "Must have been a good call. You look a lot happier."

"I am. I have a job interview Thursday with a great company in D.C."

"That's great. Do you want to cancel house-hunting until you see how it goes?"

"Oh no. If I get the job, I'll still want to invest in a property here. I'm not ready to think about a permanent place in D.C., even if they offer me a job on the spot. Besides, if I find the right place, it could turn out to be a good place for retirement."

"Definitely could be. You like Merlot? They carry a nice one from a local winery."

When Brenda nodded, Janie called over to the waitress, "Amy, two glasses of merlot, please."

Amy delivered them a minute later, and after Janie thanked her, she held up her glass. "I wish you luck on Thursday for a job, and for us to find you the right place before then."

Brenda grinned. "Thank you. I'll drink to that."

In spite of the good wishes, two more days of house hunting ended the same way as the previous ones. Brenda looked out over the valley again from the diner window. "I don't know, Janie. I didn't expect to find something the first time out, but I thought there'd be one or two that would at least feel possible."

"You know, that's how it goes. Sometimes, the right house is there waiting, and everybody goes home happy. Other times, it takes a little longer. Don't give up yet. There are still a lot of places we haven't seen yet."

"Well, I've got that interview in DC tomorrow afternoon, so we can pick up the day after tomorrow. I'm sorry to interrupt your plans like this."

"Don't worry about it. I'm looking forward to spending the day with my folks. Hope it goes well for you."

"Me, too."

Thursday morning, Joe and Fanny dropped Brenda at the airline terminal. "Here you go."

"Thank you. Are you sure it's not too much trouble to pick me up tonight?"

"Fanny said, "Not at all. We have some shopping to do in town, then we're going to a movie after dinner."

Joe chimed in, "There's a great little Japanese restaurant here. At home, sushi is still considered bait."

Fanny elbowed him and wished Brenda luck on the interview.

"Thanks again. If the plane's on time, it'll be in at 8."

"Don't worry. We'll call the airline to check."

Brenda waved and entered the terminal.

When she left the office after her interview, Brenda congratulated herself that everything had gone so well. Before calling for the shuttle to the airport, she stopped off at the ladies room. She was about to leave the stall, but stopped when she heard the door open and recognized the voice of the secretary of the man who'd just interviewed her.

"Can you imagine that old woman thinking she'd fit in here?"

The second girl giggled. "I don't think Jack has ever hired anyone over 30, and she's long past that."

"Yeah, and when I called to check with her last employer for him, they said they wouldn't rehire her."

"Why does anybody like that even bother to apply to a top company like ours?"

The first girl laughed, and Brenda heard the door bang behind them. She felt sick, and after washing her hands, she opened the door to the hallway a crack to make sure there were no voices in the hall before she slipped out.

Joe met Brenda at the Charleston airport and opened the car door for her. "So how did it go?

"It was okay, but there were a lot of applicants. I don't have a very good feeling about it."

"Aw, I'm sorry. Well, don't let it get to you. There'll be others."

For the rest of the ride, Fanny talked about her day and all the shopping she'd gotten done. Brenda was grateful she didn't have to do more than murmur an occasional sound of agreement.

When they got back, Fanny asked, "Want anything to eat?" She looked poised to sprint to the kitchen.

"No, thanks. I had an early dinner before the plane, so I'm fine now."

"Join us for a glass of wine on the porch?"

"I'm kind of tired. Go ahead and enjoy your wine. I'm going to turn in. Janie's taking me out again tomorrow."

"Well, if you're sure..."

Brenda nodded. "See you in the morning."

After she undressed and slipped into a nightgown, Brenda opened her computer address book and scrolled through the pages. Business contacts, one after the other. Clients, fellow employees. "Former fellow employees," she said out loud.

Emptiness settled around her. Page after page of names, and no one to call. No one to share the day with. *I was always involved with my job. There wasn't time. When I had time off, my parents needed me.*

A little voice within argued with her. *No, it's your own fault. You wouldn't reach out to meet anyone half way. You could have made time for more than the business lunch with its three minutes of preliminary how-are-you, what's-happening. But it wasn't important enough.*

The emptiness grew cold and filled the room. Too awake for sleep, with no escape from the awareness of being alone, Brenda loaded Facebook and tried searching for names of women she knew from college. No one. *You never kept up with any of them. Why would they want to hear from you now anyway?*

She pulled an afghan around her shoulders, trying to displace the chill. The inner dialogue started again. *You could have had friends. All the women you met along the way. Interesting, involved, excited about life. But you were too busy being successful. No time for casual conversation. Too busy. And what did it buy you?*

"I was a success," she whispered.

Yeah, until you failed—miserably. The inner voice fell silent.

Brenda went to the window and drew back the curtains. The back of the house looked out on a dense patch of woods with a grassy area ringed with flowerbeds and a massive herb garden. But now, she saw only vague shapes in the darkness. She tugged the curtains closed again and turned out the light. Huddled under the covers, she closed her eyes to the darkness, tormented again by her thoughts.

Brenda woke with a startle to a bright room. She grabbed her phone and realized she'd forgotten to charge it the night before. She plugged it in and dialed Janie who answered on the first ring.

"I've been calling you for an hour. Are you okay?

"I'm sorry I worried you. I overslept."

"Not a problem. Do you want to forget about going out today?"

"No. I can be ready to go in—say, half an hour?"

"How about an hour? Give you a little more time to get some coffee and breakfast, and I can run an errand or two."

Brenda pulled the first outfit she saw out of the closet. Black sweater, grey pants and jacket. Looking at the dark circles under her eyes, she chose tinted glasses instead of trying to camouflage the rough night with makeup.

Downstairs, she perked up at the rich scent of fresh coffee.

"There you are. Breakfast is all ready for you."

"Fanny, you didn't have to go to extra work for me."

"Now, don't you be telling me what I need to do. Here's eggs and toast, and fruit's on the table. Job hunting is hard work," she said grinning, "But house hunting is harder."

"Harder than I expected."

"It's all going to work out. I have to be off to a library board meeting, so just pull the door behind you when you go."

Brenda poured another cup. She tasted the omelette—ham, mushrooms and onions—and smiled. When she finished it, she sat back with a satisfied sigh. *The really hard work was fighting with myself all night.* She shook her head and took her dishes to the kitchen. She looked out at the now-bright woods and flowerbeds. *Seemed so threatening last night.* She closed the door behind her and met Janie outside.

Janie looked at Brenda when she got into the SUV. "Not your best day, hmm? How did the interview go?"

"Not as well as I'd hoped."

"It's a big change for you. Give yourself time to adjust. Are you sure you want to go out looking today?"

"Yeah. Let's do it." Her voice was anything but sure.

"We're going to go a different direction today. Prices are all good, quite affordable in fact. Some are on the county's power and water systems. Some are off-the-grid, and the first one's right here on the edge of town."

"What's it like?"

"Just one acre, so not a lot of land to look after. Two bedrooms, one bath, utility hookups. Let's see, directions say we turn here off the main road, first left and then a right into the first driveway."

"Looks tiny from the outside."

"It is small, about 800 square feet, I believe. It's been a weekend place for the owner. All the basics. Nothing fancy." Janie opened the door and stepped in and almost knocked Brenda over coming right back out.

Brenda only got as far as saying, "What..." when caught a foul stench. Gagging, she hurried back to the SUV and leaned against it to catch her breath. "What is that awful smell?"

Janie was already on the phone making arrangements for someone to clean up the place and air it out. "Just some dead mice. I'm so sorry. Are you okay?"

"I'm fine. But I am getting a little discouraged about finding a place here. Maybe this isn't such a good idea after all."

"Don't give up so soon. There's still a lot to see, even though we haven't had the best of luck yet. Come on, let's head to the next one. It's about 3 miles off the main road, at the end of a private lane."

Brenda straightened up on the drive, watching the changing scenery. "The countryside is so pretty. All these shades of green. In southern California, it's mostly palm tree green and brown in the city. The hills are the same green or brown according to the season, with an occasional flower box outside a store."

"Wait 'til you see the fall colors here. The hills blaze with red, yellow and orange. One of my favorite times to visit."

"You know, it does seem like there's something great about every season here. It might be nice to get the chance to find out more for myself."

Janie laughed and poked Brenda. "Now you're talking. You were so down this morning, I thought you were going to ask me to take you back to the airport."

"I might've done that if I had a place to go. It caught up with me last night that I'm living out of a suitcase. No family. No friends. No job." She swallowed hard. "At least I have some money in the bank to get me through, so I won't end up on the street."

"Brenda, you've got a few new friends already, and once you find yourself a house, you'll have a place to take root and find your center again."

"I hope so. I... Oh! Look at that view."

"Think you'd like waking up to it every day?"

"It's hard to believe I'm saying this, but yes, I think I could get used to it."

They fell silent driving along a graveled lane cut into the hill, slow curves winding upward. Brenda rolled down the window and breathed in the clean scent of earth and woods. She listened to the rustle of overhead branches in the breeze and caught glimpses of sunlight flashing on a small stream. Between the trees, she saw bits of a taupe-colored house at the crest of the hill.

"Is that the house?"

"Yes, this is a private road, and it's the only house on it. The property is 98 acres, wooded, except for the house and garden areas."

At the next curve in the road, Brenda saw a large cabin perched on the hillside in front of a stand of trees. She leaned forward, eager for a better look. "Tell me about this one."

Janie parked in front of the garage and read from her notes. "Two bedrooms downstairs and a loft, one bath, 1,100 square feet, passive solar, wood heat, hardwood floors. 24 x 36 garage/workshop with concrete floor, portable generator included."

Brenda hurried up the path, turning on the porch to take in the woodland panorama in front of her. "Look at the view. It's wonderful. I can't wait to see the inside."

"Then let's get to it." Janie pushed open the door for Brenda to enter first.

She stepped through into a cozy living room, empty now, but with a fireplace that made it easy to see where comfortable chairs for curling up in needed to be. A bookcase climbed one wall, and the expansive windows looked down on terraced gardens and trees on the hillside.

"The detail sheet says this side of the house faces south, so it warms the rooms in the winter, and the roof overhang shades and cools them in the summer."

"What kind of trees are those?"

"Let's see what's listed." She flipped through the pages of the listing. "Twelve apple trees. There are four garden areas, blackberry and blueberry bushes, and a stream."

Brenda walked into the kitchen, opening the doors on the big cast iron wood stove. She closed her eyes and was engulfed by childhood memories of apple pie baking on a fall day, the warmth, the spicy scent, her mother in an old-fashioned bib apron. She moved down a short hall to a bedroom.

"Nice size, but not too big."

Brenda nodded at Janie. "Not sure how I'd furnish it." But even as she spoke, she saw a sturdy four-poster cherry bed with a simple headboard with her parents' cedar chest under the window and a wingback chair next to the fireplace that shared a chimney with the one in the living room. She opened a door and called over to Janie, "Look at this. What an odd toilet."

"Oh, that's a composting toilet. Uses no water, and it has a solar panel for the fan. It's a very efficient system with no odor and very little residue. A lot of people are using them off grid."

"Is this house completely off-the-grid then?"

"Yes, but it's got plenty of capability for the essentials. It can run a small refrigerator and some lights and charge your laptop and cell phone, and there's battery backup for cloudy days and at night. There's a laundromat in town, but you could have a homemade washing machine built to be powered by the windmill if you want. I've seen a few around. "

"Windmill?"

"Yes, it runs the water pump from the well to reduce the demand on the solar power."

"I don't know. All this is a little overwhelming. I can't imagine what I need to ask about running a place like this."

"I know someone who can help you with that. Why don't we go have lunch in town, walk around a bit, and then come back again later today? Unless I'm quite mistaken, I think you're almost hooked on the idea of living here."

"I do like the house, but I'm not ready to commit to buying it yet. I'd like to see a little more of the town first."

Brenda was silent on the ride through the town, listening to Janie rattling off historical notes and family stories about the places they passed. Janie whipped into a parking space on Main Street. "This is a place you wouldn't find in L.A. Come on. I want you to meet the owner." She was halfway into the store before Brenda closed the car door.

"Well, hello, Miss Janie. Haven't seen you in a while."

"Well, hey, Mr. Barker. How you been?"

"Finer 'n frog hair. Been keeping yourself busy?"

"Oh yes, but this week I'm having some fun while I'm working. This is my new friend and client, Brenda Maxwell. Brenda, Mr. Barker's general store is where you'd come for just about anything you'd need to keep your place running."

"Nice to meet you, Mr. Barker."

"Store's been in my family for four generations. If you don't know what you need, I'll help you figure it out. Just ask. Not much I don't know about when it comes to keeping a house in order."

Brenda took in the floor to ceiling shelves, craning her neck to see down the well-lit row. She ran her fingers along a wall of plastic drawers, each with a different size or shape of screw, bolt or nail glued to the front. "This is a wonderful store. So many kinds of things." Her gaze traveled along the wall, taking in the signs over each row.

"We got yer supplies for home repairs, plumbing, garden, canning, every kitchen gadget made, I think. All kinds of appliances that you're not gonna find in the big box stores, especially for off-the-grid living. If we don't have it, you probably don't need it." He laughed, enjoying his own comment. "So whose place've you bought?"

"I haven't bought one yet, but..."

"She's looking at George Johnston's place."

"Poor George. Bless his soul. No sooner got it all finished than he passed on. Worked on it weekends and vacations for years. That's a nice property, young lady. My son-in-law Joshua Lee Anderson put in them gardens for George and took care of 'em and did the mowing, and George gave him a section to grow his own vegetables 'cause Josh's own land's all wooded. Not enough sun for a good garden. When his trees is big enough to log in a couple more years, he'll clear a proper space for growin' his vegetables."

"Do you think he'd be interested in the same arrangement if I do buy the house?"

"I'm sure he'd be right happy."

"Well, that would let me concentrate on inside the house. There's a lot I'd need to learn about. I've had a fireplace, but I've never cooked on a wood stove for one thing."

Mr. Barker grinned. "George ordered his stove through me. It's modern, but looks like a good old one—best of both worlds. Couple of burnt casseroles, and you'll figure when to take things out. The rest is pretty basic. You'd be surprised how easy it is to keep the temperature right. Lots of articles online about it, and we're always here if you have a question."

"Thank you. I appreciate that."

Janie stepped forward and hugged Mr. Barker. "Now I'd better get this woman some lunch before her stomach thinks her throat's been cut."

He laughed and patted her back. "Always good to see you, Janie. And you come back real soon, Miss Brenda."

A flurry of requests to pass greetings on to various members of Janie's and Mr. Barker's families followed. Brenda felt foreign to the rapid-fire exchange. So many connections between these two people, and she had none to anyone. Could she ever feel comfortable here? Janie interrupted Brenda's thoughts, bustling her out the door and down the street to the local café.

"Today's specials are on the chalkboard. Restroom's around the corner. Mind if I pop over and say hi to a few folks?"

"Of course not. Go ahead and take your time. I've got a lot to think about."

Janie smiled and patted Brenda's shoulder before going to the other end of the restaurant where she was engulfed by hugs from a group of townsfolk.

Brenda hurried to the washroom, grateful for an escape from yet another reminder of her aloneness. *What does it matter anyway? I'm going to get another job and settle down somewhere else. This is only for a get-away place or an investment if it's too far from where I find work.* She stared at herself in the mirror. *And what if there is nothing else?*

The door handle rattled. "Be right out," she called while she washed her hands and tried to arrange a more relaxed expression.

By the time she finished lunch, Brenda was in a much better mood. "I can't believe how friendly everyone is. In the past half hour, five people introduced themselves, welcomed me to town and invited me to lunch or dinner and to services at three different churches—and I haven't even decided to buy a house here yet."

Janie laughed, nodding her head. "That's how it is around here. Folks are scattered over a pretty wide area, but they're all part of the same community. If you're isolated, it's by your choice, not for lack of opportunities to get to know your neighbors. Townsfolk are a little easier to get acquainted with at first, because a lot of them came from the city themselves and know what it's like to be starting over in a new place. But once folks in the country see you've got a mite more sense than most city folk and that you aren't intending to try to change everything to city ways, you'll do fine with them too."

"It's a bit bewildering after living in L.A. for so long. What a difference."

"So does that mean you'd like living here?"

Brenda started to answer and stopped to considered the question. "I don't know. Maybe."

"Just think about it. You could do worse than settle in here—at least for a while." She slid to the edge of the booth and stood up. "Want to go back and look at the Johnston place again after I get some gas?"

"Okay, go ahead while I finish my coffee. I'll take care of the check."

Janie smiled and nodded. "Okay, thanks. See you over there."

Brenda watched her cross the street through the window and leaned back, coffee untouched. *What if I do get this place. Could I really fit in here?* She left a tip at the edge of her plate and got up to pay the check.

Leaving the restaurant, Brenda looked at the block of two-story shops. Some had ornate facades from the 1890's, some plain brick from ten or twenty years ago. Well-kept, inviting. She turned to look in the window next door to the diner. A patchwork quilt caught her eye. A simple repeating pattern, but something about it appealed to Brenda. People passing by smiled and nodded to her or said hello, unlike L.A. where avoiding eye contact on the street is an art form. She spotted Janie near the garage office at the corner and headed over. Crossing the garage lot, Brenda looked at the used cars, pickups and boats for sale there. She stopped short in front of a vintage Ford F-150 pickup with a hand-lettered For Sale sign. Powder blue and white, it didn't seem to have a scratch or dent anywhere. She startled at a man's voice.

"1979 with 4-wheel drive. Good for rough roads and winter in these here parts. Nice one, idn't she?"

"Beautiful. It's in amazing condition."

"Looking for a truck?"

"Maybe. I hadn't really thought about what I want to get yet." Her smile got broader the more she looked over the truck. "Is it yours?"

"Name's Robert Jamieson, but folks call me RJ," pointing to the name embroidered on his coveralls. "I own the garage here, inherited it from my daddy. You the lady staying at Fanny and Joe's?"

"Yes, I'm Brenda Maxwell." She offered her hand.

RJ pumped it up and down with a sturdy grip. "Nice to meetcha. I'm handling selling the truck for Aunt Gracie. Sweet old lady's in the nursing home. Truck's been a-sittin' in her barn the past 20 years or so, and she didn't get round much before that neither, so the truck's not got much in the way of miles. Want to take her for a spin?"

"I think I do." She let Janie know where she was going and climbed up into the cab with RJ riding shotgun.

Pulling back into the lot after driving through the village, Brenda said, "It really holds the road on turns, and it's fun sitting up so high." She climbed down and walked around the truck, appreciating its solid construction. RJ raised the hood for her, and she saw new hoses and wires, and no sign of oil leaks on the ground underneath. "Looks good. Drives good too. I like it, but I haven't decided on whether I'm buying a place here or not yet."

"Tell ya what. I'm gonna be up to my mama's over Memorial Day weekend, so I reckon I can hold onto it 'til then, give you a chance to see how the house stuff goes. If I get another offer next week, I'll let you know, but otherwise, you come see me with some cash when I get back, and the truck's yourn."

"How much cash would it take?"

After a few exchanges back and forth on the price, RJ said, "Deal?"

They shook hands. "Deal."

The rest of the afternoon Brenda poked around the Johnston place. She peered into closets and looked at storage battery indicators. She looked through the garage and checked the insulation. Climbing up into the loft, she looked out past the gardens to a gentle wooded slope with a stream meandering down the hill.

On the way back, Janie asked, "Ready to make an offer?"

Brenda held her breath a long moment before she said, "Yes."

Within an hour, they worked out an offering price and inspection contingencies. The documents were signed and the offer faxed.

"We should hear back by tomorrow if they like it. I'm pretty sure they'll be happy. Then we'll need to get the inspector out there to make sure everything's as good as it looks. I don't expect any problems though. Mr. Barker's son-in-law Josh checks on the house for the lawyer handling the estate and keeps up the gardens and mows too."

"I've got a good feeling about it. I'd better set up a bank account."

A week later, before leaving the local lawyer's office after settling on the house, Janie handed Brenda a small package and an envelope. "For your new home."

Brenda grinned and opened the envelope first. It was a gift certificate to the local shop where she had seen the quilt she liked so much. Tearing into the package like a little kid at Christmas, she found a small box with a sterling silver keychain with the keys to the house already on it. After a flurry of thanks and hugs, Brenda set off down the street.

It wasn't long before the Ford's keys were on the keychain, and Brenda was driving up to her new home.

Chapter 7

Fanny bustled into the dining room carrying a platter of waffles that gave an enticing scent of vanilla when she set it on the table. She went back to the kitchen for bowls of fresh mixed berries and just-whipped cream to complete the breakfast array. Satisfied with the arrangement, she sat down across from Brenda, handed her a plate and took one for herself.

"So when does your stuff arrive?"

"The pod will be here Friday, but I need to buy furniture for the whole house. I'll do it a little at a time as I find things."

"Sounds like fun to me, but you don't look like you're enjoying yourself. What's wrong?"

Brenda laughed, but her eyes filled with tears. "I should be happy and excited and having fun getting into the house. But I feel like I ought to be out looking for work, except there's nothing around."

"Summer's never been a big hiring time, except for teen-age kids on vacation. Things'll pick up after Labor Day. They always do. So enjoy your new place until then."

"Maybe you're right."

"Of course I'm right. Relax and eat your breakfast before it gets cold. You're going to be cooking for yourself soon. You might as well enjoy having someone cook for you now."

"Uh oh, what have you heard about my cooking?" They both laughed, and Brenda wiped her eyes.

"That's better. I know a lot's happened the past few months."

"More than I was ready for." Brenda took a bite and savored the taste of the berries and cream. "These are so good."

"You'll be able to pick your own every morning in season. Mr. Johnston used to bring me some of the sweetest strawberries."

They continued eating in comfortable silence. When Brenda finished, she poured another cup of coffee. "Well, I'll be able to make pancakes easily enough, but I guess I'll have to wait to come into town for waffles. Doubt I can spend that amount of electricity on a waffle iron."

"There are non-electric cast iron waffle makers. Have to season them right, but it's no different from seasoning other cast iron pieces. If you haven't done it before, I can show you how. Cast iron's perfect for wood stoves."

"My mom used a cast iron skillet when I was a kid, but I never used one myself. I hadn't even thought about getting new pots and pans for the wood stove."

"Mr. Barker carries a full line. Want to go shopping for cookware and furniture? I've got the morning free."

"Yes, I'd like that." Brenda's face brightened, and she smiled like a child promised a trip to the ice cream parlor.

That afternoon, Brenda brought in the last box from the truck and hung a brass oil lamp on a bracket on the living room wall. "This lamp looks like it was made for this room."

Fanny settled into one of the deep blue wingback chairs. "Oh, this is comfortable, and I love the little pattern. It's just enough to keep it from being too formal."

"They're exactly what I imagined should go here. The area rugs are coming Monday, and the side tables and bed will be delivered Thursday. Now I just need a kitchen table and chairs."

Fanny got up and ran her hand along the built-in bookcase. "Look at the craftsmanship. It's beautiful."

"There's one in every room, and look at this built-in desk in the hall between the kitchen and bedroom. I'm putting my cookbooks and how-to books here." Brenda added several new gardening books to her growing collection on the shelf over the desk.

"You might find some things at a yard sale this weekend. Paper comes out tomorrow, so you could check the ads, unless you'd rather get everything new."

Brenda shook her head. "No, I have no problem with used furniture if it's what I want. The movers have my dishes and linens, so I think you'll be losing your star boarder next week. Josh stacked seasoned wood next to the stove for me yesterday so it'll be ready for me to try my first meal on the wood stove. He showed me how to check that the solar panels are charging the batteries too. Next time he's over, he'll show me how the windmill works."

Fanny raised her eyebrows. "I didn't know you had one. Thought they were big noisy things."

"This is a small old-fashioned one, only thirty feet high. It runs the pump to draw water from the well to the cistern, and the way it's situated, the garage blocks most of the sound from the house. It's not that loud anyway. Once the water tank's full, the mechanism lets the blades run free."

"Say, that reminds me. Are you coming to the community meeting a week from Tuesday on the big wind farm project up by the interstate? The Green Wind Company wants to tell us *all* about the benefits." She rolled her eyes. "I'm more interested in finding out about noise and the potential impact on birds and bats. It'll be in the library conference room at seven."

"Okay, I'll meet you there. I would like to know more about what they're planning."

When she arrived Tuesday for the wind farm meeting, Brenda picked up a handful of pamphlets and signed in at a folding table in front of the library's conference room. Filing in behind a group of townspeople, she stepped to the side, scanning the room for someone she recognized.

"Looking for someone in particular?"

She jumped at the deep voice behind her.

"Sheriff Jim Holt." he said, offering his hand.

Brenda looked up into hazel eyes that reminded her of flecks of sunlight on a grey-green sea, and she paused a moment before saying, "Hello. Brenda Maxwell."

"Welcome. Fanny told me you're our newest resident."

Before she could reply, three men bustled in, and one nodded to Brenda and said, "Excuse me, ma'am. Sheriff, we need to talk to you for a minute before the meeting."

The sheriff shrugged in apology and left with the trio.

Brenda let out a deep breath watching him exit.

Fanny passed him coming in and gave Brenda a quick hug. "Well, see something interesting, did we?"

"Yes, you caught me looking at those gorgeous eyes. Just something so unusual about them."

"The rest of him's pretty nice too if you ask me," Fanny said, nodding in approval.

"Fanny!"

"Hey, I'm married, not dead. No harm appreciating a fine-looking man. Let's sit down while we can still find a seat."

After the presentation, Fanny shook her head. "Hmmm. I'm not sure how much more I know now than when we came in. Want to stop at the diner for coffee before you go back up the mountain?"

"I could go for coffee, but I'm only three miles from town."

"You know I'm only kidding you, but how are you doing up there on your own?"

"Pretty good." Brenda reached for the door at the diner just as the sheriff rushed out, and she took a quick step back.

Fanny said, "You're in a hurry again, Jim. Station on fire?"

"Sorry, Fanny. Didn't mean to startle you ladies. Some fool got drunk and ran into the ditch. Car's totaled. He's not hurt, but I need to pick him up and get him a bed at County Jail for the night." He turned toward the parking lot.

"Well, we'll catch up another time then."

He called back to Fanny, "Yes'm. We will."

"Very conscientious man. Too bad he was in such a rush. It'd be nice for you to get to know him."

Brenda smiled and held the door open. "That's okay, plenty of time to do that." She looked around while they waited to be seated. Three people came over to greet Fanny and meet Brenda before being ushered to their booth. The restaurant was loud with the clatter of dishes and overlapping conversations. A large group sat at three tables pushed together. Five men arrived to join them and moved two more tables over to form a line across the middle of the room.

"They're from the village bowling league, so if you want a quiet spot on Tuesday night, this isn't it," Fanny said. "But once the food comes out, it quiets down."

Brenda stood back to let a waitress balancing a huge tray of filled plates go by.

As she passed, she said, "Be right with you, Fanny. It's a bit busy tonight."

"Not a problem."

"Fanny, how big is the town? I meant to look it up."

"Oh, I'd say it's getting close to 3,200 by now."

"I think that's about how many students there were at Santa Monica High School. Did you and Joe have a hard time adjusting going from the city to living here?"

"It wasn't that bad. We'd been coming down here long enough that it felt like our second home."

The waitress returned and led them to a booth, giving them menus and a big smile. "Here you go. Be right back."

"What do you think about what they said at the meeting?"

Fanny looked up from the menu. "Not much. They gave no solid answers for how often they'll have to use backup power generators when the wind's not blowing, or how much it'll cost. Too bad there's no way yet to save up power when the wind's blowing, and power's not needed."

"Well, if they could, that'd be a whole different story. If we had better batteries, we could use them with solar too."

The waitress hurried over to take their order. When she left, Fanny asked, "Did you see anything in the handouts about the effect of tax credits on the cost of electricity, and what happens when they run out?"

"Not from the meeting, but I have some things I found online." Brenda flipped through a folder of papers and pulled one out. "$12 billion in tax credits over the next 10 years will cut the cost by a little over 2 cents a kilowatt hour. A business and financial magazine said the transmission lines and backup generator costs aren't included in the savings, so wind power will end up costing more than using natural gas plants. I'm not sure how current this information is. I read something else recently about the tax credits being phased out over the next few years."

"Here you go, ladies." The waitress slid a platter with assorted appetizers onto the table. "If you need anything else, let me know."

After thanking her, the two women were quiet for a few minutes while they read through the wind power information sheets and nibbled fried onion rings and cheese sticks.

Brenda sighed, wiped her fingers and put her papers back into her folder. "You know, it's one thing to be riding through the California desert on I-10, with eight or ten lanes of traffic in what amounts to a canyon below the wind farms, and see the turbines spinning—or at least some of them. They look exotic against the sky, and you can't see much of anything from the highway there anyway."

Fanny nodded. "Yes, but stick a row of 350 or 400 foot towers here on top of a West Virginia mountainside, and it goes from exotic to ugly. Who wants to come here to look at hills and forests and get wind turbines instead? The way the economy here is going, tourism may be the only industry left."

"Well, we're not going to solve this tonight, and I need to get home. Josh is planting more vegetables tomorrow."

"What's he going to plant?"

"He's planned a whole assortment and started them indoors so they'll start bearing sooner. Some I've never eaten, like crowder peas, but he tells me they're really good cooked fresh, and you can dry them for the winter too. "

"They are good. I never had them before I moved down here either, but they're one of my favorites now."

They paid and walked out to the parking lot.

Fanny said, "Remind me to send you my local recipes. Might save you from some of the internet mistakes I tried."

"Thank you. I appreciate all you've done to help me."

"Oh heck, it's what others did for me when I moved here. I'm just paying back the favor. It's how we do things in these parts." Fanny hugged Brenda. "Now watch out for deer."

"I will. Talk to you soon."

Brenda headed back to the cabin, slowing down and smiling at three deer browsing at the side of her road who stopped eating to look up at her. At the top, she stood outside the house for a few minutes watching the stars. A shooting star flashed by, but she couldn't decide whether to wish on it for a job in a big city or wish that she didn't have to get one.

In the morning, Brenda's phone buzzed with a reminder: "Get your West Virginia driver's license." Getting the license was one of the last pieces of the disconnection from her California life. *Okay, I've put this off long enough. Let's see. Passport and social security card. Proof of residency? Hmm. No utility bills. No West Virginia tax records yet. No mortgage.* The thought caused a ripple of sadness. *I used to have one of those—and a place I called home. This isn't really home. It's a place where I'm staying until I find my life again.* Her inner voice kicked in. *Get over it!* She forced herself back to the list.

Ah! Homeowner insurance documents. What else can I use? No pay check stub, professional license. Okay! My temporary registration card for the truck.

When Brenda arrived at the DMV regional office just after 10, the line snaked around the room. She filled in the license application form while the line inched forward. At noon, two of the three clerks at the counter closed their windows and went to lunch with three people still ahead of Brenda. When her turn came, the clerk took her paperwork and looked over the answers. She stared at Brenda.

"You moved to Chestnut Springs from California?"

"Yes."

The young woman shook her head. "Wouldn't see me doing that. Okay, cover your left eye and read this chart."

After the eye test and a photo that was about the worst Brenda ever had taken, she left with her temporary license. She sat in the truck thinking about the clerk's reaction. *I don't really belong here. Even if I wanted to stay, would the people ever accept me?*

Chapter 8

Cooking on the cast iron wood stove was a lot easier than Brenda expected, but in the month since she moved in, she'd learned that nighttime breezes made summer cooking a lot more comfortable. Twice a week, she baked two or three small loaves of bread to have with her meals, and the smell of baking bread filled the kitchen now. She stirred the cut up onions, carrots and celery sautéing in the soup pot on the stove and added garlic to the fragrant combination. When the garlic had softened, she added water to the pot for the broth along with green beans, tomatoes and potatoes and tossed in a dried bay leaf before she turned to the counter where she kept bunches of fresh cut basil, thyme and parsley in an open jar with a little water. She hummed while separating the greens of the herbs from the stems. *Not enough parsley. I meant to pick more this afternoon. Well, there's plenty in the garden.* She slid her shears into her pocket and reached for a wicker basket from the top of a cabinet before she took down one of the kerosene lanterns hanging on the wall.

Moonlight lit up the open spaces beyond, but the house cast a deep shadow on the garden. Brenda located the parsley and set the lantern down on the path. Moving a few steps in, she bent over to clip a handful of parsley and walked a few steps further to get some more thyme for tomorrow's chicken dinner. Just as she laid it in the basket and stood up, she heard a heavy shuffling noise from around the corner of the house. A black bear ambled into view. A cold chill ran down Brenda's back. She dropped the basket and hurried to pick her way back to the path and side-stepped her way to the lantern. Picking it up, her shaking hand made the light bounce, but she held the lantern up high, waved the other hand in the air and yelled at the bear. "Go away! Shoo! Get out of here!" She prayed that she had remembered the correct thing to do, because the bear just sat there looking at her. For another long minute, nothing happened, and she started to walk backwards to the door, a step at a time. The bear took a step forward, then stopped. Brenda screamed and stopped too, her mind and body frozen. And then the bear snorted and walked back around the corner of the house.

Brenda almost collapsed with relief, but she walked as fast as she could to the back door, looking over her shoulder the whole time. She slammed and bolted the porch door and hung up the lantern before she grabbed a heavy flashlight from a shelf to look out every window to see if the bear was still near. A second look all around convinced her the bear had taken off for the woods. She slumped into a chair in the living room and started to relax when she smelled something burning.

Running to the kitchen, Brenda opened the oven door to find her loaves of bread crusted with charcoal. She pulled the wastebasket over and threw the bread in and slammed the oven door shut. Her shoulders sagged when she realized she'd dropped the basket with the herbs on the path during the encounter with the bear. Halfway to tears, she put a heavy flashlight in her pocket and picked up a small frying pan and a heavy wooden spoon. On the porch, Brenda banged on the pan to make as much racket as she could before going outside. Her flashlight beam danced along the house, down the path and across the garden, but Brenda saw nothing of the bear. She ran to the basket and gathered the spilled herbs before retreating to the kitchen to rinse the parsley and finally get it into the soup.

Too late to start more bread now. Brenda mixed up a small batch of baking powder biscuits and put them up to bake, setting the mechanical timer before she made a pot of tea. Sitting at the table waiting for the tea to steep, the adrenaline from the bear encounter wore off, and Brenda started to shake. Tears welled up, and she gave in and let them come. Putting her head down on her arms on the table, she cried off the fear and the relief. At the same time, the knot of insecurity and loneliness from deep inside started to dissolve. When the timer went off, she took a deep shuddery breath and wiped her face with the dishtowel before grabbing a paper towel to blow her nose. The timer had stopped chattering by now, and the resulting quiet was a relief. She reached for potholders on a hook on the cabinet to take out the biscuits.

She broke off a bit of one and blew on it to cool it before she tasted it. *Just like Mom's.* She smiled, remembering all the times she'd made biscuits with her mother and the meals that followed. She stirred the fragrant soup and decided even if it needed to cook a little longer, she was hungry now. Filling a bowl, she sat at the table and ate. Each spoonful of soup, each bite of biscuit gave her an inner warmth and comfort she hadn't felt for a long time.

Finishing with a deep sigh of satisfaction, she set the Dutch oven on a trivet so that the soup would cook overnight at a slow simmer and added some more carrots and a handful of dried beans. She turned down the wick in the kerosene lantern and blew it out, taking the teapot and a mug with her to the bedroom.

The tinny clanging of the wind-up alarm woke Brenda. She yawned and went through her morning routine and stumbled to the kitchen, still only half-awake. Opening the Dutch oven, she stirred the rich soup and ladled some into a bowl and put up water for tea. She broke up a couple of the biscuits from the night before into the bowl and sat on the back porch to eat her breakfast where she could see the garden.

It looked like a well-fitted jigsaw puzzle of more shades of green than she could count. One color and shape merged into the next—lacy plumes from the carrots, dark spikes from the onions and garlic, round heads of cabbage with huge outer leaves. Summer squash and cucumber vines climbed up on a net trellis. The cherry tomatoes were turning yellow and pink, and the larger tomato plants filled their supporting cages, their green fruit still forming. Rows of beans and field peas sparkled with the white and yellow accents from their flowers. Red-edged beet greens stood out in front of the towering okra stems set along the north side so they wouldn't shade the next rows. *This is really all mine.*

The wonder of it carried through as she washed up the dishes from this morning and last night and carried the vegetable trimmings from the soup ingredients out to the compost bin. She stopped for her shears and a basket before she wandered through the rows, pulling a weed here and there and checking that the drip irrigation lines were working. She gathered more herbs and a few beets, carrots and green onions before going back in.

After filling a mason jar with soup for Fanny, Brenda put the rest in the refrigerator. She washed off the beets and carrots and set them to dry off on the drain board while she changed to go to town. She called Fanny and looked out the window while waiting for her to answer.

"Hi, Fanny. Did I take you away from something?"

"Not at all, I was just having a cup of coffee on the porch, watching people walk by."

"Still up for lunch?"

"Come on down whenever you're ready."

"I'm on my way." Brenda smiled and went to the kitchen and put the mason jar of soup in a round basket and piled onions, beets and carrots around it before she wrapped up an assortment of herbs in foil and placed them on top. A few minutes later, Brenda pulled up in front of Fanny's house.

The women hugged in greeting.

"Well, that didn't take long. How are you?"

"Good. These are for you."

"Thank you. The vegetables look terrific. Joe will enjoy the soup too. Come in with me while I put them in the kitchen. Are you enjoying your house?"

"I never imagined it would make me so happy to grow my own food." Laughing, she followed Fanny into the house. "But at lunch, I have to tell you about the bear I met last night."

Chapter 9

After the waitress refilled their iced tea and cleared the lunch plates, Fanny said, "You are going to be more careful about going out at night?"

"Definitely. I'll do my herb picking in the daytime from now on. I have to see if there's a way to make Mr. Bear feel a little less comfortable about visiting my garden though. He could eat up quite a bit if he had a mind to."

"That's something I haven't had to cope with here in town. Maybe the sheriff could give you some ideas about that. That would be a good reason to chat with him. I'm sure he'd be glad to. He asks me how you're getting along every time I run into him."

Brenda shook her head at Fanny's grin. "I'm not interested in the sheriff."

She laughed at Brenda's sudden blush. "Now did I say anything like that? Although you could do worse."

"There's no room in my life to be thinking about a man now. Just too much else I have to work out."

"Like what?"

"Like where I'm going to find a job or what I'm going to do with the rest of my life."

"Still no leads on jobs?"

"Worse. Besides nothing new in the wind, I've gotten back rejection letters on every résumé I've sent. That should worry me, but I felt relieved that the last few places weren't interested."

"So if they weren't what you wanted, you must have some idea of what you do want?"

Brenda took a deep breath and sat lost in thought, staring out the window.

"You okay?"

Brenda blinked and came back to the moment. "I'm sorry. I keep going around in circles in my head over this."

"So talk to me. What's got you so wound up?"

"I don't know if I'm just avoiding what I should be doing, or if I really should take off in a different direction."

"Such as?"

"Such as not going back to work somewhere else. Maybe I could just stay here, come up with some kind of a small business idea or take a part time job when one comes up in town, and not go back to city life at all."

"And what would the worst case be if you did that?"

"I might not have enough in my pension fund if I don't go back to work at a regular job. And if I changed my mind, it would be that much harder down the road."

"But since nobody's knocking at your door with a job now, is it such a big risk?"

Brenda sat back considering the idea, then shook her head. "No, I suppose it's not."

"You seem to like being here."

"I do, and I like the people I've met so far. Most have gone out of their way to be friendly. Although I did overhear one fellow in the diner who didn't seem thrilled to have another come-here in town."

"What makes you say that?"

His buddy told him, "Jest you wait, she be outta here after the first snow." And the first fellow said, "Well, gonna be an early winter, idn't it?" And they both had a good laugh over it."

Fanny laughed now. "Don't worry about what they said. Some people from the city get here and want to change everything. But you're not one of them."

"I have no reason to change anything. I love waking up and looking out at the hills and trees, and going out and tending the gardens. I don't mind cooking on the wood stove. In fact, I enjoy it, although I think I'll enjoy it more in the winter."

"Yes, that heat will be welcome then." Fanny thought for a minute. "How about now? Do you have a grill for cooking outside so you don't heat up the house cooking?"

"No, and you know what, it never occurred to me to get one. Maybe I'll stop at Mr. Barker's before I head home today."

"I think you've made up your mind already about what you want. Try saying it out loud a few times and see how it feels."

"I don't know. It feels strange to think about deciding to change my whole lifestyle—and just do it. Am I just avoiding dealing with the job situation and fooling myself about staying here? I think I need to give it some time and see how it goes."

Chapter 10

The weather radio woke Brenda while it was still dark. Groping for it on the nightstand, she turned up the volume. "The National Weather Service has issued a severe thunderstorm warning...." A distant rumble of thunder punctuated the announcement's listing of all the nearby counties. "Meteorologists are tracking a severe thunderstorm capable of producing half-dollar-size hail and extreme damaging winds in excess of 100 miles per hour. For your protection, move to an interior room on the lowest floor of your home or business. This storm has the potential to cause serious injury and significant damage to property."

Her heart started pounding, and Brenda jumped out of bed and dressed as fast as she could. She shoved her phone into a pants pocket and grabbed her computer and hurried to the built-in desk in the hallway between the kitchen and bedrooms. The laptop showed the storm was expected to reach her area in twenty minutes. She watched the growing red and orange areas of intense activity on the weather radar image. The winds outside already sounded louder than the 35 or

40 miles an hour of Santa Ana winds that Brenda knew from when they came in from the desert to Los Angeles. *But the Santa Anas never brought hail.* She shivered and turned off the computer, wondering how much damage this storm could do to her house.

As if her fears became reality, she heard pinging noises on the roof that turned into louder thumps. *Hailstones make that kind of racket?* Brenda found her anxiety rising with the shriek of the wind and ear-pounding thunder punctuated with crashing noises of other things hitting the house.

After minutes that seemed more like hours, the sounds declined, turning into an ordinary thunderstorm with frequent thunderclaps and lightning before moving away. Brenda took a deep breath and went to the windows at the front of the house, but saw only darkness and sheets of the continuing downpour. She kicked off her shoes and climbed back into bed to wait for daylight, but fell asleep.

When Brenda woke, she ran to the window. Her orchard trees had lost a lot of leaves, but only a few branches. She gasped at a strip through the woods on the hillside by the stream that looked like a giant had run a lawnmower over the trees and left them flattened, snapped off at the base or roots pulled up out of the ground, all pointing in the direction the wind had gone.

She stopped to put on socks and shoes again and shoved her phone in her pocket before going outside to check the house. Melting golf-ball-sized chunks of ice were strewn everywhere. Somehow, none of her windows had broken, and the roof looked okay from the ground.

I have to ask Josh to go up and check it out. Josh. Was his family okay? What happened in town? Fanny and Joe?

Brenda dialed Fanny first and waited for the phone to ring, but she only got a series of clicks and pops before the call ended. Josh's number returned a recording saying all circuits were busy and try again later.

Trying to push aside her concern, she walked around to the back of the house and turned her attention to the gardens. One look and she burst into tears. Part of the garden looked more like a garbage dump than yesterday's neat rows of flourishing vegetables. Plants still stood here and there amid piles of broken green debris. The sight of the windmill still intact and turning gave her a lift. *Better go look up what to do with what's left of the plants.*

She went inside and poured a glass of sweet tea before going to her little library of garden and homesteading books. *Seven months ago, tomatoes in pots on my balcony were the only vegetables I'd ever grown. Now, I'm trying to save a whole summer's supply.* She went through half a dozen books looking for information about how to deal with hail damage before sitting back and reading through the two that discussed it. *I'm not sure I'm up to this.*

Shaking off the doubts, she went out through the workshop door and put an assortment of hand tools for pruning and trimming in a bucket and gathered gardening gloves and a few empty 5-gallon buckets to add to her collection.

Wheeling it all outside, she looked down the rows at the extent of the damage. *Should I start with the least damage or the most? Maybe I can save more from the part with less.* That decision made, she set the buckets on the ground and put on her gloves. Tossing broken stems and torn leaves into the wheelbarrow, row by row, she left the small zucchini that just had nicks and scrapes. The books said they'd finish growing, even if they weren't beautiful. Once the damaged outer leaves of the cabbages were off, some of the plants didn't look too bad, but others probably wouldn't make it. The eggplants were a total loss, leaves shredded and stems snapped off at the base.

She cut back the herbs, but saved the trimmings to check what could be dried and used. Green tomatoes on the ground went in one bucket, ripe ones in another. Squashed ones to the compost bin. The cucumber vines seemed to have escaped serious injury once the netting was tied up to the garden stakes again, and the beans under them looked fine. The far end was another story, and Brenda made trip after trip to haul away the torn and crushed mess.

Brenda worked until mid-afternoon before she turned to go back in. The phone rang just as she reached the workshop door.

It was Janie. "Are you okay? How bad was it for you?"

"I'm okay and so's the house, I think. Looks like it just tore out a piece of the woods and wrecked half the garden. How's your family?"

"Oh, Gram's fit to be tied. She lost some of her chickens when the coop blew over, but the house is fine. My aunt's okay, and she said Fanny and Joe are too."

"That's a relief. I was worried about them."

"They'll be glad to know you got through it okay. Well, I have a couple more calls to make. Are you still okay with staying on there?"

"I suppose. Storms happen everywhere. At least you don't have earthquakes here, but wow, what a wake-up call."

Janie chuckled. "It sure was. You take it easy. I'll catch up with you when I'm in town next month."

Brenda went back inside and built up the fire in the stove before she set the griddle on the burner and mixed up a batch of pancake batter. While it heated, she turned on the radio, but got nothing but crackly noises and broken bits of music. She had better luck with the laptop and learned that while many areas had property damage, there had been no deaths from all of last night's storms. She logged off and turned to make her breakfast just as a raucous noise came from the bottom of her driveway. *Josh on his ATV.* She pushed the griddle back from the heat and went outside to meet him.

"Hey, Miss Brenda. How ya doin'?"

"Pretty good. Is your family okay? I couldn't call out, but Janie got through and let me know about her folks and Fanny and Joe. I couldn't pull in the local radio station this morning to check what happened in town, and the internet news doesn't cover local events."

"Yeah, the station antenna got hit by lightning, so it'll be a day or two before they get back on the air. But it looks like we got off easy this time."

"I looked at the gardens, and most of the hail missed yours. There's some wind damage, but it's not too bad. I cleaned up a lot of mine. I'm guessing more than half should survive." She pointed from the garden to the woods. "That's the only big damage I've seen here."

"It could have been a lot worse, that's for sure. I don't see any roof damage from here, but I'll go up and check the roof and solar panels." He dragged out the extension ladder from the workshop and scrambled up to the roof. A few minutes later, he was back down and put the ladder away. "It all looks fine. Mr. J. put in the best stuff. These panels have a film over the collectors. Makes them a lot more resistant to hail, and in the winter, you just use the big soft rake and squeegee to get the snow off."

"So none of them were torn loose?"

"No. You'd know if they were. They're bolted right into the roof beams. Only way they'll go somewhere is if you lose your roof."

"I'm glad that didn't happen. Thank you for coming over to check. I feel a lot better now that I know nothing's damaged. Say, I was just making some pancakes. Join me?"

"Thanks, but I'll take a rain check. Still have a few folks to check on. Is it okay with you if I bring someone over to check if it's worth trying to salvage any of the downed trees in the woods for pulp or lumber?"

"Thanks, I hadn't thought about that. Sure, that's fine. Do what you think is best."

"Well, it won't bring in much, but it'll open up the space so you can decide later if you want to replant or just let it regrow on its own." He started toward the ATV and called back, "Oh, you weren't planning to go anywhere today, were you?"

"No, why?"

"You've got some trees down across your road. My cousin Arthur'll be by with a few of the guys from the fire and rescue squad. They'll bring chainsaws and a tractor to clear the trees off the road for you. I hope you don't mind that we put you on our list of folks living alone that we check on after a storm. It's something we do here."

"Mind? No, I'm grateful for the help. I'm still learning about the place. I have no idea yet about what to do in situations like this."

"If some of those old oaks come down or split in an ice storm or big wind, it'll be more than we can handle. You'll have to call the tree service guy. He's got a big crane, and his prices are good. I'll bring you his card next time I'm over. Smaller stuff though, we can take care of for you."

"Josh, thank you so much. Can I offer you a little something for gas?"

"Nah. I'll just pretend you didn't say that. This is something neighbors do for each other." He grinned at her. "Tell you what you can do for me. You could make some of those chocolate chip cookies like you had the other day."

"They'll be waiting for you."

"Okay, I gotta go. When you hear the chainsaws down the hill stop, you'll know the road's open again." He jumped on the ATV and waved as he rode off.

She watched him zoom down the hill and into the woods before she went back in and started heating the griddle again. Eating her pancakes with strawberry jam, she tried to remember if her neighbors in L.A. had ever stopped by to check on her and couldn't think of a time any of them stopped by, even once.

By mid-afternoon, Brenda heard the chainsaws buzzing like giant bees. When the sounds lessened, she picked up two jugs and the basket of muffins she'd made after Josh left. She drove halfway down the hill and walked the rest of the way to where a group of six men were working. As she watched, the one on the tractor pulled the last downed tree off into the woods and parked the tractor on the side of the road. A couple of the men lit up cigarettes.

In the quiet after the engine stopped, she called out, "Hi, guys. Thank you so much!"

"No problem, ma'am." A burly man with a wild red beard down to his chest stepped forward, pulled off his gloves and shook her hand, introducing himself and the others. "Glad to help out."

A young man stepped forward. "Hi, I'm Josh's cousin Arthur. Sorry to be meeting you like this. Miss Brenda."

"I really appreciate your help. I brought down some muffins, sweet tea and water."

"Thanks. A cold drink sounds right good about now."

A chorus of thanks echoed from the group. One of the guys dressed in camo with a hunter's cap grinned and reached for another muffin. "You're a good cook."

"Thanks. My mom started me cooking when I was three, but I'm rusty now."

"Couldn't prove it by me. Well, we need to move on to the farm down the road."

Brenda thanked them again and headed back up to the house. Once she'd dropped off the basket and jugs in the kitchen, she picked up her pruners and the long pole with the pruning hook and blade and went out toward the orchards. She trimmed broken branches so they could heal over and stacked the detached limbs off to the side to be cut up for kindling for fires this winter. When she finished, she looked at the pile and shook her head. "Guess I'd better plan on getting those chainsaw lessons sooner than later."

The next day, down at the bottom row of fruit trees, Brenda looked over to the woods at trees turned into giant pick-up sticks. She shivered at the strength of the winds that could break grown trees off that way and breathed a little prayer of thankfulness that the house had been spared. The sound of a truck coming up her road caught her attention, and she walked back and recognized the county emblem on the big pickup's door. *Sheriff Jim Holt.*

He climbed down from the truck and stretched. "Hey. How's it going?"

"Fine. Cleaning up a bit. Guess you've been busy today."

"It's been a long day. The Fire and Rescue Squad boys let me know you were okay, or I'd have been by sooner."

"Have time for some coffee or iced tea?"

"Coffee would be great. If the power's not restored in town by the time I get back, it's going to be a long night ahead. I'll need to arrange for a delivery of ice and water for tomorrow. Emergency services is part of my job."

"I didn't even think about the power being out in town. That's one advantage of me living up here with my own. Come on in. Have a seat while I put up a pot of coffee."

Jim followed her in and looked around. "Well, you fixed this up real nice. Last time I was up here, Mr. Johnston had a little folding bed on one side of the fireplace and his easy chair on the other. When he wasn't working on the house, he was out hunting or fishing. After a while, he couldn't go hunting any more. Didn't get out much at all toward the end."

"It's a shame he didn't get to enjoy it longer." Brenda cranked the coffee grinder, and the rich smell of the ground beans filled the air.

"He passed away this time last year. Heart finally gave out. Tell you the truth, I think once he finished building this place, he didn't have a reason to keep on going. Outlived his wife and kids, friends too. He was more than ready to go."

Brenda shook her head without saying anything and sighed before putting the coffee pot on to perk.

"Your folks still around?"

"No," she shook her head again and swiped at an unexpected tear that trickled down her cheek. "Dad died last November. He was the only one left of my family. It wasn't a very big one to begin with, and my mom died young."

"I'm sorry. Didn't mean to upset you."

"That's life. Can't do anything about it but keep going."

"If you don't mind my asking, will you be leaving after Labor Day?"

"I don't know yet. I'm still sending out résumés, although it's not looking great for getting another job right now." She put a small container of cream on the table and poured a mug of coffee for each of them. "I'm thinking about staying and not going back to the city."

His eyebrows rose over the mug he'd just raised to his lips. He gulped the mouthful of coffee down in surprise. "Really? Never thought you'd consider that."

Brenda laughed and set her own mug down. "Now what's so strange about me staying?"

"It's one thing to play at living off-grid for the summer, but it's hard work in the winter. Do you have any idea of what you'd be getting into?"

Brenda bit back a sharp response and waited a beat before saying anything. "I may have grown up in the city, but I was a Girl Scout and went tent camping a lot. I've worked hard all my life, and besides, living in this house is far from roughing it."

"I didn't mean to give offense. I'm just surprised. Most city folk can't do without all their fancy appliances."

"Yeah, I traded in some luxuries like a hairdryer, but I've got some state-of-the-art equipment here too. My computer takes the place of a TV and a stereo system. I get movies by mail and download music I want. Not much else I really need. I'm not a purist. I do my light wash in a little hand-operated machine, but I use the laundromat in town for sheets and towels. Grew up hanging clothes on a line outdoors, and there's something to be said for that fresh air smell when you bring them in. I love cooking on the wood stove, and I'm pretty sure it'll keep the kitchen nice and warm in the winter. Speaking of cooking, can you stay for a quick supper?"

He hesitated, and Brenda pretended not to notice while she refilled their mugs. As if on cue, his radio crackled with a call. "Excuse me a minute." He stepped into the living room to answer it, but was back after only a few words.

"Actually, if it's not too much trouble, I'd enjoy staying. That was one of my deputies. Power's back on, and everything's quiet for the moment."

"It's no trouble at all. Let me run out and pick some vegetables, and I'll be right back."

"I'll come with you. Did you lose much in the storm?"

"It could have been a lot worse. I think that half of the garden will do fine. For the rest, I'll have to wait and see."

Following her down to the garden, he watched her pull carrots and pick some kale. "Did you put all this in yourself?"

"Joshua Lee did. He set it all up, and now it's pretty easy to keep it going."

"Nice job."

She wasn't sure if he meant that for Josh or her, so she just smiled with a nod and went back inside and rinsed off the vegetables. Once the carrots were in the steamer and the kale ready to cook, she chopped and sautéed onions in a little butter in a cast iron frying pan before adding cut-up chicken from the night before with a pinch of salt, a bit of parsley, basil and a splash of wine. While that simmered, she started a second pan and sautéed the kale with garlic and a bit of cooked bacon.

A salad with tomatoes and onions and a balsamic vinegar dressing was next. Jim sat back watching. "It's nice to watch a woman who enjoys cooking. Did you entertain a lot back in the city?"

"Gosh no. I was always working. Maybe that's why I'm enjoying cooking so much now."

"You miss city life?"

She put a foil-wrapped packet in the oven before she turned to him. "Sometimes, I miss the bustle and excitement, but not for long. Would you like a glass of wine with dinner?"

"I would, but I can't. I'm off duty now, but still on call."

"Coffee or iced tea with dinner then?"

"Sweet tea if you have it, please."

She put glasses and a pitcher on the table and laid out bright orange placemats before she set the table. She opened the foil packet of cornbread which soon sat on a plate on the table with a knife and butter dish nearby. Two plates with chicken and vegetables followed, accompanied by the tomato salad. Brenda sat across from Jim. "Would you like to say grace?"

He took her hand and bowed his head. "Heavenly Father, thank You for bringing us safely through the storm and for this wonderful meal and the cook who made it." He gave her hand a quick squeeze and smiled before he released it.

Brenda felt her cheeks grow warm and hopped up to get the salt and pepper shakers, hoping Jim didn't notice her blush.

He did though and grinned at her while he buttered a piece of cornbread. He took a bite and stopped, his eyes wide. "Who taught you how to make this?"

"I found the recipe online. Is something wrong?"

"Wrong? No! This is just like Mom's. Forgive me, I just never expected a city girl to know how to make it that way."

They ate and talked about the weather and the town.

"Did you know George Johnston well?"

"I was just a kid when he started coming up for hunting and fishing weekends. He had a camper on his truck that he stayed in when he came up. He gave me my first fishing rod and showed me how to use it down at the river. I used to help him every summer on his vacations when he started planning this house. He cleared the land and put in the orchards and berry patches first. That way he always had something to take home. Then after he retired, he started in on the house. He loved this place."

"It's such a shame he didn't get more time in it. Everything is so well made. It's a pleasure living here." Brenda cleared the dishes and set out a bowl with almonds, dried figs and tangerines.

Jim said, "My mom always liked almonds."

"My mom's best friend was Italian, and she always had them, and Mom did too, especially for company meals where we'd sit and talk for hours."

"I've missed times like that. Haven't been many since my mom passed."

"Was that recent?"

"Been a couple of years now, but I still miss her. Used to go every Sunday for dinner."

They nibbled on almonds and fruit and shared stories of growing up. At sundown, Brenda lit a lantern and hung it on the living room wall and set another on the table before she served coffee and cookies. "You have other family?"

"I got married, but that ended after my second tour of duty. No kids, but I've got a brother who's married with a couple of kids, a sister with three, plus a few aunts, uncles and cousins. But it's not the same as it was when Mom was around."

"Have you always lived here?"

"Born here and traveled around the world in the military. Retired after 22 years, and I came back. But I wasn't sure I was going to stay. Things were different when I got back."

"Had the town changed so much?"

"It wasn't the town. It was more the people. The old folks had died off or gotten too frail to get around the way they used to. Guys I grew up with who hadn't died young had mostly gone off to bigger cities, some all the way across the country to get jobs. Didn't really feel like home any more, except Mom needed me around. I wasn't sure what I wanted to do anyway, so I stayed, and then the sheriff job came up three years ago. Last sheriff decided I'd make a good replacement." He shook his head and chuckled. "Seemed like the thing to do at the time. So here I am."

It was full dark when Jim said, "I'd better be getting back. Gotta be in early tomorrow." At the door, he turned to her. "I enjoyed the food and the company. Thank you."

"You'll have to come over again some time." Brenda said, looking up. Standing, he was a full head taller.

"Say, would you like to go to the fish fry at the American Legion a week from Saturday?"

"That sounds good. Sure."

"Pick you up at six?"

"Okay, I'll see you then."

"I'll look forward to it." His grin echoed his words.

Chapter 11

Brenda followed Jim across the large open room at the American Legion, crowded now with long folding tables and abuzz with people engaged in lively conversations. They moved along a row of serving tables and filled their plates with fried fish, French fries and coleslaw.

"There's a couple of seats over on the other side." Jim led the way, answering a flurry of hello and how-are-you's and set his plate at the empty seat across from Brenda's.

"Hey, guys, this is Brenda Maxwell. She just bought George Johnston's place." He turned to Brenda, "Lemonade okay?"

"Sure." She watched Jim work his way through the crowd and back with the drinks, stopping to answer greetings every few steps.

The petite brunette seated next to Brenda chuckled. "He's a popular guy, all right." Her husband, tall and slim with short blond hair, smiled and nodded, but didn't try to interrupt his wife who kept talking without a pause. "I'm Millie. This is my husband John. So what brings you to Chestnut Springs?"

Brenda launched into her upbeat explanation about being down-sized and taking a little vacation before getting back to serious job-hunting.

John saw through the story in a flash. "Don't feel bad. It's going around a lot these days. Company I worked for folded last year when half a dozen mines we supplied shut down."

Millie nodded. "Yeah, we had to do some adjusting, but we're okay. Folks in these parts are good at coping with trouble."

Brenda glanced up and was startled to see two women about her age glaring at her from across the room. She looked down at her plate and took a bite of fish.

John looked over his shoulder. "Uh oh. You did it now." He grinned at Brenda's confusion.

"Oh, stop teasing her. Brenda, Sallie Ann Miller and her sister Lucille went to school with Jim. Sallie was in the same grade, and Lucille's a year younger. They both had their eye on him, but he married someone else, so the girls went with their second choices—and they all ended up divorced. So when he came home from the service single again, they thought maybe one of them would get another chance, but he still wasn't interested in them or anyone else local."

He nodded. "Yeah, really must frost their butts to see you walk in with him tonight."

Jim's return with a pitcher of lemonade and a foil-topped bowl changed the subject. "Got some of my sister's mac and cheese. Pulled rank as big brother to get us our own supply."

"Good job, Jim." John thumped him on the back and reached for the dish.

After a meal accompanied by good-natured conversation, the four shared a sampling of the home-baked desserts. Jim finished his coffee and shook his head. "I hate to break up the party, but I need to be in early tomorrow."

On the way out, Brenda was relieved that Sallie Ann and Lucille had already left.

Back at Brenda's home, Jim walked with her up to the porch. "You found some nice old rockers." He settled into one, and Brenda in the next.

"Yeah, I got them at the consignment shop last week. I love the curve of the seat and the back. It's like they were made to fit here."

"It's a classic design. There's just something that feels right when you set yourself down in one of these. You can rock your troubles away, and let 'em go with the breeze."

"That's a nice way to put it." She rocked without speaking for a minute. "You know, I really enjoyed this evening."

"Not the fancy L.A. cuisine you're used to."

Brenda laughed and shook her head. "It definitely was not one of my usual frozen food aisle selections. It was real, and fresh, and tasted like home, and…" Sudden tears choked off her next word. She put her hand across her eyes, willing the tears to stop.

Jim reached over and laid his hand on her other arm. "I'm sorry. I-I didn't…"

Brenda interrupted him. "No, no, it's not you. It's been so long since I've been part of anything that felt like home and friends and family."

"No friends in the city?"

She shook her head. "I've always been too busy working so I could have enough money to help take care of my parents. I was lucky and had enough to have nice things for me too, but I never had time to just be a friend."

"No man in your life?"

"Once upon a time. After he left, it didn't seem worth the effort to start over."

Jim moved his hand down her arm to briefly squeeze her hand. They rocked, side by side, listening to the frogs and night bird songs.

"I never heard a bird with a song like that before. So unusual, almost like a flute."

"That's a hermit thrush. The males sing a lot in the morning and at night."

After a long pause, Brenda sighed and said, "I'm not sure what I should do. I'm afraid to give up trying to get my old life back, but staying means… I don't know what it means, how I would change, if I'd be happy."

"I won't pretend to know exactly what you're feeling. I went through something like that when I came back home from the Navy. But I was coming back home, so I knew what the life would be like. And I'd had enough time out in places around the world to know what I'd be giving up to do it. It's hard for folks who've never been in that place to understand. You know you can make a life for yourself either way, but it's a tough choice."

Brenda nodded. "Harder than I expected."

Jim stood up. "Guess I'd better be getting back, but you need to remember, you're not alone anymore. No matter what you decide, you've got friends here now, including me." He leaned over and gave her a quick kiss on the cheek and hurried out to his truck.

Brenda watched until his taillights disappeared around the bend in the road down to the highway, not sure what importance to attach to that peck on the cheek.

The following Monday, the crunch of gravel from a vehicle moving up the driveway caught Brenda's attention. Curious, she watched a white Blazer turn at the last curve and caught a glimpse of the Green Wind Company logo on its side door. *What in the world do they want?*

Two men got out. Brenda watched as the one with a briefcase spoke a single word, and the one with a clipboard nodded. Something about the set of his jaw put her on alert. But his face shifted, with just a hint of a smile.

Brenda felt a shiver of unease, but before opening the door, she used her own sales experience to project a pleasant neutrality in her greeting.

"Hello, gentlemen. What brings you out this way?"

"Good afternoon, Ms. Maxwell. We represent the Green Wind Company." He offered his business card saying, "I'm Jerry Jones, and this is my associate Tommy Ryan. May we take a few minutes of your time? We have something to discuss which you might find quite interesting."

She opened the door wider and gestured for them to enter, leading them to the dining room table.

After fifteen minutes of taking turns pitching the benefits of wind energy for the area and the country, the company reps got down to the point of their visit.

"The project plans are nearly complete. We have a few details to wrap up, and we'll be ready to move ahead with the next phase of construction. And this is what we're here to discuss."

Like an actor with a well-rehearsed script, the second man continued without missing a beat. "Yes, we would like to purchase a 160-foot strip of your property to use for a transmission line. If you look at this map, we've marked out the area we're interested in. There'll be a little extra traffic and some construction sounds while it's being built, but we'll resurface your driveway after it's done and repair any landscaping that's affected. We've added a figure as compensation for the inconvenience. He slid a small stack of papers cross the table. Here's the contract for the offer."

Brenda took the papers without speaking. Her mouth fell open at the number on the third line. "That's a lot of money."

"Green Wind Company wants to be a good neighbor and show their appreciation for your help with the project."

The first man offered Brenda a pen. "Just sign and date the last two pages of both copies. We'll handle all the details and have your check drawn."

After reading through the rest of the contract, Brenda picked up the map, looked at it and put it on top of the contract on the table. She shook her head and pushed the papers back. "No, I'm sorry. I'm not interested."

Jones sat back startled. "Don't you agree that it's a generous offer?"

"It's a very generous offer, but I'm not sure I want to sell my land to you."

"May I ask why?"

"I'm not convinced that wind power is a viable option for this part of the country for openers."

"If you come to one of our meetings in town, we go over the value of these installations to the country."

"I have been to one, and I've read all your material. You didn't convince me." She shook her head and ticked off points on her fingers. "The output is unpredictable. The highest production is at night when it's needed the least, and no one's solved the problem of how to store energy that's not immediately needed. You have to have traditional power plants running as backup for when the wind isn't producing power. So how much do we save in the long run?"

"Aren't you concerned about energy independence for our country?"

"I think I'm doing my part. In case you didn't notice, this is an off-the-grid property. I use solar for my household needs and a small windmill for my water."

"So you use wind power. Then you know its value. We're going to do the same thing, but on a larger scale."

"The scale is part of the problem. No one wants to wake up in a beautiful place like this and see transmission power lines instead of woods or a mountain. If the project goes bust, as so many have, we'll be left with massive high iron tower monuments to the failure instead of our mountain views." She pointed to the construction area marked on the map. "That's where one of the springs this area's named for becomes the stream that runs down the hillside on my land. Putting your transmission lines and towers there would destroy it."

"You haven't been here that long, and we've heard you may decide not to stay anyway, so why not take advantage of our offer?"

"That's interesting. I haven't made up my mind yet, so maybe your sources don't know as much as you think they do. And even if I don't stay, why would I want to see the beauty of this place destroyed?"

Jones shrugged. "Either way, a little nest egg couldn't hurt."

Brenda pushed back from the table. "Even if I considered it from a purely financial point, it's a bad deal. It would ruin the resale value of this place. But it's more than that. No, I'm sorry. I can't help you. Some things are worth more than money." She started toward the door and turned back toward the men.

A moment later, they followed. Their expressions showed this was not the result they usually got. Jones said, "I left the papers on the table. Take some time to think it over, and I'll check back with you."

Ryan clenched his jaw. "You know, we can find another way to run the lines, so you might as well get something out of it."

Brenda felt a touch of malice in his words, but nodded and opened the door. "Thank you. Good day, gentlemen."

When she left to go into town, she locked her doors, something she'd never bothered doing before.

A week later, Brenda checked her post office box for mail and found a yellow notice of a parcel that needed to be picked up at the desk. She handed it to the post mistress.

"Hi, Mrs. Barker. How's your husband?"

"He's fine, thanks. Here you go. I didn't want to fold it to squeeze it into the box."

"Thanks." Brenda started back to her truck and ripped open the thick white envelope. She flipped through the pages of the report it contained and looked up just in time to avoid walking into Fanny.

"Whoa, girl. What kind of story's got you so interested?"

"Not a story, at least I hope not. It's the water testing report on my well and on the spring up on the hill."

"What's it say?"

"They both have a good assortment of natural minerals, but nothing that shouldn't be there. No bacteria. No man-made chemicals."

"Why were you worried? There aren't any mines around here."

"I know, but I just wanted to be sure there wasn't anything that shouldn't be there."

"Well, I'm glad you have one less thing to worry about. Let me grab my mail, and then come on over for some tea. I have something to show you."

"What's that look for? What are you up to?"

"You'll see," Fanny called over her shoulder before the heavy door closed behind her. "I have one more quick stop to make, so if you get there before me, relax on the porch for a minute. I won't be long."

Brenda finished reading the report at Fanny's and slid it back into the envelope next to her on the old metal glider. With her eyes closed, the slight squeak of each move forward and back and the scent of roses in the air made her feel like she was moving back in time.

"Earth to Brenda. You look like you're a million miles away."

"Just relaxing and letting my thoughts wander." Brenda took one of the shopping bags from Fanny and followed her to the kitchen.

"Now, what is it you have to show me? You've got my curiosity up."

"Sit down and meet my foster baby, Fuzzy. Here, hold him while I get his food ready."

She pushed a kitten into Brenda's hands. The little ball of fur started to climb up her shirt, sniffing her hair and neckline. Brenda pulled him down and started petting him. "What a tiny kitten."

"He's eating wet and dry food now, but the poor little thing is still underweight. He was the runt of the litter."

"What happened to his mama?"

"The vet didn't know. Someone left half a dozen kittens in a box at his back door. The others were much bigger and wouldn't let him get to the food dishes, so he wanted this little guy to get some extra feeding and loving. Other than being small, the vet said he's healthy. You can bring him over. I've got his food ready now."

Brenda untangled him from his third attempt to climb up onto her shoulder and set him down next to the dish. "He's a sweetheart."

"He already uses the litter box and is even starting to use the scratching post."

The kitten finished his meal and started washing himself, then wandered off into the closet to his litter box. A minute later, he came back, stretched and rubbed against Brenda's leg. She reached down and picked him up. He snuggled against the crook of her arm. "Oh, he's purring!"

"I think somebody likes you. Maybe you should adopt him. He's ready for a home."

"I don't know. I've never had a pet."

"I can teach you the little bit you need to know to get started."

"Yeah, but what about when I go back to work? He'd be alone all the time."

"The truth is, cats sleep a lot. They'll race around a bit, eat, wash up and go back to sleep. You can get toys that will occupy him when you're not around."

"But what about taking care of him? Don't they need a lot of care?"

"If you start trimming his nails now, he may not like it, but he'll get used to it. You have to brush him, but most cats love it. Once a year, get him checked by the vet and get his rabies shot. Mostly, you play with him and enjoy having him around."

"I don't know."

"C'mon. I can't keep him because some of my guests don't like having animals around or are allergic. He needs someone to love him, and you can see what a lovebug he is. He'll repay you every day with snuggles and purrs."

"You're making it very hard to say no."

"Say you'll give it a try then. Keep him for a week, and if you really don't like having him around, bring him back, and I'll try to find someone to take him as a barn cat at a farm somewhere."

"A barn cat?"

"Farmers take in strays to keep rodents away from their livestock feed. The farm animals don't mind them. Some seem to enjoy having them around. The cats form their own little colony. Trouble is, being so little, this fellow might have a rough time with other cats. He probably wouldn't get a lot of personal attention, but at least he'd be alive."

"How can I say no?"

Fanny laughed. "You can't. So set him in his bed and drink your tea. Afterwards, we'll get his stuff packed up, and I'll give you the notes on his food. Another month, and he won't need the extra feedings." Fanny put a plate of cookies on the table with a grin. "Now I want the inside story on your date with Jim. The cashiers at the market have been buzzing about it all week."

Brenda slid out of bed, careful not to disturb the curled-up kitten sleeping next to her. After she'd brought him home from Fanny's last week, she worried the first few nights about rolling over on him or knocking him off the bed, but he'd taken to sleeping snuggled up at the small of her back and scooted out of the way if she moved too close, so she was at ease about sleeping next to him now.

She smiled at the ball of fur and went about her morning routine, pulling on jeans and a tee shirt. She frowned though, when she moved to the computer for the first of her dreaded checks for job listing updates. She logged in two or three times a day to try to catch new postings right after they appeared. *I can't keep hanging in limbo like this.* She connected to the internet through her mobile hot spot. *Yeah, but I'm not ready to give up on a job yet either.*

Her fingers flew across the keys, bookmark to bookmark, checking for changes. One new listing popped up. A contract administrator for a company in Huntsville, Alabama. *Sounds like the job my credit rating scuttled when I first started looking. Hope that's all squared away now.* Brenda hesitated, but went through the too-familiar ritual of filling out an online application and attaching a résumé before shutting down the computer and thinking about breakfast.

The novelty of using a wood stove had worn off as the summer temperatures rose, and Brenda had added a two-burner propane cooktop to the kitchen. She kept a small cast iron frying pan on one burner for frying up eggs or other quick meals and used the other for the teakettle. The little windmill in back kept the cistern filled with spring water, and a few up and down pumps on the old-fashioned handle at the kitchen sink filled the kettle.

A strike of a wooden match, and both burners flared blue and hot. Brenda took out a covered dish of diced onions and a left-over potato from the propane-powered refrigerator, the most recent kitchen upgrade. The kitchen filled with the scent and the sound of an old-fashioned breakfast. Brenda refilled the cat's water bowl, and he came running at the sound of the lid being pulled from a tiny can of salmon in gravy cat food. He started eating as soon as the dish touched the floor. In no time, two fried eggs and potatoes were ready for Brenda to enjoy while she caught up on the top news stories on her phone.

She still fired up the wood stove once a week to bake bread and make a soup at the same time, but a propane grill outdoors was perfect for her summer meals. *Let's see. Chicken with potatoes, sprinkled with fresh thyme and basil, wrapped in foil, that'll work.* Brenda pulled out a white paper-wrapped package of chicken from behind the egg basket in the refrigerator and set about making three foil packets for separate meals. She still couldn't adopt the local custom of keeping fresh eggs on the counter. Once when Josh was refilling her kitchen wood supply, he saw her putting eggs away and teased her about her city ways. She tried to deflect him by saying she didn't know when she'd be using them. He'd just grinned and said, "Sure thing, Miss Brenda."

She had to remind herself now and then that there weren't many secrets about everyday life in the country. The chicken farmer was Josh's uncle, so Josh probably knew exactly how often she bought eggs. *Even as polite as Josh is, he has to tell his family a little about how I'm doing on my own.* She washed up at the sink and put the foil packets in the refrigerator to cook later on the grill.

A loud mewing erupted from the bedroom. Brenda ran in, calling, "Fuzzy, where are you?" A plaintive yowl came from the top shelf in her closet. She pushed the sliding door all the way back and looked up as a frantic kitten cowered and looked down at her.

"Now how did you get up there, you silly animal." He put one paw forward, then pulled back and tried the other before Brenda reached up on tiptoe and pulled him down. He buried his face against her arm for a few seconds, then jumped down and ran to the hallway. "Don't know how a little fluffball can make the house feel like home," she said as she went after him to put him in her bathroom while she went out to weed the garden.

A pleasant breeze carried a hint of a sweet fragrance and a soft sighing from the trees beyond the clearing while Brenda pulled weeds and checked the drip irrigation lines. At noon, she wiped her face with the bottom of her tee shirt and fired up the propane grill. After getting the chicken and putting it up, she grabbed a basket from a cabinet on the porch and picked tomatoes and greens for a salad.

She rinsed off her salad fixings and drank a tall glass of cool spring water before she opened the bathroom door for the kitten. Fuzzy stretched and yawned and rubbed against Brenda's ankle. She picked him up and settled into the wingback chair in the bedroom, petting him. His whole orange and cream striped body vibrated with his purring. There was something so calming about touching his soft fur and feeling the contented rumbling.

The kitchen timer woke Brenda and the cat. Fuzzy jumped down to grab a few bites from his food dish and run off to explore his home while Brenda went out to retrieve the chicken from the grill. She left two of the packets to cool to be put away in the refrigerator and fixed a plate for her lunch.

Maybe I'll go into town for the mail and sign up for quilting classes now before a job comes up. After she ate, she took a quick shower and used a small battery-operated pump to refill the shower container to be warmed by the solar panel above for the next time and dressed for town in tan slacks and a colorful cotton top.

Chapter 12

In town, someone was coming out of the craft shop with an armful of purchases, and Brenda stepped forward to hold the door for her. Once inside, Brenda browsed through some of the new items and picked up a quilted placemat to put under the kitten's food and water dishes. She heard laughter and chatter from the back room where a group of women worked together, quilting on a big frame. Brenda continued browsing, planning to call over to Maggie, the shop owner, once she was done, but a shrill voice caught her attention.

"Yeah, Miz La-dee-dah Maxwell thinks she's so high and mighty with her designer clothes."

"Why's your nose out of joint, Sallie Ann? What'd that woman ever do to you?"

"Oh, Maggie," Sallie's sister Lucille piped up. "You know Sallie's still got a thing for our sheriff. She just can't abide the thought of some outsider getting close to him when he won't give her the time of day."

Brenda put the placemat back in the display basket and edged toward the door before anyone noticed she was there and realized she'd overheard them.

"The way she…"

Brenda pulled the door open hard, so the bell jangled, then pushed it shut to make it seem like she'd just entered. *Sallie Ann. The woman who was looking daggers at me at the American Legion dinner.*

Brenda went back and picked up the same placemat she'd chosen before as Maggie, a white-haired sprite of a woman a little over four feet tall, came out of the back room.

"Hi, Brenda. The loom you ordered is here, and I put together the selection of yarn and threads you asked for too. "

"Thank you. I'm looking forward to trying weaving. I'd like to get this too." She took her selection to the counter.

"Are you ready to sign up for weaving or quilting lessons? We have a lot of fun working together."

"No, not yet. I may have a job interview coming up."

"Well, you let me know whenever you're ready. And if you need help with the weaving, I can always make some time for a few private lessons too."

Brenda smiled and thanked her, pulling out cash for her purchases. A few more pleasantries and Brenda was out the door with Sallie Ann's hostile words still echoing in her mind.

As she stepped out of the shop, she bumped into one of the men from the Green Wind Company. He caught her as she stumbled.

"Thank you, Mr. …"

"Jones. Nice to see you again, Ms. Maxwell."

"Sorry, I didn't see you."

"Here, let me help you with those bundles." He took some of them from her and carried them to her truck at the curb. "I've been planning to get in touch with you to follow up on our conversation. Do you have a few minutes now? We could chat over a cup of coffee."

"I don't know what good it will do to…"

"We got off on the wrong foot last time. Give me a chance to sort things out with you."

Brenda hesitated.

"Come on, the coffee at the diner's not half bad, and it's right next door."

His grin reminded her of a cartoon wolf's. "Okay, I'll hear you out, but I don't expect to change my mind."

Mr. Jones immediately launched into a history of how many projects the company had brought to out-of-the-way places and how much they had benefited the communities. "You know the unemployment rate here is pretty high. We're providing a lot of jobs with the construction of this wind farm." He held the door for her and gestured for her to go in first.

Brenda slid into a booth and ordered coffee from the waitress who seemed to materialize at her side.

The Green Wind man leaned toward her. "Sure I can't talk you into a piece of pie. They make some of the best I've ever had."

Brenda shook her head.

The waitress beamed at him. "Our pies are all home-made. What kind do you want, Sugar?"

"Apple, warmed up with just a little vanilla ice cream on the side and coffee please."

"You got it. Be right back."

He turned his grin back to Brenda. "So why don't you believe in wind power?"

"After what, 20 years or more and billions in tax subsidies, wind power still only produces, what, five percent of the country's electricity? So how much is that really adding to the energy picture?"

"That will grow a lot in the next few years. It's good business to invest in clean energy. Fossil fuel use has to be reduced to save the planet." He pushed the ice cream against the pie and ate a forkful of each. "Sure you wouldn't like some pie?"

She shook her head. "But the cost in human terms, lost jobs, whole towns losing their economic base—it'd make more sense to find ways to clean up the use of fossil fuels. But how much is being invested in that?"

"That's just trying to hold onto the past. We need to move to the future, and wind power is the way to go." He nodded, taking another large bite of pie.

"I don't know how you can say that when the biggest drawback is the wind mostly blows at night when it's least needed. Seems like it's a great deal for the investors, but no one else."

Mr. Jones looked at his watch and beckoned to the waitress for the check. He took one last bite of pie. "As much as I'd enjoy continuing our conversation, I have to meet someone. Maybe we can pick up from here at another time."

Brenda let that pass without comment and stood up.

"I need to be going too. Thank you for the coffee." She hurried out the door while he was settling up with the waitress.

That evening, Brenda turned from stringing green beans to answer her phone and almost tripped over the kitten who had decided to stretch out next to her. "Fuzzy! Move over!" She gave him a little push with the side of her foot and looked at the caller ID.

"Hi, Fanny. What are you up to?"

"Checking in to see how it's going with you and the kitten."

Brenda pulled a bent straw from the locally-made broom and sat down dangling it over the kitten. "We're fine. He's already such a part of my life, I can hardly remember what it was like without him."

"Think you can leave him for a day and go rafting with us? I have a newlywed couple coming in tomorrow for a few days, and they'd like to go on a day trip Friday. The end of September and beginning of October dam releases on the weekends make for a great experience. And it won't be as cold now in September as it will be in a couple of weeks."

"We talked about it when I first got here, but I don't know. I'm not sure what I need to wear or how it works."

"Come on. It'll be fun. I'll send you a link to a website where they'll tell you all of that. They even have videos so you'll know what to expect. I need one more person so we can get a raft with just us and a guide. Say yes. You'll love it."

Brenda gave in and wrote down Fanny's directions on what to wear and where to look online to get a sense of what the trip would be like.

An hour later, with the kitchen fragrant with sautéed garlic, onions and herbs, she served herself green beans and mixed greens with strips of chicken cooked with a splash of soy sauce and wine. A pot of tea and a piece of cornbread with butter and a drizzle of honey completed her meal. Brenda shook her head. *Having my own garden. Cooking without a microwave. What a change from just a few months ago.* After eating, she picked up the kitten and let him lick a bit of butter from her finger. "Okay, Mr. Cat. You go play while I check for work." She put him down, and he settled down to groom himself before he jumped up and started racing from one room to the next.

She turned on the laptop and checked her email. A response to a job application was waiting. Her heart raced while she opened and read through the message and re-read the last line. *Are you available for a video conference interview on Skype Monday afternoon at 3?* She sat unmoving, hands poised over the keys. With a deep breath, she typed a reply and agreed to the time and provided her Skype contact information. An automated acknowledgment came through less than a minute later.

She sat back, thoughts tumbling over each other. *I've got an interview. What if I don't get the job? It's going on ten months looking now. And what if I do get it? Is that the life I want? But can I afford not to take it if they offer?* She shook away the circling thoughts. *This is pointless. I'm not going to find the answer tonight.*

To distract herself, Brenda turned to a series of videos online about whitewater rafting. She wasn't sure whether the whitewater experience would be fun or terrifying.

People do this every day and survive, and Fanny's been good to me since I got here. If nothing else, I owe it to her to go for all she's done to help me settle in— at least this once.

The late summer light was fading to twilight. Brenda struck a wooden match and lit the kerosene lamp on the wall next to her bed before changing into a cool cotton nightgown. Peaceful night sounds came through the window. The sounds varied depending on the temperature and whether there'd been a recent rain. *Wonder where the frogs go when it's been dry for a while? Or do they just sing more when it's wet?* She sat at the computer again and googled about frogs. *Huh, they burrow into the soil when it's hot and go into a dormant state until it rains again. Well, now I know.* She grinned at her new-found knowledge and shut down the computer and hooked it up to recharge the battery, She padded out to the kitchen, pausing to click on a small battery-powered night light that was just bright enough for her to see and not bump into anything once it got full dark. After she washed up her dinner dishes, she filled a tall glass of tea and got a dish of salted almonds to nibble while she read a book in bed. By the time she finished her book, Fuzzy was ready to join her in curling up to sleep.

The next morning, Brenda dug out a pair of old sneakers and looked through still packed boxes to find her bathing suit and a windbreaker. She tried on the two-piece suit and turned one way, then the other checking how it looked in the mirror. *Not perfect, but still pretty good.* She took off the suit and got dressed, feeling pleased with herself.

On Friday, Brenda woke before the alarm. The early morning air was cool through the screened window, but the clear sky promised it would warm up later. She cleaned Fuzzy's litter box and put out fresh food and water in the bathroom before moving the sleeping kitten from her bed to his plush bed near his food dishes and putting down a few toys.

She put on her swimsuit under a pair of shorts and a long-sleeved shirt. The rafting company would provide wetsuits for the chilly water. Sunscreen, bug spray, a hat and sunglasses went into a waterproof bag. A towel and a change of clothes and shoes for after their excursion completed her packing, and she slipped into her windbreaker before going out. She stood on the porch and looked to the east at the sun just peeking above the wall of trees on the hillside. The birds were trying to out-sing each other, and Brenda closed her eyes and took a deep breath of the fresh morning scent as Fanny drove up the hill to pick her up.

Brenda climbed into the Explorer. "Thanks for picking me up."

"No problem. I'd rather drive up and get you while Joe's checking that the windows are closed in case it rains than stand around waiting. The newlyweds are running late."

"Well, it gives me a chance to tell you my news now."

"News?" Fanny turned and took a quick look at Brenda. "Okay, so tell me already!"

"I have an online interview Monday afternoon for a job in Huntsville, Alabama."

"Oh, my. I wish you all the best—I think. I'd hate to lose you as a neighbor, but you know I want what's good for you."

"I haven't been able to decide what I want, but I need to talk to them. Maybe that will make up my mind one way or the other."

Fanny pulled up in front of the bed and breakfast. "We'll have to talk more later, but here come the honeymooners now."

Brenda climbed down from the front seat using the chrome running board while Fanny came around to introduce her to the bride who had just come down the steps.

"Brenda, this is Tiffany Abbott."

"Hi, nice to meet you."

"Likewise," the twentyish blond said, climbing up into the Explorer without looking at Brenda.

"... and this is her husband, Charlie. They're from South Carolina."

Brenda looked up at the tall man with grey sideburns as he turned from helping Tiffany up into the vehicle and folding the other seat forward for Brenda to climb into the back row. Their eyes locked, and Brenda felt the blood drain from her face. "Charlie," she said in a choked whisper. He glanced up at Tiffany.

Joe boomed out, "Let's get going. Everybody get in and buckle up."

Brenda took the opportunity to get in back without saying anything more. Mercifully, the vehicle was noisy, and no one expected her to engage in conversation. She turned to the side and closed her eyes, as if napping, but she was fighting off the assault of long-ago memories. Charlie. A little heavier, streaks of grey in his hair, but the same Charlie who abandoned her thirty years ago after she lost the baby.

The scope of old memories played against her closed eyelids. The remembered physical pain and the overlay of being abandoned by her lover and losing the chance of ever being a mother brought a stream of silent tears. Brenda shifted further to the side against the seat and pulled the hood of her windbreaker over her face. Over the years, the cauldron of time had changed the pain to white-hot anger expressed in dreams of shredding Charlie's face with her nails, but in the end, the heat had cooled to icy distance between Brenda, her feelings and the world. She reached for that frozen wall of anger now.

Chapter 13

After what seemed like hours to Brenda, Joe flipped the turn signal on. "I'm going to take this exit to fill the tank while you guys take a quick rest stop."

Charlie opened the door and helped Tiffany down. Neither of them looked back at Brenda before they strolled to the welcome center entrance, arm in arm. Fanny came to the open doorway and caught a glimpse of Brenda's reddened eyes before she could slip on her sunglasses. "Are you okay? What's wrong?"

Brenda shook her head. "It's something from a long time ago. I can't talk about it now."

"But...."

"Please, I promise I'll explain, but not today. I just have to get through today."

"Come on. Let's see what we can do to keep the others from asking questions." Fanny opened the rear lift-gate and wrapped some ice from the cooler in a paper towel. She handed the wrapped ice to Brenda with a few extra paper towels. "Here, get back in before the others come out, and press this against your eyes. By the time we get there, it should undo most of the damage. And you owe me a story, right?"

Brenda nodded and hugged Fanny. "Thanks." She climbed back in and curled against the seat, cold compress in place, hood pulled up, just as Tiffany's bubbly voice echoed from the doorway of the welcome center.

At their destination, Brenda was last out of the vehicle, but waved Fanny over, away from the others. "Can you keep Tiffany from Charlie for a few minutes? I have to say something to him, and I'd rather she weren't part of the conversation. He's helping Joe unload our stuff, so now would be a good time."

"He's behind the story?"

Brenda nodded.

"Well, at least your eyes aren't going to give away how upset you were." She turned and walked over toward Tiffany. "That is such a lovely top. Walk down the hill with me to sign in, and tell me where you got it."

Brenda waited until Tiffany was moving down the path and Joe had started after them before she went around to the back of the SUV and stepped in front of Charlie. "Hello, Charlie. It's been a long time."

He stared at her for a few moments without speaking. "What are you doing here?" He looked over his shoulder to see where Tiffany was and back at Brenda. "You're looking good."

"Listen, you're the last person on this earth I want to be around, but I'm not ruining this trip for my friends, and I suspect your sweet little wife wouldn't enjoy hearing what a wonderful supportive person you were 30 years ago. You pretend you don't know me, and keep out of my way, and I won't tell them all how you walked out on me without a word while I was still in the hospital."

"Oh, don't be so dramatic. Women have miscarriages every day."

Brenda clenched her fists, shaking with the effort not to hit Charlie. "Dramatic? You bastard. You never even asked about me. You just packed and left. The pregnancy was in the cervix, and it ruptured. They had to do an emergency hysterectomy, and even then, it was touch and go for a couple of days. And I had to go through it alone. You weren't man enough to even say you were going. You're a pathetic worm, and I regret not realizing it all those years ago." Without waiting for his reaction, Brenda grabbed her bag and ran down the hill. She saw a picnic area off to one side with no one around and moved to the table furthest from the trail. The running had helped with the adrenaline rush from the confrontation, but did nothing to help the surge of emotions. She leaned against a table and tried to use deep breathing to regain control.

A quiet voice came from behind her. "Hey, lady. Who is it I have to take my badge off for and beat the snot out of for you?"

Brenda turned, laughing and crying at the same time while Jim wrapped her in a hug.

"I don't know, woman. Seems like I bring out the waterworks in you."

"Jim, you don't know how good it is to see you." She stepped away and took a deep breath, wiping her eyes.

"I don't know what's going on, but I'm glad I'm here then. You okay?"

"Yeah, I am now."

"You want to cancel this trip? Fanny said you might not be feeling up to it. She already talked to the guide, and he can find another couple to take our place if you just want to head back in my car."

"She tell you anything more?"

"No. If you don't want to say anything else, it's okay."

"For now, let's just say I knew Charlie back in L.A.—a very long time ago. That son of a bitch isn't going to ruin one more minute of my life."

Jim grinned at her cussing. "Sounds about right to me."

They got to the staging area just in time for the guide's explanations and directions. Fanny and Joe looked relieved at her arrival. Charlie avoided looking in her direction, and Tiffany cracked her gum like a teen-ager through the guide's presentation.

Once the ride began, Brenda forgot about Charlie and the past. The rush of the raft through the swirling water, following the guide's paddling instructions past rock formations and flying downstream took her a state of sheer exhilaration. During a quiet stretch, they could look at the rock formations and trees along the shoreline, and Brenda grinned when she turned to look at the opposite bank and caught Jim looking at her. He grinned back and gave her hand a quick squeeze before getting ready for the next challenging section of the river. The hours flew by as fast as the scenery. Nearing the end of the run, the guide called out, "Bump!" Everyone leaned forward with their paddle handle down just as they had been instructed, except Tiffany decided to lean to the side instead to see what was ahead. The raft flew up and crashed down into the churning water, and she lost her balance, almost falling over the edge. Charlie grabbed her life jacket and pulled her back into the raft, but the end of Tiffany's paddle smacked into the side of Brenda's face.

Brenda nodded yes to the guide's and Jim's inquiries if she was okay, but she saw red and black stars of pain.

Fanny rushed over as soon as they got out of the raft. "Are you okay?"

The guide came over too, squeezing a chemical cold pack. "Here, let me take a look, then keep this on for about 20 minutes. It will help keep the swelling down." He gently felt along Brenda's cheekbone and nose while Fanny hovered to the side.

"The good news is it doesn't look like anything's broken, but you are going to have a Grade A shiner. Have your doctor check it out if it's still swollen in a day or so, or if the pain increases."

Brenda thanked him and said, "Great timing. I have a job interview on Monday."

"Well, it'll give you something to open a conversation with. Good luck!"

Fanny took charge and ushered Brenda along to shower and change. "I can't believe she never even apologized. She's all upset that she almost fell overboard."

"I have a feeling she's the center of her world, and there's not much room in it for anyone else. Here she comes now."

Brenda ducked into one of the shower rooms, leaving her towel and dry clothes in the little area outside the stall. She wanted to be done and out before Tiffany, so she hurried to finish and dress. In the outer room, when she looked in the mirror to comb her hair, she got her first look at the growing bruise on her face.

Fanny stepped up next to her. "Have you got a good concealer?"

"I can tone it down some, but I don't think there's going to be any way to hide this. I'll just have to brazen it out. Either they'll like that I'm adventurous, or they'll be appalled."

"Jim asked if we minded if he took you home. I told him I'd let you know he offered. He really is a good person."

"You don't have to sell me on him, but I still need to decide what direction I want my life to take before I can even think about getting involved with anyone."

"That's up to you, of course. But you could do worse."

"Fanny, I already have."

Both women laughed at that until Brenda grimaced at the impact on her injured face.

"Let me get out of here so I can avoid having to talk to Tiffany. Say goodbye to both of them for me. I don't ever want to talk to Charlie again in this lifetime."

"How about if I come up tomorrow and bring lunch? Our guests will be leaving in the morning."

"Sounds great."

Fanny shook her finger at Brenda. "But I expect to hear the whole story."

"Don't worry. I'm more than ready to talk about it now."

Jim was outside waiting. He winced when he saw Brenda's face. "Man, does that hurt a lot?"

"It probably looks worse than it feels."

Jim shook his head. "I sure hope so."

"You know, I heard a certain nice guy might be willing to offer me a ride home."

Jim's smile spread ear-to-ear. "Give me your bag, and let's go. I already arranged with the shuttle driver to take us back to the parking area and have someone else take the others." They were quiet on the ride back, and Jim gave the driver a generous tip before they walked to his car.

Once they got in and buckled up, Jim turned to her. "Now what's this about an interview? And who's this Charlie guy to you?"

"Give me a minute, and I'll explain." She waited until they got on the road to start talking. "Remember when you asked if there was a man in my life, and I told you there was someone a long way back?"

"Yes, but you didn't say any more."

"Well, Charlie was that guy."

"And it still bothers you after all this time?"

"I was young and in love, and I thought I was going to marry him. There's a lot more I'd really rather not go into right now, but I can see I lucked out that he ran out on me. He's no better now than he was then."

"He must have been a fool then, and he still is. I'm sorry he hurt you so much."

"Thanks." Brenda stared at the passing landscape, but it was more like watching the years of her life roll by.

Jim waited a few minutes before he asked, "Anybody special in your life after him?"

"No. I dated a few men over the years, but nothing ever developed, and then, my parents needed me. At least until my dad passed away last year."

"So you were an only child?"

"Yeah. My mom had me when she was almost 40. I don't think my parents were planning to have kids, but along I came. They couldn't wait until I outgrew being a kid."

"What do you mean?"

"They took good care of me, but they weren't comfortable with me until I was an adult, then we got along great."

"How about your grandparents?"

"Never knew them. In fact, neither did my parents. They were both orphaned as toddlers when their parents died of the Spanish flu. My mom left the orphanage to go to work in a hotel laundry at 14. My dad was one of the kids sent west on an orphan train."

"I've heard about those trains. Was he adopted?"

"No. He said the couple that took him as a foster kid treated him okay, but they were older and more interested in having a boy to help them around the house and on their farm. He said he had to work hard, but at least he had enough to eat during the Depression years. His foster father died when he was 16, and his foster mother died the year after. Relatives came and sold the farm, and everything in the house. They gave him a few dollars, dropped him off in town and said he was on his own."

"What did your father do?"

"He never wanted to talk about those years. Only thing he'd say was he wanted to get as far away from life as a farmer as he could, so he joined the Navy." Brenda smiled remembering. "He loved the sea."

"I can understand that. I still miss it sometimes myself, but I've got a good life here. I thought you were getting to feel that way about living here too. What about this interview. When did that come up?"

"Just this week."

"You haven't said where this job is."

"Huntsville, Alabama."

"A bit far to commute."

"Yes, it's back to either here or there, not both."

"So you've decided to go back to the city?"

"I haven't made up my mind yet. I'm hoping what happens Monday will help me choose one way or the other."

Jim kept his eyes fixed on the road ahead. "I'd kind of hoped you liked it well enough to want to stay."

Brenda couldn't read anything from his expression. "I have been thinking about staying—a lot. But I don't know if it's the sensible thing to do."

"Do you always do the sensible thing?"

Brenda paused, thinking about the question. Jim glanced over, and seeing her intense look, waited for her answer.

"I can't remember the last time I made a decision that I couldn't say was sensible, except maybe going on this trip."

Jim laughed. "Well, maybe it's time to start letting life happen instead of calculating every step, in spite of the occasional smack in the face."

They both laughed, but Brenda was serious when she continued speaking. "Just letting things happen is asking a lot of a woman on her own in the world."

"You don't have to do everything alone." He reached over with one hand and squeezed hers.

She didn't answer, but held tight to his hand, heart pounding, afraid of misunderstanding. They didn't let go until he needed to make a turn.

Brenda sighed. "It's not an easy choice. If I stay, I won't have any income until I'm old enough for Social Security. And the way things are going, who knows if I can even count on that. I have a retirement account, but I'll lose a lot in growth and taxes if I dip into it early. And I planned to add to it for a few more years before I started taking money out."

"Would you consider doing something else? Taking a job in these parts? I know it wouldn't pay as much as a city job would, but it doesn't cost you as much to live here either."

"I don't know. I keep turning it over and can't settle on a definite answer. If the people on Monday don't make me an offer, I guess I'll have to start thinking about staying."

"If it's that unpleasant an idea, maybe you should keep looking."

The sharp edge in his voice caught her off-guard, and Brenda stared at the set of Jim's jaw.

"Staying's not an unpleasant idea at all. In some ways, it's everything I ever wanted, but I need to be realistic about my future. I've got no one to depend on but myself."

"It doesn't need to be that way, you know?"

"Jim, we've only been out together a few times, and…"

"You're right. Forget I said anything. It's not my place."

Brenda sat silent, not finding words to address the hurt on Jim's face and in his voice. He stayed silent too until he pulled up at her door and went around to help her out and get her things from the back.

"Hope that doesn't hurt too much tonight." He put his hand alongside her face and brushed it with a gentle touch of his thumb.

Brenda almost broke down in tears at the simple gesture. She held his hand in place and pressed her cheek against it. "I'm sorry. I wasn't trying to push you away. I just don't know what's the right thing to do. I've been trying to sort it out for weeks, and I'm no further along than the first time I thought about not trying to pick up on my old life."

"Hey, it's okay. I'm not used to caring about anybody this way. It's been a long time since I had anyone in my life where it mattered if they stayed or went. The idea of not getting a chance to see where it might go…" He broke off and held her close which said more than words ever could.

"I know. Let's let this interview play out, and we'll talk before I make any decision. Heck, they might not even want me."

"If they've got a lick of sense, they will. Now you get in and take it easy tonight. Okay?"

Brenda picked up her things and smiled up at him. "I think that sounds like a plan."

"I'll be working or on call from tonight through Monday. Can I call you Monday night?"

She nodded. "Please do. Maybe we can talk some more then?"

He kissed the top of her forehead and watched until she turned at the door to wave before he got in his car and headed back to town.

Brenda watched through the window until Jim's car went around the curve in the drive. She opened the bathroom door for the kitten. He stretched and watched while she refilled his water bowl, rubbing against her leg. She picked him up and sat in the rocker with him, petting him until the lump in her throat went away.

Just before noon the next day, Brenda hurried out to the driveway when she heard Fanny's car coming up the driveway and waited for her by the steps. "Hi, what can I help you with?"

Fanny opened the back door and took out a tray. "Here, you take the cobbler while I get the casserole."

Brenda peeked under the foil. "Blackberry?"

"Uh huh. You like it, don't you?"

"Love it! We could start with dessert."

"What, and deprive you of my spinach lasagna? I made the noodles myself."

Brenda hurried ahead to hold the door and caught a spicy tomato scent as Fanny walked past. "Oh, that smells good."

Brenda set the cobbler on the table and took serving pieces from the kitchen drawer. Fanny cut two pieces of lasagna while Brenda poured glasses of a California Cabernet. They ate the savory food, chatting about the news and weather. By the time Brenda cut the cobbler, Fanny couldn't hold back any longer.

"Now, what's the rest of the story about you and Charlie?"

Brenda got the coffee pot and two mugs. Pouring the coffee, she said, "I've never told anyone the whole story before." She sighed. "I didn't want my parents to know, or anyone else for that matter." She launched into the background of her life with Charlie and their last days together. Her face was pale and her hands shaking by the time she finished describing what happened in the hospital and coming home to a half-empty apartment.

Fanny was suspended between compassion for Brenda's plight and outrage at Charlie's behavior. "And he never came to the hospital to see you?"

"No, when they found his name as my emergency contact in my medical records, they called him at work and let him know I was there. He went back to the apartment and got my purse, put my keys in it, and left it with the hospital administrator. That was the last I heard of him until yesterday."

"Are you very upset about running into him again—and with a young wife?"

"It was a shock when I saw him. All those memories and feelings came flooding back. Things I hadn't thought about for years. But after I talked to him, I realized I was lucky he walked out on me then." She took a long sip of coffee, staring into the past. She shook her head after a moment and said, "Just wish I'd realized what he was really like a lot sooner."

"Brenda, I'm so sorry. I never would have invited you on that trip with him if I'd known. In fact, I would have told him we were booked up and couldn't accommodate him and Tiffany."

"Don't feel bad about it. I did enjoy the trip— well, most of it." She grinned, touching the edge of her multi-colored bruise.

"What a shame you never met anyone special since then."

"I dated a few guys, but I never gave them a chance to get close. It wasn't the hurt as much as it was I couldn't face telling them I could never have children. The men I liked were the kind who would want to have a family someday. Maybe it was more I couldn't face it head-on myself. It made me feel less of a woman. If I didn't have a man in my life, I didn't have to think about it. It was easier that way."

"What did you tell Jim yesterday?"

"Not much, and I'd rather he not know anything about all of it now. It's enough that he knows about Charlie in general, and that I haven't gone through a series of bad relationships."

"I won't say anything to him, but how did he take the news about the interview?"

"I can't say he was happy about it. I've got mixed feelings about it myself. I did say I'd talk to him afterwards. And you get that cat-ate-the-canary grin off your match-making face!"

Fanny laughed and held up her hands in mock innocence. "Now would I do something like that?"

"I just bet you would."

"You know the saying, 'Every pot has its cover.' And I like a neat kitchen—or a well-matched couple. Speaking of which, it's time I got back to my other half."

"You and Joe do seem to be happy together."

"It took some effort over the years with a little give and a little take and a lot of love, but it did work out for us. And you can't blame me for wanting people I like to have that in their lives too."

"We'll see. I'm not ready to go there yet."

As they walked to the door, Fuzzy dashed into the room and leaped to the back of a chair and started grooming himself. "You weren't sure about the kitten either, but it looks like I was right about putting the two of you together."

"I'll give you that, but Jim's not an orphaned kitten."

"He could be just as good for you."

Brenda laughed. "You're impossible. Thank you for lunch and the visit. I enjoyed both."

"Me, too. Let me know what happens Monday."

Brenda experimented trying out different ways to explain the red, purple and blue discoloration all afternoon as she pulled weeds and raked leaves in the garden.

Monday morning, Brenda checked her appearance in the mirror one more time. Sleeping on extra pillows to keep her head elevated hadn't helped reduce the black eye. *What are they going to think? What can I say?*

Chapter 14

After lunch, she worked on using makeup to conceal the bruise, following instructions she'd found online. By the time she finished, only one small area along her cheekbone showed purple in the mirror through the layers of makeup. But when Brenda turned on the camera in her computer, it looked a lot worse.

No way they'll miss this. Watching her image in the viewer, she moved the computer screen a little further back and changed the angle a bit one way, then the other. *A little better, but I am going to have to say something.* She turned off the camera and opened the Skype program. Her thoughts were interrupted by the Skype signal. She clicked the button to accept the call, and the image of a man with salt and pepper hair and a pleasant expression filled the screen. Brenda felt like she'd swallowed a flock of butterflies greeting the caller with what she hoped was a confident, "Good afternoon."

"Hello, Ms. Maxwell. I'm Greg Abernathy. May I call you Brenda?"

"Of course." She smiled and noticed an uncomfortable look pass over his face. *Uh oh.* Um, Greg, before we get started, I'd like to get something out of the way."

"Yes?"

"I went whitewater rafting on Friday and had a bit of an accident." She touched her cheek and grinned. "I wanted you to know I'm not in the habit of getting black eyes."

Greg laughed. "Thank you for explaining that. I couldn't help but notice, and I was looking for a polite way to inquire. Was it a good trip otherwise?"

"Oh, it was great, but I think I might sit up front next time so I don't have to worry about the person in front of me forgetting how to handle her paddle."

They shared a laugh at that before Greg continued.

"Well, Brenda, I have some notes here from your interview with our L.A. office last spring. They were very impressed with your background in international sales and exports. The notes say you'd do well as a contracts administrator for us, and the only reason they didn't hire you was your credit score was too low to get a security clearance. Let me see, yes, that's all cleared up now, so I just have a few questions to fill in some details."

The rest of the interview was casual and relaxed. Brenda's answers seemed to fall in line with Greg's pattern of questions, and Brenda noticed how often he seemed to nod a bit after she'd replied. His expression turned serious when he asked about her ability to relocate.

"I'm planning to keep my property here in West Virginia as either a vacation home or an investment, so I'm free to relocate for work."

"Excellent. Well, that wraps up all my questions. Do you have any questions?"

"Yes. How long is this project expected to run?"

"It's for five years, with a possible extension depending how things go."

"That's good. When do you anticipate making a decision?"

"We have a few more people to talk to, and we'll make a decision this week or next, so we can move ahead on the project. We'd like to have it underway in about a month. Anything else?"

"Thank you, I think you've covered everything. Your company certainly has an excellent reputation, and from what you've told me, it sounds like a great place to work."

"I think so. I'm here 28 years now. Well, Brenda, it's been good talking to you. We'll be in touch."

After the call concluded, Brenda sat back thinking about the conversation. *I don't think I could have done any better, and he seemed to approve of my answers.*

Brenda turned off the computer and put up the kettle on the propane cooktop for a pot of tea. *So if he offers the job, do I take it?* With no answer by the time the tea was ready, she poured a cup and grabbed a black wool shawl from the hook on the kitchen wall on the way out to the porch.

She sat rocking, looking out over the hillside at the orchards and forest beyond, glad for the warmth of the cup she held. She pulled the shawl closer around her shoulders. There was a sharp nip to the air.

The temperatures had been dropping, and most of the trees had already changed color. *Such a difference from the palm tree greens and the brown grasses of California after the hot summer months. The fall colors here are so intense. Yellow, orange, red against the green of the hemlocks and spruce.*

Even the indefinable scent of outdoors had changed from the rich overlays of summer fruit and flowers to something plainer. Clean, fresh, but distant, signaling the approach of winter. A chill breeze made her shiver.

Boy, we got that rafting trip in just in time. Going inside, she stopped to light a fire in the fireplace between the living room and bedroom before putting her empty cup in the kitchen sink and hanging her shawl on the hook. She repeated the steps to start a fire in the woodstove. A few minutes later, the crackle of the kindling accompanied the dancing flames licking at the hardwood stacked over it. Brenda paused to watch the fire spreading through the glass-fronted firebox. The flickering light and growing warmth made her feel content. The chiming tone of her phone echoed from the bedroom, and she hurried to answer it. After a glance at the number, her heart skipped a beat.

Trying to sound relaxed, she answered. "Hi, Jim. How are you?"

"Fine, thank ye, fine." One of his usual responses, delivered in the local style of speech, almost as one word. "How was the interview?"

"I think it went well, but I'm still not sure what I want to do if they make an offer. Would you have time to come over tonight so we could talk about it?"

"I'm on 'til seven, and I'll want to run home and change out of my uniform. Eight okay?"

"That's fine. Should I make something for you to eat?"

"Nah, just coffee. The diner's bringing dinner over at five."

"Okay, I'll see you later."

"'Til then."

Brenda broke the connection and left the phone on the desk. Back in the kitchen, she lit the lantern over the table before she pulled out a bowl. She put a couple of handfuls of self-rising flour in the bowl, poured some sugar on top and sprinkled a healthy amount of cinnamon, a little less allspice and a smidgen of Chinese Five Spice powder. She beat in an egg and some milk with a splash of vanilla and a dollop of oil until a thick tan batter formed.

She used her finger to take a bit off the mixing spoon, tasted it and nodded before she scraped the batter into a small round nonstick baking pan and slid it onto the middle shelf of the oven. With the timer set for fifteen minutes, she washed up the dishes while the spice scent of the baking cake filtered through the room. The aroma of coffee beans from the hand-cranked coffee grinder mingled with the spice in the air as Brenda poured the ground coffee into a covered container for later.

Think I'll just have some ham and eggs for dinner. A few minutes later, after adding slices of one of the last red tomatoes from her garden.

she sat down to her simple meal. The timer went off, and Brenda checked the cake with the tip of a finger. Not quite done, so she gave it another five minutes while she finished eating. Checking the cake again, it sprang right back, and she slipped it out of the pan onto a cooling rake on top of the stove.

I have time for a quick shower. It'll be good to get this makeup off my face. With the propane line she'd installed, she had hot water without depending on the solar panels. In the city, hot water on demand was something that used to be taken for granted. Now it was a delightful luxury.

Wrapped in a towel and standing at the open closet, Brenda realized she hadn't dithered over what to wear in a very long time. *Why am I acting like a school girl? Just because he's got eyes that change color like the sea and it feels like you could drown in them...Stop it!* She shook her head and grabbed a soft blue sweater and jeans. A flip of the brush through her hair and a dab of musk oil, and she headed back to the kitchen.

After a moment's thought, she opened a jar of peach preserves and spread a thin layer across the top of the cake before she cut it in half and made it into a two-layer half round. She dusted the cake with a sprinkle of powdered sugar and put it on a plate on the table. With a kettle of water up to boil, Brenda set up a coffee carafe with a drip cone and filter before going to the computer to check her email and the news.

At quarter to eight, Brenda heard a truck coming up the drive. When she met Jim at the door, a blast of wind entered with him, and

Brenda pushed the door closed as soon as he was inside. "Wow, the wind is picking up."

"Pretty cold out." Jim rubbed his hands together to warm them before he took off his jacket and laid it on the chair by the door. "Wouldn't be surprised at an early snow this year."

"Really? It's just barely October." She led the way to the kitchen.

"Wouldn't be unusual around here, but the big snows don't come 'til later in the winter. Hmm, something smells good."

"Just a little spice cake. Sit down. I'll make the coffee."

Jim watched her as she put the ground coffee in the filter and poured the hot water over it.

She turned and asked, "Want some cake?"

"Sure thing."

She smiled and cut a wedge of still-warm cake for each of them and brought the coffee to the table and poured it before sitting down.

"Thanks." Jim reached across the table and touched the side of her face, running his finger along the side of her cheek. "How's it feel? It looks a lot better."

Her breath caught at his touch, but she tried to keep her voice steady. "It's okay. Starting to clear up."

"We had a traffic jam on the road outside town today."

"Really?"

"Yeah, a flock of goats found a weak spot in their fence and trotted off down the road. Owner has a new border collie puppy who decided to take on the whole group." He chuckled. "He couldn't quite get them back to the farm, but kept them bottled up on the road, blocking both lanes."

Between bites of cake, Jim told Brenda about having to give a ticket to Fanny's new guest at the bed and breakfast for speeding on Main Street. "Gave him a warning yesterday, and today, he was going even faster so I wrote him up. Oh, I meant to ask, did you get yourself some winter boots yet?"

"No, tell you the truth, I hadn't thought about it."

"Well, Mr. Barker tries to keep a good selection, but I'd recommend getting in there this week in case he has to order your size. You ought to get a pair for mud and another for deep snow."

"Thanks, I'll have to do that."

"That was good." Jim pushed back the plate, finished his coffee and smiled.

"Would you like some more?"

"No, thank you, but would you mind if we took advantage of that nice fire in the other room?"

"One of my favorite things. Come on." Brenda added another log to the fire, sparks flying as she adjusted its position with the fireplace tongs.

They settled into the small sofa in front of the fireplace, sitting close together, and Jim put his arm around Brenda's shoulders. She rested her head against him, watching the fire.

He cleared his throat. "So, how'd the interview go?"

"Pretty good. Once I explained about the black eye, it all went well. Actually, I think it broke the ice, so I was a lot more relaxed than usual in an interview."

"Then, you do want the job?"

She felt him tense up when he asked the question, and she looked up at him. "I don't know. I'm still not sure what I really want. It makes sense to work for another five years if I'm offered the job, but that means putting off finding a different life here until then. If I turn it down, there's probably no going back. It'll be a final decision."

"I came here planning to tell you to forget about it, to stay here, but then I figured no matter what I say, you have to decide that for yourself."

"Thank you. I didn't expect you to say that. I thought you'd try to convince me it's not worth considering the job in the long run."

"Well, I do want you to stay, but you're a strong-willed woman, and no matter what anyone says, I'm pretty sure you have to find the answer yourself. Besides, I'm trying to be good, but all I can think of right now is how much I want to kiss you."

Brenda laughed and hugged him. "To use one of your phrases, seems like that might be the thing to do about now."

He held her tight and kissed her softly on the lips, then harder, telling her as no words could how much he desired her. Brenda lost herself in the kisses. She felt the room spin, and the old icy wall inside melted. Their kisses fed the touch hunger they both felt, satisfying and creating a need for more contact at the same time.

Jim moved one hand along Brenda's shoulder and down the side of her neck, pausing to gauge her reaction before beginning to slide further down.

A flying ball of fur landed between them. After the first shock of the interruption, they both broke into laughter.

Jim picked up the cat and petted him. "Cat, you've got lousy timing."

"Aw, he just doesn't like being left out of the cuddling."

"Well, I guess I can't blame him for that."

Fuzzy pushed away and jumped down to sprawl on the hearth and smooth his fur before curling up to take a nap.

Jim pulled Brenda back close against him and whispered in her ear, "If you do decide you have to go, promise me you'll come back?"

She nodded, face against his chest, and they sat without speaking, watching the fire.

After Jim left, Brenda washed the dishes and went through the routine of turning the wall lanterns down low. She added some wood to the fireplace in the bedroom and watched until it caught. After undressing by the light of a small battery-powered lamp, she put on a warm fleece nightgown, the soft fabric soothing against her skin. In front of the fireplace with her eyes closed, the crackling warmth of the blaze reminded her of Jim's arms around her, and her growing feelings for him. *Maybe I should have asked him to stay. But how could I, when I don't know whether I'll be leaving soon?*

Brenda pulled the edge of the window drape back, and the cat came running to see what was behind it. With nothing of interest to him, he turned and stood up with his front feet against her leg, meowing to be picked up. Cradled in her arms, Fuzzy rewarded her with a rumbling purr as Brenda looked out at the rows of silhouettes backlit by moonlight in the terraced orchards. *So very different from my old view in the city.* She set the cat down on the bed, moved the lamp over to her desk and took out the folder with her financial statements. For a few minutes, she sat still, folder closed on the desk in front of her.

Leaning back, she picked up the folder without opening it. She knew the numbers by rote now. *What if I decide not to play by the old rules?* She got up and tossed the folder on the desk. Pacing back and forth, Brenda tried to sort out her thoughts. *I'm getting nowhere this way.* Stopping short, she turned and went to the kitchen and made a pot of tea from the big iron teakettle she kept simmering on the stove and returned to her desk with a supply of strong black tea. After the first cup, she opened the folder and flipped through the pages, making notes on the laptop. By the time she'd finished, the teapot was empty. Stretching, she turned out the lamp and climbed into bed. *The job will pay enough for me to be comfortable in the city. If I don't get it, I can still manage with what I have now, and later, on Social Security because the costs here are so much less.* Brenda plumped up her pillow and settled in for the night with a satisfied yawn. She'd just drifted off to sleep when she woke with a start. *But if I go back to the city, I'll be alone again.* Sleep was a long time returning.

In the morning, Brenda started wrestling again with the what-ifs of getting a job offer in Alabama or not getting one. She decided to wait until she heard from Greg Abernathy before trying to come to a decision.

A week after the interview, Brenda was up early and used her hand-operated machine to do some laundry. There was a stiff breeze when she hung it on the clothesline. After lunch, Brenda brought her wash in and rehung a few things that were still damp on a drying rack in the kitchen. *I don't know. It feels awfully damp today, even if they're not predicting rain. It's getting colder too.*

After checking the weather forecast online and finding out a Midwest storm system was headed east, Brenda checked her pantry and added a few things to her shopping list. Cat food and litter. Hot chocolate. Milk. Bird seed. *I'd better get those boots today too. Hope they have my size.* She tucked the list in her purse and put on her coat. Ten minutes later, she was in the market collecting her listed items.

She was putting the last bag in the truck when it struck her. I almost forgot the boots! Brenda left the groceries in the truck and walked over to the general store.

"Hi, Mr. Barker."

"Brenda! Good to see you. What can I do for you today?"

"Jim Holt said you're the man to see for boots."

"That I am. Let me show you what we've got. We've got them with ducks, horses, soft colors, bright colors, dark colors. Take your pick."

Brenda chose pink rain boots and insulated black knee-high snow boots and brought them to the register at the front of the store. She grinned and told Mr. Barker, "You weren't kidding about your selection. This is the most fun I've had with necessary shopping in a while."

"Glad you came on in, and bet you'll be glad too when this storm hits. Do you have everything you need?"

"I think so, but I'm afraid this will be one of those times when I won't know I should have gotten something until I need it."

"Just give a holler if you do. I can always send Joshua up with it."

"Thanks, Mr. Barker. I appreciate that."

After Brenda put the groceries and other supplies away, she left the rain boots in the storage corridor next to the kitchen and put the snow boots in her bedroom closet. She checked the news and weather reports half a dozen times before bedtime. The storms weren't following the usual pattern according to the forecasters, and no two agreed on what they might do.

Chapter 15

Wednesday afternoon, Mrs. Barker finished bundling the last tray of outgoing mail and slid it on top of the stack already on a cart. The cart wheel squeaked under the weight as she wheeled it out the back door of the post office. Her nephew Arthur leaned against the 24-foot truck he drove to the regional mail distribution center.

"Right on time as always, Arthur."

He grinned and loaded the trays into the truck. "Yes, ma'am, Auntie Sanna. My daddy always set great store on us kids being on time. Now I don't know any other way to be."

"Your father's been like that since he got his first watch for his tenth birthday. You be careful today. Smells like snow."

"I will." Arthur climbed up into the cab. "See you tomorrow." He waved as he drove off.

Arthur pulled in at the diner on the highway outside of town and put on a blue and white parka before he dashed inside. Sounds of an upbeat country song mingled with lively conversations were punctuated by hearty laughter.

"Hey there, Art. How ya doing today?" The dark-haired waitress reached for the thermos he'd just placed on the counter.

"Fine, but it's getting colder fast."

"That it is." The waitress filled the thermos with coffee as she did every trip. "I'm afraid you're going to need this tonight. Weather report gets worse every hour."

"Yeah, it might take me a while to get home if the roads get slick. Better get moving while I can." Arthur picked up the thermos, along with the paper sack next to it, his standing lunch order of a ham and cheese sandwich and some cookies. He counted out cash for the bill, plus a generous tip as always.

"Thanks, Arthur. You be safe now."

He grinned before he turned to leave. "Always try to be."

Back in his truck, he waited for an 18-wheeler to pass before he pulled out. The first large flakes of snow clotted on the windshield. Arthur flipped on the wipers, defroster and headlights as he fell into line behind the big rig. The sullen sky looked ready to release a furious curtain of white. *This is not going to be a fun trip.*

After a few miles, the road steepened with a series of switchbacks as it rose, wrapping around the mountain. The speed limit for trucks dropped, with signs directing them to the right lane. Near the crest of the hill, a small white car screamed past Arthur's mail truck on the left. *Crazy people. Speeding in this weather.* A gust of wind rocked his vehicle. *Holy Jesus.* Arthur eased up on the gas, putting more space between him and the truck ahead. Through the snow, he saw the white car tailgating a red pickup in the left lane. As the pickup drove past the big rig, the white car swerved to pass the pickup on the right.

Caught between a prayer and a curse, Arthur gripped the wheel and down-shifted, waiting for the inevitable. It came in a flash.

The accelerating white car spun out of control on the new layer of snow and slid sideways into the right lane, front end first in front of the 18-wheeler. The truck driver tried to avoid it, but clipped the small car, bouncing it like a cue ball into the back of the pickup. Both of the smaller vehicles went down the slope across the wide median strip, but the white car rolled over twice before it came to a stop.

The wind chose that moment to gust again, and the trailer ahead of Arthur rocked as the driver fought to pull out of a skid. He almost made it, but the momentum of the trailer kept it moving forward, forcing the cab into a jackknife. In slow motion, the driver's door slammed into the side of the trailer, while the whole rig slid toward the shoulder.

Arthur glanced back, relieved no other vehicles were coming up fast behind them. He breathed a prayer in earnest and swung to the left lane to avoid the jackknifed truck.

"Please, Lord, help me now," he said through clenched teeth applying his brakes as his truck continued sliding toward the median. He managed to scrape past the jackknifed truck, ending up on the left shoulder inches from the embankment. He put his emergency flashers on and climbed down to the ground on shaky legs. Only his grip on the door saved him from falling on the snowy pavement.

Arthur looked over at the 18-wheeler. The trailer had stopped on the shoulder, but its front outer wheels perched over the edge. His thoughts were with the driver, but if he didn't alert oncoming traffic, they'd all be at risk from more crashes. Grabbing his emergency reflectors and flares, he ran as fast as the slippery road allowed, dropping reflectors behind his truck and flares in a diagonal line across both lanes.

Arthur saw headlights coming nearer and moved even faster, sliding with every other step. He lit the last two flares and waved them, one in each hand, arms outstretched. Three approaching cars stopped. The drivers put their emergency flashers on and ran toward Arthur.

Arthur continued toward them, calling to the nearest driver, "Dial star-seven-seven. Tell them there's a pickup and a car down the median embankment and a jackknifed trailer on the road. Don't know about injuries yet."

"Will do," the man called back.

The other two drivers headed for the smaller vehicles that had crashed. One man, wearing a dark green raincoat, ran toward the white car. The other man, in a black overcoat, headed toward the pickup while Arthur hurried back to the jackknifed trailer whose driver was just climbing down from the cab's passenger door.

"Hey, Bud. You okay?" Arthur helped ease the man to the ground. The driver groaned and leaned against Arthur before sitting on the cab's step. "My shoulder's messed up, maybe a broken collarbone, but I think that's the worst of it. I called it in. Go ahead. See if you can help the others."

"Take it easy. Help will be here soon." The icy wind bit at Arthur's face as he turned to check on the drivers in the median. He pulled up the hood on his parka as he went and watched the man with the green raincoat walking away from the undercarriage of the twisted white wreck toward the red Dodge pickup. He looked up at Arthur, shaking his head. "He's gone," he called across the space between them.

The wind grew to howling blasts, one after another. Arthur turned at a sound behind him, stunned to see the wind pushing the 18-wheeler's trailer closer to the edge. It slid, inch by inch, until it rolled off the shoulder, dragging the cab along. Metallic crunching and the cracking and snapping of brush and small trees preceded a louder crash of metal on metal that echoed up the hill. A shower of sparks like defective fireworks flew up and flickered out. A new screech of bending, breaking metal erupted, ending in a loud crash as the cell tower buckled from the impact at its base and fell.

"Oh, hell," Arthur muttered to himself. He rushed to the driver whose truck had gone over the edge.

The man's face was ashen, staring at the wreckage. "I was sitting there, and it started to move. I stood up and watched it go over. My rig's gone. The tower's gone. All because that jerk was in such a big hurry."

"C'mon. Let's get you over to my truck. It'll block some of the wind." Arthur guided him back to the mail truck as a far off wail of sirens grew louder and blue flashing lights approached. "I've got a blanket here behind the seat."

The other driver just stared out into the storm. Arthur tucked the blanket around him.

A few minutes later, state troopers arrived and checked on everyone's condition before they started writing up reports. Twenty minutes later, red flashing lights announced a fire truck and two ambulances pulling up to the scene. Arthur walked back to his truck after giving his statement. More blue flashing lights came from the other direction, from town.

The ambulance crews tended to the big rig and pickup drivers, while the firemen made sure there was no danger from leaking fuel. Yellow lights from two tow trucks joined the scene. The combined flashing lights created a kaleidoscope of colors against the snow, but the howling gusts were the only sound.

Arthur stood back and watched while the EMT's helped the truck driver onto a gurney before placing him in an ambulance.

A trooper came back to Arthur. "Your truck good to go?"

"Yeah, I lucked out. Nobody hit me."

"How about you? You all right to drive?"

"I'm good, Officer. I just want to get out of here."

"Here's my card in case you need to get in touch. If our investigators have any questions, they'll give you a call. You can leave as soon as the plow gets here from the interstate. Follow it out. It's already pretty deep up that way." He nodded and walked away toward the tow trucks.

Arthur had picked up his reflectors and stowed them behind his seat when red lights flashing and sirens from ambulances moving away toward the interstate drew his attention. He caught sight of Sheriff Jim Holt walking toward him.

"Arthur. Helluva night."

"Hey, Sheriff." Arthur shook his hand and said, "How's the truck driver?"

"The EMT said the driver's in shock, but they're taking care of him. The pickup driver got a burn from the airbag, but it's not too bad. The guy who caused it all didn't have a chance. The car flipped, and he wasn't wearing a seat belt. You get hurt?"

"No, I'm fine, thanks."

The sheriff clapped Arthur on the shoulder. "I'm glad to hear that."

"Yeah, me too. How bad's the cell tower?"

Jim shook his head. "Whole thing's gone. No one's going to be able to get out there for a few days with this weather. And no telling how long before they can get something up and running again."

"Let my aunt know I'm okay, please? My dad'll get in touch with her when I don't call him tonight."

"Don't worry. I'll have someone let both of them know. Thanks for your help with the flares. That was good work."

"Glad I could help with that at least." Arthur smiled when he heard the sound of snowplows clanking toward them. "Looks like I'll be out of here pretty soon so I can get this mail moving again."

"Get off the road as soon as you can. There's a blizzard coming in. Governor's already declared a State of Emergency."

"Soon as I get this mail delivered to the distribution center. I'll stay with friends up there until the roads are clear enough to get home."

"Call the station on a landline if you can. I'll see your family gets the message."

"Thanks."

Both men moved toward their vehicles. A trooper called Jim over before he reached his. "Just got confirmation that all cell service is out for your neck of the woods." The trooper grinned. "Guess you already figured that out."

"Pretty much. Now I have to work out getting the town through the next few days."

Chapter 16

Brenda scrolled through the subscription TV program guide for Wednesday on her computer, skipping over the daytime game shows. She checked for concerts or programs scheduled on public TV to watch that evening, then clicked for her usual five o'clock news and weather report. It was still a few minutes before the end of a popular medical show, and she heard the program's guest say something about using a coin to find the answer to difficult choices.

She turned up the volume and listened for a while. *Hmm. So all I need to do is flip a coin. Heads mean yes. Tails mean no. And if I'm happy with the result, that's what I really want to do. If I'm not, then I should listen to my gut and go with the opposite choice.*

In a way, it made sense. It cut out all the dithering over possibilities and trying to make the right decision when two options were both reasonable. *Should I use that to decide whether to take the job if it's offered?* Brenda shook her head. *No, I'm not going to let chance make such an important decision.*

The lead-in for the news show interrupted her thoughts and caught her attention. The weather radar map showed the bright blue of heavy snow headed toward Brenda's area. The voiceover said, "The snow storm is moving in hours ahead of schedule with high winds and heavy accumulation expected. This could be a rough one. Stay tuned for details next."

Brenda didn't wait for the news to come on. She hurried to put on her new lightweight rain boots and bundle up before going out to bring in more firewood. For forty minutes, she moved armfuls of wood from the covered wood rack outside and stacked it in the garage. By her last trip, daylight was fading as fast as the snow was falling. She slammed the door against the rising wind, stamped the snow off her boots and shook it from her knit hat. *Hope that's enough. I don't want to run out of wood in the middle of a snowstorm.*

She stopped to take off her coat and shake it out before going into the corridor between the garage and kitchen. The area made good use of the space with storage shelves and insulated doors to the garage and kitchen. A battery-powered light mounted on the wall provided enough illumination to check the storage battery monitors and locate anything on the open storage shelves. Sitting on the bench there, Brenda pulled off her boots and set them on a raised rack over a tray to dry and hung her coat and scarf on hooks on the wall.

A welcome warmth enveloped Brenda when she stepped into the kitchen, and she slipped on the sheepskin-lined slippers she wore around the house before she sat down to get an update on the weather. When she clicked on the bookmark for the news station, part of a running banner scrolled across the screen. "… declares state of emergency as state readies for winter storm." The breaking news link opened to pictures of snow-covered roads, but before she could get any details, the internet connection failed. When she couldn't re-establish the connection, Brenda reached for her cell phone. No service. *Now what do I do?* Brenda shut down the computer. *The storm must have interrupted service.* She pushed away a trickle of fear. *You're in the mountains. It happens. My weather radio! Where is it?*

Brenda looked on every shelf and counter in the kitchen, then moved to the bedroom, looking on the desk, in drawers, in the closet. She went to the living room and looked on all the bookshelves. *This doesn't make any sense. When was the last storm?* She sat down on the sofa and tried to calm herself. *Okay. It was at night. I was in bed. The night table!* Brenda ran back into the bedroom, got down on the floor and looked under the bed. She caught sight of the edge of the radio between the night table and the wall. With a sigh of relief, she retrieved it and sat on the bed while trying to get a clear channel. Fuzzy jumped up and watched while she listened to the weather report, then reached out and tapped her hand with a front paw.

Setting the radio on the night table, Brenda picked up the kitten. "Well, since we're staying in, a little snow and wind isn't going to bother us. Now what is it you'd like?" The cat let her pet him for a minute, then twisted away and jumped to the floor, looking back over his shoulder. "I get it. You want your canned food now. Okay, come on."

The cat followed her to the kitchen and sat on the rug next to his dry food dish and water bowl while Brenda opened the can. When she put down a plate with chopped salmon in gravy and petted his back, Fuzzy rubbed against her leg, then turned to lapping up the cat food.

"You are so pleased with the simplest things. Maybe that's the secret to happiness."

She smiled and left the purring cat to make her own dinner, warming up a pot of leftover beef stew. "Now this is the perfect meal for me today. It's always better the second day." While it warmed, she went through her twilight ritual, lighting the hanging kerosene lanterns in the kitchen, pulling the insulated drapes closed in the living room and bedroom, and building up the bedroom fire. Brenda came back to cut a thick slice of the bread she'd baked the day before and ladled a bowl of the hearty stew.

Instead of her usual mealtime reading on gardening or country living, she concentrated on her notes about her solar panels and batteries. When she finished eating, Brenda washed up the dishes and put up water for tea. *I really don't use the batteries that much, so I should be fine for a few days before they run down.*

Reassured once more about being alone in the coming storm, Brenda showered and put on a fleece jogging suit to sleep in. She took one lantern from the kitchen to the bedroom and hung it on the wall hook near the bed. *Wonder if the internet's back on?* She powered up the computer and found the internet service was not back yet, but some emails were waiting for her to read from the connection earlier in the evening. Most were notices that statements for various bills had been posted online, along with the usual junk mail. But one message caught her eye. It was from Greg Abernathy.

Hello Brenda,

It's my pleasure to let you know that we think you'll be a great addition to our team, and we would like to offer you the position as our contracts administrator for the new project, effective the second of November. Details of the compensation package are attached.

Please confirm your acceptance of our offer as soon as possible so we can complete final arrangements for the project contract. Once we have your acceptance, our Human Resources Manager will be in touch and will be happy to assist you with relocation information. We will reimburse half of your moving expenses after six months of employment.

I look forward to working with you,
Greg
Gregory Abernathy, Regional Vice President

Brenda sat back stunned. *I got it. I got it. After trying all year, I got a job.* She grabbed up her cell phone to call Fanny, only to find there still was no service. *Damn. Well, it'll wait until tomorrow.* She yawned, tired from hauling firewood into the garage. *May as well turn in.* She tried not to think of the other call she'd need to make, but she heard Jim's voice as he asked her to promise to come back if she took a job in the city. A tear rolled down her cheek. She swiped it away, but the thought wasn't as easily dismissed.

When Brenda pulled back the drapes Thursday morning, she stared at a curtain of white falling on a foot-thick layer of snow. After enjoying the beauty of the landscape for a few minutes, she closed the drapes to keep the heat in the room. As soon as Brenda sat in the rocker next to the fireplace, Fuzzy yawned and stretched on his corner of the bed before he leaped onto her lap.

"Oof…you're getting big, kitty. We're going to have to take you down to the vet in a few weeks to get you fixed. Good thing you don't know what I'm saying." The cat purred and turned his head so Brenda could scratch under his chin. A moment later, the mercurial pet jumped down to race to the kitchen and down the hall. Brenda laughed and leaned back watching the glowing embers left from last night's fire

After a trip to the bathroom, she got dressed and turned on the computer. *Oh no, still no internet?* When she reached for her phone and again found no signal, a sinking feeling settled in the pit of her stomach. *What is going on? I can understand the internet being out, but the phone too?* She scolded herself out loud, "Stop it! It's not even a whole day yet." She shook her head and went to the kitchen to make breakfast.

Pancakes with strawberry preserves and some crispy bacon and a pot of hot chocolate gave her something to focus on. After she ate, she stood near the kitchen window, sipping from a large mug while she watched the snow fall. *Even though I stay around the house for two or three days at a time, and it doesn't bother me at all, not being able to go to town chafes. And being without my phone and the internet makes me feel more confined.*

After casting about for something else to do, Brenda settled on cleaning out the old ashes from the fireplace between the living room and bedroom. The small metal container she kept in the bedroom for the ashes was almost full, and she took it out to the garage and emptied it into a galvanized trash can to save for adjusting the pH of acidic soil in the garden next spring. She pushed the still glowing coals to one side and put the colder ashes into the metal container and covered them before she rebuilt the fire.

After washing up, Brenda settled into the rocker in the bedroom to read the latest Caroline Leavitt novel, taking a break to make some tea. She stretched and yawned before checking her phone and laptop. Still no connection. She shook her head. *I never realized how much time I spend on the computer every day.* She shrugged off the sense of being adrift.

After dinner, Brenda looked out her bedroom window. Flakes were beginning to fall again. She closed the drapes and went to bed early.

Reading and cooking filled her next two days. She had to check her phone to make sure it was Saturday. With no outside contact, the days blurred from one to the next. *Now I know why prisoners scratched marks on the wall to track time.*

The refrigerator was full of leftovers, and the cookie tin was full. The cabin sparkled from all the cleaning she'd done.

As a diversion, she set up the loom she'd bought at the craft shop during the summer and set aside. *Weaving should be a pleasant way to keep busy in the winter if I can figure out how to get started.* She shook her head. *That's if I stay here, but I could take it with me to the city too.* She kept busy all day reading a how-to book and learning to wind the warp threads.

Before she went to bed, she looked out at the snowdrifts on her driveway. *Why hasn't the plowman been here yet? Can't even call to ask.*

Sunday morning, the sky looked like more snow might be coming. Brenda settled on making a batch of bread to occupy herself for a while. She built up the fire in the wood stove and set out the ingredients. By the time she mixed the hot water and some flour and added the sugar, oil, yeast and salt, Brenda's unease had subsided. She sipped hot chocolate while she waited for the bread mixture to get bubbly. When it was ready, she added the rest of the flour and started kneading the dough. The motions and the change in the texture of the dough as she worked it calmed her. When it was ready to set aside to rise, she covered the bowl and put it on the warming shelf at the back of the stove.

An old Star Trek movie on DVD filled in the time until the dough was ready to punch down. Brenda set the bowl on the warming shelf again.

If I get the snow off the solar panels now, maybe it'll help keep the batteries charged. She put on her rugged waterproof knee-high boots and got suited up to go out. *I remember Josh telling me about doing it, but I never thought to ask how often or when to do it.*

In the garage, the roof rake hung length-wise from hooks along one wall. It was a simple device with a telescoping pole and an adjustable angled connector with a hard foam piece that looked like the end of a sponge mop. The rake was light, but it took a few minutes to get the length adjusted. The snow was fluffy powder and came off the panels with a light motion of the rake.

The soft accumulation slid down from the lower panels. When Brenda pulled against the snow on the next row up, it worked well at first. She moved the pole over to the next panel, and it triggered a small avalanche from the higher tiers and from the upper part of the roof. Before Brenda could get out of the way, the cascading snow hit her in the face and chest. She put up her arms in front of her face, but the snow knocked her flat on her back and piled up on top of her, covering her face and upper body.

The shock of the cold weight stunned her for a moment. She wasn't hurt, but she felt like a turtle on its back. Brenda pushed the snow on top of her away a little at a time, but the heavy clothing hampered her movements. She finally got enough snow off that she could sit up, but two feet of soft snow under her provided no traction to turn over. She rocked back and forth and managed to flip over and pull her knees up under her. Her feet kept sliding as the snow shifted, and she couldn't get to a standing position. *I need something to grab onto.* Face down, she inched forward until she could reach the rake and dragged it over, its length awkward to maneuver from her position.

The rounded end of the pole slid every time she tried to use it to give herself a balancing point. Giving up on that approach, she scraped away the snow on the ground with her hands. Once she'd dug down to grass, she was able to get one foot planted on solid ground. She picked up the rake again and set it on the nearly bare spot, and levered her way up on her feet again.

Using the pole as an oversized walking stick, she worked her way back to the garage door, falling twice and struggling to her feet again. She stumbled into the garage and dropped the rake on the floor inside, but the snow piled up against the door had fallen in and blocked the door from closing. Shivering from the snow that had gotten inside her coat and melted, Brenda looked around and found a snow shovel on a hook at the far end of the garage. Pushing the snow out took only a minute, but her fingers were numb from the cold and wet.

She slammed the door and hurried to the storage corridor leading to the kitchen to strip off her sodden gloves, coat and scarf. Even her sweater was wet, and she pulled it off, her teeth chattering. She hung everything up on hooks to dry and struggled to get out of the boots. *Why can't I get these off?* She put one foot on the heel end of the other boot and used her leg to push at it. It finally slid off. She tried reversing the positions, but her stockinged foot kept sliding on the wet rubber surface. She finally caught the boot at an angle just above the heel, and it popped off. She flung herself at the kitchen door and the warmth beyond, going straight to the bathroom where she fired up the propane heater. The water took only a few minutes to warm, and she stripped off her clothes and thawed out under a hot shower. *How will the storm affect my water supply? How much water is in the cistern if the windmill doesn't pump more? It doesn't matter. I need to get warmed up now.* After a few minutes, she relaxed and turned off the water, wrapping herself in one thick towel and putting another around her hair to pad out to the bedroom for dry clothes.

Still feeling chilled, she put on heavy pajamas and a robe. Her sheepskin slippers helped her feel warmer, even though her fingers still stung. Hoping something had changed while she was outside, Brenda checked her cell phone. No service. She slid a log into the bedroom fireplace, watching to make sure there were enough embers and heat for it to catch. She added some smaller pieces of wood just to be sure.

When Brenda checked the fire in the stove, she realized the bread dough had risen past the top of the bowl and concentrated on getting it punched down and dividing it into loaf pans for a second rising. After she put linen towels over the pans and set them back on the warming shelf, she went to the kitchen corridor where she gathered up the clothes she'd taken off and put them on hangers to dry so they wouldn't get musty waiting for her to do the laundry in town.

Back in the kitchen, she looked in the refrigerator, settling on a container of soup. While it heated, Brenda stayed near the wood stove, still craving heat. *Is this what it's going to be like in every snowstorm? Why didn't anyone tell me the phones go out? What else didn't they tell me? What didn't I know to ask?* She poured the hot soup into a large mug and took it to the bedroom, settling into the rocker in front of the fireplace. The rich chicken broth was from her mother's recipe, and Brenda remembered all the times she'd helped her mother make it.

Cleaning the chicken and covering it with water. Peeling a big onion and cutting X's on the ends. Scraping carrots and stringing celery and tossing them in. Adding a handful of parsley and a couple of bay leaves and letting it cook until it became Mom's chicken soup. *And I have no one to pass it on to.* Sadness replaced the initial warm feelings.

An angry little voice in the back of her mind answered. *Whose fault is that? So what if you couldn't have your own kids. You could have found a nice guy to love and adopt a child.*

Brenda almost dropped the soup mug. Why had it never occurred to her before? Was she so blinded by self-pity, she couldn't find another way to be a mother? *Too afraid to take a chance on trusting anyone again is more like it.* Brenda went to the kitchen, trying to get away from the thoughts. But the door to the vault where she kept her feelings was open now, and she had no way of slamming it shut.

How many other things have you run away from? Like an annoying internet ad that interrupted programs without warning, a memory from high school wormed its way to the surface. The day she won her first debate, and afterwards, the boys on the team attacked her for using emotion instead of reason to make her point. *They were so upset with me. I didn't know how to deal with it.* She felt a wave of the confusion and loss memories of that day always triggered. *So what if I quit. They didn't want a girl on the team anyway. But I made sure to use facts and reason to win my arguments from then on.*

Somehow, that wasn't a very satisfying response, and Brenda took the mug and what was left of the now-cold soup back to the kitchen. She poured it back into the pot to warm it up again and checked the bread dough. Sliding the pans into the oven didn't give her the usual pleasure of finishing a task. She poured the rewarmed soup into her mug and sat at the kitchen table, sipping until it was gone, revisiting all the times success had ended up leaving her separated from those around her, not knowing how to fit in.

"Brenda, I've got some good news for you."

"What is it, Dad?"

"Would you like a job starting right after graduation?"

"Of course. I've been applying all over, but haven't had any luck yet."

"You remember Mr. Jonas? He owns the company next door to where I work?"

Brenda smiled. "Sure, he always bought ten boxes of Girl Scout cookies from me and set up a card table in his lobby so I could sell more. Such a nice man."

"His clerk is going to have a baby and wants to take a year off. He knows how smart you are and said if you're interested, you can fill in for her. Instead of starting college in the fall, you can work until his girl comes back, and you can start college next year with a little cash in the bank."

"Did he say what the pay would be?"

Brenda's father grinned. "The minimum wage goes up to $2.65 this month."

"That's good."

"What's even better, is he'll pay you $3.00 an hour."

"Wow. Why would he do that? I don't know anything about how his office works."

"Don't you worry. Mr. J said he'll teach you what you need to know. He was worried about hiring someone and having to let them go when his girl returns."

"His girl, Daddy? That's kind of old-fashioned. She's a woman, not a girl."

"Now don't get all smart-mouthed like that with Mr. J."

"I won't. I'll keep my opinions to myself."

"You better."

Brenda went to her father and hugged him. "Yes, Daddy. Thank you. "

He grunted in response, but looked pleased. "Go help your mother with dinner."

The job was easy enough, answering phones, typing letters, making deposits, filing invoices. Negotiating the minefield of personalities and the other workers' suspicions was another matter. If Brenda finished her assignments too quickly, she was the target of sharp tongues and snide remarks about trying to impress the boss by making the others look bad. When the bookkeeper told the biggest gossip Brenda was making as much as half of the older women, the comments took a nasty turn about why the boss was giving her special treatment—and what else that might involve. Brenda didn't catch what they meant right away, but when she did, her face turned scarlet, eliciting snickers from the other women. She had no idea how to cope and couldn't imagine asking her mother about what to do.

When she arrived at the office, she did her work and counted the minutes until she could escape at lunchtime to eat in the park. After lunch, she continued counting down to closing when she could escape before the others. Working there felt like a prison sentence.

When Brenda started college classes the next year, she was an outsider again. She didn't know anyone from the high school class after hers, and those who had started college the year before had a circle of new friends. Her relief at being out of the hostile office was replaced with a dogged determination to survive this new environment until she got her degree in business. With her year's work experience though, she was able to get a part-time job in a small machine tools manufacturing company.

Brenda was studying for her senior year finals when her mother knocked on the bedroom door. "Come in the living room please. Your father and I have something to tell you."

"What's up?" Brenda followed her mother to the living room.

Her mother sat on the couch and waited for Brenda to sit down too. She took a deep breath. "Your father has decided to retire, and we want to move to Florida. It doesn't cost half as much to live there, but we don't want to leave you here alone."

"I never thought about you retiring and moving somewhere else. A lot of people do go to Florida. Do you think you'll like it there?"

"We're going to take a trip to see what it's like, but we think so."

Brenda's father sat forward in his chair. "One of the guys I worked with retired last year, and he wrote and invited us down. Says it rains a lot more, but he's enjoying being there."

"Would you come with us?"

Brenda looked at her mother and thought for a minute. "I don't know. I have to think about it, but I probably will stay here. I have some money saved up, and I'll get a job once I graduate, so I can afford to get my own place." She got up and hugged her mother. "Don't worry about me. It's time you both got to enjoy life. Guess I had to grow up and get out on my own some day. Seems like as good a time now as any."

It was two years after they moved and I'd gotten my own place when Charlie found me. He saw how awkward and lonely I was. I fell in love with him, maybe because he seemed to understand me. I thought he loved me, but was he ever capable of loving anyone, or just going through the motions?

The timer went off, and Brenda shook off the memories and checked the bread. It gave a satisfactory *thump* when she tapped it so she pulled it out to cool. Sitting down again, Brenda flipped through last week's Sunday *L.A. Times,* refusing to let her thoughts go back to Charlie again. The room was growing darker by the moment. The sun had already moved behind the hill, but the moon hadn't risen yet. *Must have spent more time daydreaming than I realized.* She lit the lamps in the kitchen and bedroom and was surprised to find she was hungry.

While the cast iron frying pan heated, Brenda poured a little olive oil and sliced a small onion into it before adding the drained contents of a small can of mushrooms. After she added a small steak to the pan, she put up a kettle of water for tea and instant mashed potatoes. A small baking dish of sliced apples with cinnamon and nutmeg in the oven wrapped up her meal preparation.

Being in this kitchen made Brenda feel safe and at ease, more so than any place in her life had done before. The food was soon ready, and while she ate, Brenda worked on the *Times* crossword puzzle. She rarely completed them, but enjoyed the effort. After dinner, Brenda turned on the computer hoping to connect. No internet. No service on the phone either. *What in the world happened?* She turned down the lanterns to a low glow and curled up on the bed, burrowing under the covers.

Brenda woke shivering; her face felt frozen. When she sat up, the room looked darker than usual. A few seconds later, she recognized what happened. She'd forgotten to build up the fire before she went to bed. Still half-asleep, she went through the motions of scraping some of the now-cold ashes into the covered metal pail on the hearth and laying crumpled paper under the twigs and small branches she used for tinder and kindling. She piled up larger branches and topped them with heavy sections of logs before lighting the paper. She crawled back into bed and was almost asleep when she jumped up in alarm. Grey smoke was building up in the fireplace and seeping out at the top into the room. She closed the fireplace insert, but smoke still crept out along the top edge. *What did I do wrong? What's happening? Is the snow blocking the chimney?* Any other time, Brenda would go online to look up a problem and what to do about it. *Still no connection.* Panic grew with each wisp of smoke wafting out of the fireplace. *What should I do?*

Brenda opened the insert. She choked on the smoke and used the fireplace tongs to pull the heavy logs to the sides. The logs hadn't caught well at all and were just smoldering, putting out smoke and no heat. When she moved them, some of the tinder and half-burnt paper flared up. Still, the smoke continued to rise from the heavy logs and seep into the room. Trying to turn one log caused it to break open where the fire had started to burn along one edge and glowing bits of bark flew up and floated out onto the hearth rug. Brenda snatched it up, folding it in on itself and ran to the bathroom and threw it into the shower and ran water on it.

She ran to the bookshelf over the small desk in the kitchen and clicked on the battery-operated light. *Which book?* The first three yielded no clues. The fourth had an answer: Cold air was heavier than warm. Brenda hadn't made a tall twist of newspaper and lit it and held it up the flue to warm the cold air settling downward from the roof when she had added the logs earlier in the evening. She grabbed the *Times* off the kitchen table and ran back to the bedroom.

Pushing the smaller wood together in the center of the fireplace, she twisted the newspaper before lighting it and held the burning end up inside the flue. The newspaper burned down toward her shaking hand, without any change in the smoke. She dropped it and sat back, not sure what to do next, but bits of tinder flashed into flame, and Brenda concentrated on adding more, a bit at a time until some finger-thick branches caught too. She pushed the two big logs back into the fireplace into a V-shape. Balancing more wood like a teepee against them and over the kindling, she closed the insert and watched. *It's working. The smoke is going up now.* Afraid to trust that she'd resolved the problem, she pulled the comforter off the bed and wrapped it around herself, sitting in the chair in front of the fireplace.

There's so much I don't know. What if I couldn't find the answer? What would I have done? Maybe I'm not cut out for this life. A wave of sadness washed over her and settled deep inside. Slow tears rolled down her face.

Quitting again? Running away again? She jumped up. Anger pushed fear and sadness aside. *I'm not going anywhere.* And the relentless little voice whispered at the back of her mind. *So you're going to turn down the only job offer you've had in a year? Is that sensible?*

Brenda shook her head and checked the fire one more time. She went to the kitchen and added some wood to the fire in the stove, just to be sure it would hold until morning. She muttered under her breath, "Sensible. Sensible. My whole life has been sensible, and where am I? Alone in a cabin I really don't know how to run in the middle of a snowstorm."

Fuzzy came running to her. She picked him up. "I wasn't talking to you, sweetie. But I bet you wouldn't mind having some of your fish now, would you?" She put him down and opened a small can of food for him. He rubbed against her ankles waiting for her to put it down.

Brenda ran her hand the whole length of his back a few times as he started to eat. His purring grew in volume. "You do put things in perspective for me, don't you, cat?"

Leaving him to his midnight feast, Brenda washed her hands before going back to the bedroom to put the comforter on the bed. The after-effects of the excitement caught up with her, and she yawned and settled in again to sleep. This time, the little voice stayed silent, but her dreams took her back to the past again.

School-age Brenda, always reading and learning about something new for the next Girl Scout badge, faithfully attending every meeting, working with, but never connecting with any of the other girls. Nose buried in a book during recess and before class started and every spare moment at home between chores. Books were her teachers, her passions, her lifelong companions. They never made fun of her thick glasses or pudgy cheeks. She rode on wild ponies in the surf, climbed snowy mountains, swam in tropical blue waters.

Traffic sounds turned into the music and bustle of a medieval fair while she carried a basket and looked through the wares on display for a blue ribbon to tie up her long blond hair. She galloped on a tall black horse through the woods to carry a message and save a town until her mother called her back to their small apartment to peel potatoes for dinner.

The tinny clanging of her wind-up alarm brought Brenda back to her mountain cabin. She hurried to look outside. The snow had stopped, but drifts covered the driveway. Except for the skeletal outlines of her fruit trees in the orchards below, nothing looked familiar. She shivered and reached for a heavy robe from the chair near the bed before she pulled on her fleece-lined slippers.

Following her usual pattern, she slid into her computer chair and opened the laptop. Still no connection. Still no phone service. A tiny spot of fear spread like ice through her chest. Brenda pushed away from the desk and went through the routine of cleaning out some of the ashes in the fireplace and building up the fire.

How long does the snow last? How much usually falls in the winter? People lived alone in little cabins through the ages. What did they think about as they went through their day, gathering enough wood to build their fires and hauling water?

Fuzzy came running over and stood up on two legs and stretched up to tap Brenda and remind her to set out his breakfast. "At least we don't have to do that, and we don't have to go out in the snow to hunt for food." She laughed and picked up the kitten. "I'll bet those people had someone like you or a big old dog to talk to, or maybe both. A nice cat to keep the mice out and a dog to go hunting with."

The cat rubbed his face against her arm and twisted around to jump to the floor and dash to his food dish, waiting for Brenda to catch up to him. "Boy, do you have me trained." She filled his dish and watched his dainty and thorough approach to every morsel of fish.

Brenda adjusted the fire in the wood stove and set about getting dressed to go outdoors. Bundled against the chill, she took the extension pole out through the back garage door. The previous day's avalanche had cleared some of the panels, but snow still covered others in drifted piles. This time, she stood to the side and tried to use the panel scraper at an angle. She did succeed in getting the tallest drift piles to slide to the ground, but couldn't completely clear all the snow. *I guess I'll have to let the sun on the dark panels do the rest when it warms up a little.* She retreated to the garage, not happy about the results, but hoping it would be enough to let the batteries charge before they ran down too far. *Still so much I don't know—like how long the charge will last, or even how much I need for my basics. But I'm not using that much, am I?*

With her clothes drier than the day before, getting out of her winter gear was a lot easier. Before going into the kitchen, Brenda took down a jar of preserved green beans and another of peaches from the storage shelf to use for dinner. Leaving the jars on the counter, she checked the phone. Still no signal. Brenda looked up at the fireplace and saw soot stains from the previous night's smoke. With a sigh, she plugged the phone into the charger and went back to the kitchen. One of her homesteading books described ways to clean off soot, and Brenda filled up the tea kettle using the pump at the sink. She set the kettle on the stove to heat while she half-filled a small bucket at the pump. After spreading a stack of old newspapers around the fireplace hearth, she gathered cleaning cloths, a sponge and a small scrub brush. One more trip to warm up the water in the bucket with the hot water in the kettle and pick up a can of foaming bathroom cleaner, and Brenda was ready to work on cleaning off the dark stains.

It took a few trips to get clean water and more scrubbing than Brenda had done in many years, but by noon, the bricks and the mantelpiece were clean. Fuzzy rubbed against Brenda's legs, and she bent to pick him up. "Hello, cat. You had your breakfast, but it's way past time for mine." She petted him for another minute then carried him into the kitchen and put him down. "Okay, my turn to eat." Brenda put up a pot of tea and sliced two pieces of bread. She let the slices warm on the stove while she set the table and poured herself a mug of tea. "Now, all I need is some plum jam and butter." Both were soon enhancing the warm bread, and Brenda closed her eyes enjoying the first bite. *Have to ask Josh's mom what spices she used in this jam. Or maybe it's a secret? Well, if it is, maybe I can trade her something else for more next year.*

Next year. Brenda froze at the thought that her decision on the job would decide what happened next year and maybe every year after.

Brenda turned on the computer, barely noticing the lack of internet connection. She switched into business-mode, ignoring her feelings, and opened two new files, side by side. She started typing.

TAKING THE JOB

Picking up my life where I left off in L.A.

Building up my cash reserve for when I retire.

Job pays for health insurance.

May not get another offer.

New city. Might like or not like.

No guarantee of how long the job will last.

Upfront cost for moving and apartment.

Half repaid if I stay 6 months.

Don't know anyone there.

STAYING IN CHESTNUT SPRINGS

Continuing the new life I started here.

Have some friends already.

People look out for each other.

Growing and cooking my own food.

Living in a clean environment.

Can learn crafts.

Costs less to live here.

Still a lot I don't know about this place.

Less money to retire with.

Have to pay medical insurance.

Brenda sat back and read through the lists. Her inner voice reminded her of one big omission: Jim.

She turned on her phone. *Maybe if I talk to him, it'll help me make the decision.* No service. Brenda pushed away from the desk, angry that the choice might be made by whatever random event had interrupted her connection to the world outside her cabin.

Chapter 17

Brenda turned back to the desk to save her notes before shutting down the computer. She moved through her daily chores in a bad humor, savagely scraping some of the old ashes from the bedroom fireplace into the metal can. She rebuilt the fire stabbing at the embers from last night's fire to set the tinder and kindling alight.

The wood stove was next, and she treated it as roughly as the fireplace. When she finished, her mood had settled into resignation. She glanced out the kitchen window and saw some birds scratching and pecking at the ground where she'd scraped away the snow earlier in the week. *Poor things. I forgot to put out more birdseed!*

She ran into the bedroom and changed into warmer clothes. Brenda put on her boots in the pantry corridor and grabbed the birdseed from the shelf. She set it on a workbench and took the snow shovel from its hook. The small door to the side of the overhead garage door opened inward, and snow spilled in when she opened it. Brenda wrapped her scarf across the lower part of her face and pushed the snow back out and away from the opening. It took a few minutes to find a rhythm, but once she did, a path soon emerged from her efforts up to the porch with a clear way to the front door. She returned the shovel to the garage and took a broom and the bag of birdseed to the porch. After she'd swept the remaining snow from the steps and from the cleared area of the porch, she took down the bird feeder. It was shaped like a wooden cabin and hung from a big hook on a chain next to the porch pillar. It had rails on two sides where the birds could perch.

That task completed, Brenda realized she was hungry from the cold air and exercise and hurried to hang up her outdoor clothes and get back into the kitchen. She adjusted the stove to raise the temperature and went back to the pantry to pick up a few sweet potatoes. She poked them with a fork so they wouldn't explode and put the potatoes on a piece of foil in the oven.

From the living room window, she looked out at the porch. Birds were busy pecking at the seeds from the perches, while others were on the porch floor picking up seeds the ones above knocked down.

Fuzzy came galloping into the room and jumped up on the chair that was next to the window to look out. His tail twitched back and forth while he watched the birds, tracking their movements.

"Good thing you can't get out there." Brenda started to pet him, but he twitched away from her hand, still intent on the birds. "Okay, enjoy your bird-watching. I'm going to work on dinner."

Brenda opened a mason jar of sliced apples and put them into a baking dish with some cinnamon and nutmeg and dotted them with butter before putting them into the oven. She put green beans from another jar in a pot before taking a vacuum-sealed plastic package of ham steak out of the refrigerator. The center bone with a little meat around it went into the pot with the green beans over a low heat. Brenda put the rest of the steak into a frying pan ready to heat when the potatoes were near done. She yawned and decided to stretch out on the bed for a nap before dinner, taking the timer with her to be her alarm clock.

It was dark when the timer went off, but something else had started to wake her, a distant noise, somewhere between the whine of a leaf blower and the growl of a chainsaw.

"What in the world?" She ran to the front window and looked out at a flicker of light in the woods. The light showed more often as the sound grew louder, and then she caught a glimpse of a snowmobile through the trees. She watched as it emerged from the woods and came across her yard to stop in the snow-covered driveway in front of the garage near the path she'd cleared earlier. When the rider shut down the engine, dismounted and took off his helmet, Brenda broke into a grin. It was Jim.

She opened the door as he approached.

"Nice night for a ride?"

He stomped off the snow from his boots and came up the steps, closing the door behind him. He hugged Brenda. "Glad to see you survived on your own up here. I've been worried about you."

"It's good to see you. I can't believe you rode all the way up here."

"It's not that far. I've had my hands full in town, or I'd have been up sooner."

"Can you stay for dinner?"

"You don't have to do that. I can eat when I get back to town."

"Nonsense. I always cook extra so I have leftovers to use the next day, so there's plenty. It'll be ready in a few minutes."

"It does smell good. Have you got room in the garage for the snowmobile?"

"Sure. I'll go around and open the door for you from the inside."

Brenda grabbed her coat and hurried to open the main garage door. He drove to the doorway and came in to check where to put the snowmobile.

"Great, you still have the old rug Mr. Johnston used for his machine. I'll park it right there. Go ahead in. I'll shut the door."

Brenda waited in the pantry corridor for Jim to come in. "You can hang your coat here, and if you want to take off your boots, you can leave them here too."

"Thanks." Jim took off his outerwear and sat on the bench to take off his boots.

"I'm going to check on the food, so hurry in and tell me what's been going on with the phone and internet."

Jim followed her into the kitchen a minute later. Brenda smiled at him and put the frying pan on the heat and filled the kettle.

"The plowman was upset that he had no way to let you know he had engine trouble before he could get to your driveway. He won't be able to get here for another couple of days. RJ figured out the problem, but he has to wait for parts from Charleston to fix it."

Brenda said, "I figured he was busy with all this snow and would eventually get to me, but not having the phone hasn't been fun. Do they have service in town?"

She put the kettle onto the burner and ground coffee beans for the drip carafe while Jim explained about the accident on the highway above town.

"We have landline, but no cell service. They were out today working to get a temporary cell tower up, but it's still going to be another two or three days. We've been busy at the station going out to check on people and relaying messages to worried relatives. I was planning to come up yesterday, but I had to take a woman in labor to the hospital."

"Is she okay?"

"Oh yeah. Her son was eager to make his entrance a month early, but he's fine and so is she. Not so sure about the dad though. Worried him half to death."

"I can understand that. I managed to scare myself a couple of times this week. I'll tell you about that while we eat. Would you light the lantern on the wall there for me please while I set the food out?"

Once their filled plates were on the table, Jim said grace holding Brenda's hand. When he finished, he said, "Now tell me what happened," and gave her hand an extra squeeze before letting go.

While they ate, Brenda described how she buried herself in snow clearing the solar panels and about the smoky excitement with the fireplace. She stopped for a moment and bit her lip, not sure how to tell Jim about the job offer.

He watched the change in her expression and asked, "What's wrong?"

"Just before the phone and internet went out, I got an email from Alabama offering me the job. I've been going back and forth since Wednesday about what to say.

Jim's expression froze, as if he'd put on a mask. "And what did you decide?"

"That's just it. I haven't decided. I'm not sure what I want, any more than I was the last time we talked, right after the interview. More coffee?"

Jim nodded and Brenda cleared their plates and moved the kettle over to heat more water.

"Do you have time to stay for a while so we can talk about it?"

"Yeah, sure. I'm off duty until tomorrow evening. My deputy is covering for me."

"That's good. Let me straighten up here, and we can have coffee in the other room."

By the time the water was hot, Brenda had finished washing the dishes and putting things away. She lit another lantern to take into the living room where she hung it on one side of the fireplace. She lit the matching lantern on the other side of the brick structure and turned as Jim brought two mugs of coffee in.

He gave her one mug and said, "Thank you for dinner. I do enjoy your cooking."

She sat on the sofa in front of the fire and smiled at him. "I enjoy the company."

They drank the coffee in comfortable silence, watching the fire.

Jim set his mug down on the side table and held out his arms to Brenda with a smile, "Want to settle back in like when we were talking last time?"

She smiled back and moved closer. "Don't mind if I do, but we need to talk this through."

"What's keeping you from knowing your own mind on this?"

"I know I can do the job, but you never know about how government projects will go. I've read stories online that sometimes, once the contractor gets the go-ahead with the people they hired for a specific project, they'll turn around and let some of those people go. And other times, they keep to the original plan and employ them for the length of the project, which in this case is supposed to be five years."

He pulled her close and rested his cheek against the top of her head. "So there's no guarantee which way it will go."

"None at all, but if I do go, and the job lasts the full five years, when I come back, there's no guarantee about how things will be between us. And if I stay, same answer."

"That's true, but if you go, there's no guarantee you won't find someone there or change your mind about this lifestyle and not want to come back."

Brenda pulled away and looked up at Jim. "I keep going around in the same circle, but what good is having more financial security when you're all alone without any friends nearby? But then, if you're on your own, that's exactly why you need to have your finances in order."

Jim took both Brenda's hands in his and looked her in the eye. "I'm attracted to you, and I'd like to see where this goes, but I don't want to stand in the way of your career. I'm not going to try to tell you what to do. It has to be your decision."

"You know, if I really wanted to go, I don't think it would have been this hard to make the choice." She stopped and nodded. "Let's find out how it goes with us. I'm going to turn down the offer and stay here."

"Just like that? Are you sure?"

"For the first time in quite a while, I'm sure." Brenda reached up to touch Jim's face, and he held her hand to his lips, kissing her palm.

They talked until the fire was glowing embers. Jim said, "I'd better head on back to town."

"Maybe you should wait until morning. I don't have a guest room set up yet, but you can share my bed, if..." Brenda broke off, not sure exactly what to say.

Jim finished the thought for her. "If we just cuddle and sleep?" He laughed. "I'm capable of being a gentleman."

"Okay, then let's get the fire built up in there." She turned down one lantern and took the other into the bedroom. "I'll put more towels in the bathroom and get ready for bed. You can hang your clothes in the closet there. I'll be right back."

Jim added wood to the fire before he undressed. Brenda came back into the room and looked at him standing next to the fireplace in his white long underwear. "They look smooth. What are they made of?"

"Silk. Very soft, and they keep you warm without a lot of bulk or weight. You should get some for yourself."

"Let me guess. Get them from Mr. Barker?"

Jim grinned at her. "No, not this time. I get mine at L.L. Bean from the internet."

Brenda turned down the bed. "You have a preference for which side of the bed?"

"Yeah, but it's your bed, so you get in first. Back in a minute."

When Jim came back from the bathroom, Brenda was waiting under the covers. Jim got in and said, "Spooning acceptable?"

"I'd like that very much." She turned on her side and moved over toward him. He kissed the side of her neck and put one arm across hers. They talked until yawns punctuated their conversation.

Brenda adjusted her pillow and said, "First one up gets to make coffee or tea."

"Sounds like a plan. Good night."

Brenda woke to the smell of fresh-ground coffee and bacon cooking on the stove. She grinned and stretched before getting up and putting on a robe. She stood in the kitchen doorway and watched Jim as he sliced bread and placed it on a sheet of foil on top of the hotter area on the stove top and folded the foil over the slices.

"I see you know your way around a kitchen."

"Hey, good morning, sleepy head. Yeah, but I don't get to cook for anyone else very often. How do you like your eggs?"

"Over easy, please." She put mugs and silverware on the table along with creamer, butter and a jar of blackberry jam before she got the pot and poured the coffee.

Jim flipped the toast and put the bacon and eggs on their plates and brought them to the table. He leaned over and gave Brenda a quick kiss on the forehead. "Let me grab the toast, and we can eat."

Jim said a quick grace before they ate.

"You'll have to show me how you did the toast. I haven't managed that yet. It's usually as dried up as croutons when I try it." She laughed. "The birds like it though."

"Do you fold your foil over the bread?"

"No, I just put it on top of the foil. So that's what makes the difference?"

"Yeah, keeps it from drying out."

"As much as I've learned, there's still a lot I don't know about living out here."

"I think you're doing a pretty good job of it—now that you know to stand to the side when you pull snow down off the panels."

Brenda gave him a playful shove when he broke into a chuckle. "I shouldn't have told you about that."

He put his hand on top of hers. "There's nothing you can't share with me. I hope you'll come to know that."

Before Brenda could answer, Fuzzy came bounding into the kitchen from the living room. He jumped up on the chair next to Brenda and let out a plaintive meow.

"Don't worry. You'll get your breakfast in a minute." She took a can of cat food down from a shelf and put it on a dish. Fuzzy rubbed against her ankles before settling in to eat.

She came back to the table and nodded yes when Jim held up the coffee pot. "Would you send an email to the people in Huntsville for me when you go back to town?"

"Why don't you ride down with me and send it yourself? I've got another helmet in the storage compartment, and the second seat is pretty comfortable."

"I'd like that, but then you'd have to come back up here again."

"And the problem with that is?"

They both laughed, and Brenda said, "Okay. After we finish eating, we can head out. I'm curious about something though."

"What's that?"

"How do you cross the roads on the snowmobile?"

"You don't have to up here. There's a snowmobile trail that winds around coming up from town and it passes right by the edge of your property. Maybe you'll get one yourself."

"Maybe. I have to see what it's like first."

"You haven't been into winter sports?"

"I used to ski, but haven't gone for years."

"Well, we've got lots of opportunities for that here too."

Brenda grinned at him. "One thing at a time. I'm going to get dressed for my first snowmobile experience."

"Okay, I'll go warm up the engine after I finish my coffee and bank the fires."

"Thanks."

Twenty minutes later, Brenda was seated behind Jim riding down the hill through a postcard landscape.

Jim pulled up behind Fanny and Joe's bed and breakfast and turned off the engine. He turned to Brenda. "So how'd you like your first snowmobile ride?"

"It was great. I'd like to do it again."

He grinned at her. "This afternoon be soon enough?" He opened the snowmobile's storage compartment and put their helmets in. Before he turned around, Fanny was waving from the back porch.

"Brenda! I'm so glad to see you. How you doing, Jim? Come on up here. It's cold out there."

Jim called to Fanny, "Hey, I want to check in at the office, and then I'll come by. Okay?"

"Sure thing. That'll give me a chance to catch up with Fanny."

Jim looked down at Brenda. "I'll be back as soon as I'm done. Need anything from the market?"

"A quart of milk?"

"You got it. Mind if I hug you in front of Fanny?"

She shook her head, and Jim wrapped his arms around her and gave her a squeeze. "See you soon."

"Hey, you two!"

At Fanny's call, they laughed and broke apart, and Brenda hurried up the walk to the porch.

"Well, well, well. Let me give you one of those too. I've been so worried about you." She swiped away tears of relief and hugged Brenda. "You don't look any worse for wear, but what's with you and your riding companion?" She bustled Brenda inside and shut the door after her. "Are you hungry?"

"No, we just finished breakfast before we came down. Get that look off your face. Nothing happened, just talk and food…and a little cuddling. But I wouldn't mind a cup of tea."

"How about some hot chocolate?"

"Oh yeah, that'd be great."

"Hang up your things here in the kitchen so they'll be nice and warm when you leave. Did you do okay up there alone?"

"A couple of minor events. Nothing too dramatic, except no phone or internet. I didn't realize how much I depend on the 'net to look things up, and how many things I still don't know about living off the grid."

"Do you want to check your email while you're here?"

"Oh gosh! I almost forgot. That's why I came down."

Fanny laughed. "To check your mail? Laptop is right there. Help yourself."

Brenda gave her friend a playful shove. "No, silly. I didn't tell you the news yet."

"And I thought you only talked and cuddled?"

"Fanny! You've got a one-track mind. If you don't mind, I'd like to use your phone first. Something I need to get done, then I'll fill you in."

"Go right ahead while I make the chocolate."

Brenda pulled out her phone and looked up Greg Abernathy's number and dialed on Fanny's landline. Greg was in a meeting, so she told his secretary she'd send him an email.

Fanny poked her head around the corner. "Go ahead, I'm dying to know what's going on."

"I'll be just a minute." Brenda logged into her webmail account and sent a brief note to Greg to thank him and decline the job offer. She ended it saying, "Six months ago, I'd have been on a plane on the way there. It wasn't an easy choice, but being on my own in this blizzard showed me I've already made the transition from city to country life, and my future is here." She read it over once more and pushed the send button. "That's it. All done."

Fanny put two mugs of chocolate on the table, and Brenda joined her there. "So, what's the story?"

"They offered me the job in Alabama."

"Oh." The smile disappeared from Fanny's face. "And you're leaving us?"

Brenda shook her head. "No, I'm not, but I needed to let them know. I've had no way to contact them, but if I hadn't gotten down here today, I think they'd have figured it out. Although they wouldn't have thought very much of me for not telling them."

"I don't know what to say. What made you decide?"

"The offer came in an email just before the service went out. At first I was happy to get an offer after so many months of looking. But I kept going back and forth about what to do. I was still undecided until Jim rode up yesterday to check on me."

"And what did he say that settled it?"

"It wasn't so much what he said as the way the picture shifted for me while we were talking. Things are different here. I can have friends who care about me, and I don't need to be alone the rest of my life the way I've been for so long."

"You do have friends here, that's for sure, and there are lots more who'd be glad to get to know you too."

Brenda took a long sip from her mug before she spoke again. "When Jim said he didn't want to stand in the way of my career, I realized I don't care about making a name in another career or earning a certain amount of money. None of that counts when you don't have anyone to share what really matters to you." Her eyes filled with tears. "Before I lost my job in L.A., I had everything I could want. But when my father died, there wasn't one person I could call."

"Maybe while you were there, you didn't want to think about what you might really want?"

"It goes back further. What Charlie did hurt me so much, I didn't want anyone to ever get that close again. And instead of getting over it, I walled off that part of me. I gave up on depending on anyone but myself."

"You have to know Jim would never treat you like that."

"I do know that, but it's too soon to know if we can have a life together."

"Have you really looked deep into his eyes? That man is smitten with you."

"I don't know if I can be who he needs or wants me to be."

"Give it some time. Don't be afraid to try. If it's not meant to be, you'll both know soon enough, but I think that spark between you is about to turn into an open flame."

The sound of laughter came from the front of the house, and the door opened. Joe called out, "Hey, look who I found wandering around."

Fanny got up. "Come on in, Jim. What can I get you?"

"Not a thing, thanks. I need to be taking Brenda back home."

"What? You just got here."

"I'm sorry. I heard the weather report at the market. The wind's going to pick up, and her gear won't keep her warm enough for that." Jim handed Brenda a small shopping bag. "Try this on."

She took out a winter face mask, and Jim helped her put it on. It covered her head and came down over her face and neck and shoulders.

"It's called a balaclava. It's not very pretty, but it'll keep you warmer on the way back, and on really cold days, you'll need it."

"Thank you. She touched the mask. "It feels strange, but it's really warm."

Fanny shooed the men toward the door. "Why don't you guys head out back while Brenda gets her coat on. We'll be right out." As soon as they left, Fanny said, "You remember what I said, okay?"

Brenda finished pulling on her gloves and nodded, "I will."

Jim took a more direct route on the way up to Brenda's than he had that morning. When they reached her driveway, she waited in the open garage door until Jim brought the snowmobile in and lowered the overhead door again.

"Can you stay a little while?"

He looked at his watch. "I do have to work tonight, but not until eight. I hope you're not angry that I dragged you out so fast."

"No, I'm glad you did. You'll have to tell me what kind of clothes I should get for the really cold weather. Plus, I'd like to spend a little time with you before you go back."

Jim opened the storage compartment and took out a bag before putting the helmets in. "I remembered the milk and got some lunch too."

"Thanks."

Once they'd taken off their outdoor clothing and hung it in the entryway, they moved into the kitchen. Jim put the bag in the refrigerator. Fuzzy came running to Brenda, meowing loudly. She picked him up.

"Poor baby. Your feet are cold. Were you standing on the windowsill?"

"He was probably watching the birds. I'll build up the fire in the living room."

"Thanks, I'll take care of the stove." She added wood to the firebox. "That should warm things up pretty quickly."

Jim came back and washed his hands at the kitchen sink before he stood behind Brenda and wrapped his arms around her. "I don't know what you must think of me, wanting to hold you close all the time."

"Umm, I don't remember complaining."

He turned her to face him. "Talk like that, and I might be tempted to do something like this." He bent to place soft little kisses along the side of her face and neck. When she smiled and closed her eyes and pressed against him, he kissed her on the lips, a soft touch that grew more insistent.

She slid her hands up along his chest and around his neck, returning his kiss, adding a little bite on his lower lip. "I think we should go in the other room." She pulled away and walked across the kitchen.

"I'm sorry. I didn't mean to…"

"Shh. Come with me." She moved to the doorway. "If you want to, that is."

He crossed the room in two long strides and reached for her.

She grinned and stepped into the bedroom, waiting for him to come in before she closed the door behind him. "I think we should leave the cat out of this." She closed the door to the bathroom, leaving the hallway door open for the cat to get to his box.

Jim held out his arms. "It's been a long time since I've been with anyone."

She moved close and looked up at him, eyes bright. "Longer for me, I'm afraid, but I think we can still figure out how it works."

Clothes puddled on the floor in a wild flurry.

They fell back against the pillows, breathless, with mellow smiles and drowsy half-closed eyes. Jim held her hand tracing the outline of each finger. She sighed, content in a way that was new to her. He pulled the covers around them and held her close. They watched the flames in the fireplace, and soon Brenda heard his breathing ease into the slow rhythm of sleep.

She grinned and slipped out of bed and into the bathroom. After she washed up, she pulled on a robe to go into the kitchen. Fuzzy came running as if she'd been away for days and rubbed against her legs purring. She opened a small tin of wet food for him, and he transferred his attention to his chopped salmon meal.

"What do you think, kitten. Maybe I should get a people lunch ready too?" Brenda took out the contents of the bag Jim had placed there earlier, two sandwiches on rolls, a plastic bag of lettuce, sliced tomatoes in one deli container and pickles in another. Two more containers held potato salad and cucumber salad. "Well, all we need are napkins, plates and some mustard and mayo." With everything set out on the table, Brenda pulled vegetable soup from the refrigerator to heat, along with a kettle of water for coffee.

She poured the water over the coffee grounds to drip, and Jim came into the kitchen with a sheepish look. "Coffee smells good. Guess I fell asleep."

Brenda smiled when he came over and hugged her. "Yeah, I guess you did. It's okay. I know that's how men are wired. Besides, it gave me time to set out lunch. Come sit down. Do you want the ham or turkey?"

"You choose. I like them both."

"Me too." She unwrapped the sandwiches, cut them in half and put half of each on their plates while Jim grinned at her.

After she'd poured the coffee, Jim took her hand and said a short grace before they started eating.

"So now that you've made the decision to stay, have you thought about what you'll do to keep busy up here?"

"No, I haven't gotten that far. I bought a loom, but haven't worked out how to set it up yet. I might try quilting. I don't know if there's any income possibilities with that. Heck, I don't even know if I can master the skills, or if I'd enjoy them. It would be good if I can develop a little income, but with my expenses so much less than in the city, I could manage on what I have without dipping too much into my pension savings."

"You're ahead of a lot of folks, then. You've also got a nest egg in your woods too."

"How's that?"

"There are mature trees along the far side of your property. You can explore harvesting and replanting. The hardwoods are a good size and would bring a good price."

"I hadn't even considered that. Good to know, though. There's so much to learn about."

"There's no rush now that you know you're staying. But I'd better get moving and get back to town."

Chapter 18

A month after the blizzard, Brenda hopped off Josh's snowmobile, and they both stamped the snow off their feet on the porch before going in. Brenda hung her coat and scarf on a hook in the kitchen and tossed her gloves on the wire rack. "What would you like? Coffee or hot chocolate?"

"Some coffee would be good. You know, Miss Brenda, I'm really glad you're going to stay on. I've been worried about what might happen to the land if you left."

"I understand. I've been thinking about that too, about what happens when my time on this earth is over."

"It's a long way before you have to think about that!"

"Thanks, Josh. I hope so, but I don't have any family, and I want to start planning for the future. And that's why I asked you to come out here today and show me the timberland on the other side of the hill."

"Ma'am?"

"I'm thinking about cleaning up some of those dead trees scattered about from the windstorm and harvesting a few acres past them off the old logging road to pay for it."

"You could just leave them and they'll break down into compost in a few years, and it wouldn't cost you anything. More trees'll sprout up on their own to replace them."

"That's true, but clearing the space and selling some of the timber would also give me some extra income to do something else." She paused while she poured the coffee and brought two mugs to the table. "I was reading about the chestnut blight that wiped out the groves this area's named for."

"Yeah, my grandfather told me stories his grandfather told him about how chestnuts grew everywhere when he was young. Wish I'd seen those big old trees, ten-foot across and a hundred feet high." Josh looked off in the distance, the depth of his memories reflected in his face. He took a sip of coffee and sighed. "They used the wood for furniture and shingles and fence posts. The bark was used to tan leather, and they fed the hogs on chestnuts in the winter, plus what they roasted and ate themselves. Sold wagonloads in big cities for cash too."

"Well, The American Chestnut Foundation's been working to develop hybrids of American chestnuts and Chinese chestnuts that are relatively blight resistant. It's an on-going process. They're making some seed available to see if they can bring back the chestnuts."

"Wow, that'd be something if it works."

"There's no guarantee where or if it will work, but I'd like to try starting a chestnut grove. I can't do it on my own though."

"Any new orchard does take some work to get started, but once they're going, it's a lot easier."

"Here's my idea. If you help me with the planting and fencing to get the grove going, I'll pay you for your time, and whether or not it works, I'll write up a trust that the land with the chestnut grove and some of the land on the other side down to the road will go to you when I pass on—if you stick with it for five years."

"I don't know what to say."

Brenda grinned at him. "Yes would be good, because I need you to make it happen."

"Yes, yes, Ma'am. Thank you. Thank you so much." Josh almost tripped over himself getting up and putting his coat on. "I've got to get home and tell my wife. Susie'll be as happy as I am. Not just at the gift of the land, but that we can try to bring back a chestnut grove. It's going on a hundred years since they died out here. A chance to do something like this—my great-great-granddaddy'll be smiling down on us."

Caught up in the excitement of the project idea, after Josh left, Brenda spent hours re-reading all the bookmarked information she had saved. Her stomach rumbled before she remembered she hadn't eaten dinner. Fuzzy was curled up, sound asleep on the bed, and the fire was almost down to glowing coals when she renewed it for the night. She made tea and fried some eggs. Yesterday's biscuits were a little hard, but she wiped up the egg yolk with them anyway, savoring each crunchy bite. *Being on my own has really taught me to enjoy the simple pleasures.* And with a yawn, she turned down the lantern and went to bed.

Before heading to the market in town, Brenda filled the bird feeder. She sat inside with a cup of tea and watched birds come and go against a blue sky Christmas card scene with a background of evergreen trees frosted with snow. Her phone rang and Brenda took it from her pocket.

"Hey, Fanny. It's gorgeous up here today."

Fanny chuckled. "I swear, you are always so happy about something there. I wonder when it will become ordinary for you."

"I'm sure it will eventually. But now, it's so different and new, even the hard work to take care of everything seems like fun."

"Well, I'm still enjoying what we do here, so hold on to those feelings. I called to see if you're in the mood to leave wonderland for a bit and go Christmas shopping with me today? The crafts shop just put up their first displays of new items."

"Christmas! I hadn't thought about it yet. I used to love shopping for my parents. I started months ahead looking for little surprises for them. Then my mom died, and my dad didn't care about holidays any more. Seems like such a long time ago."

"Now don't go getting melancholy on me. Come on down for lunch, and let's have some fun. I've got a new apple-cranberry crisp recipe I'm testing for Thanksgiving. It's got oatmeal in the topping, so it's healthy."

"Don't know about healthy, but it sounds good. See you around noon."

After lunch, Brenda and Fanny walked to Maggie's crafts store.

"Wait until you see how Maggie dresses up for Christmas. She wears a different elf costume every day. The little kids really believe she's one of Santa's helpers, and the mothers tip her off about how the kids have behaved well and what they could use a reminder about. Maggie makes up an index card with their name and looks it up when they come in. Their eyes get so big, and Maggie gets the biggest kick out of doing it."

"That's sounds like so much fun."

"It works out for a lot of people. The moms get kids behaving very nicely before Christmas, and the kids get a treat and a little holiday wonder to believe in for a while. Maggie gets some sales out of it, and the ladies who consign things to her make money too."

In the store, Maggie was unpacking a new shipment of yarn. Brenda was drawn to a grey multi-color yarn that was textured and heavy, but soft to the touch.

"Now that would make a great scarf for a certain gentleman. I have a crochet pattern that would work well on it."

Brenda blushed and smiled. "Okay, help me with how much I need and the hook to use." She continued looking through the shop and picked up some handmade wooden toys for Jim's nieces and nephews and some decorated candles. "I think that's it for me today."

Maggie wrote up the purchases while she chatted with Fanny about the guests coming to the bed and breakfast for Thanksgiving.

The next few weeks were filled with sketches of layouts for the chestnut orchard and lists of what needed to be done. Soil samples came back with good reports, so Brenda spent time with Mr. Barker working out the best materials for fencing out deer and large animals and deciding on what protection to use against the smaller critters on the ground. When the materials were selected and the amounts figured out, it was easy to set up a budget. Once Brenda knew the amount they'd need to get the chestnut grove started, Josh worked with the forester to select and mark the trees to be harvested.

"Okay, Miss Brenda. Here are the contracts for the harvesting and for the sale of the lumber. Simpson's the best. Always leaves the site in good shape, and he's careful not to do any damage to the slope that will cause erosion with the spring rains. He's the only one my family's used for years."

"I trust your judgement on this. There's too much about all this for anyone to pick up in one season." She picked up a pen, read through the documents once more, and signed them with a flourish. "There. Our chestnut project now has its income source arranged. How about some coffee and chocolate chip cookies to celebrate?"

"Your chocolate chip cookies are still my favorite, but don't tell Susie!"

"Don't worry. Your secret is safe with me. So, do all the Barkers have a big gathering for Thanksgiving or several small ones?"

Josh dropped his cookie and looked stricken. "I'm so sorry. I never thought to ask you to join us."

Brenda patted his hand. "That's not why I asked. I was just curious. I'm going down to spend the holiday with Joe and Fanny and help her with dinner. She's having a whole crowd between her guests and local folks."

"That's a relief. My father-in-law would give me what for if he found out you were alone on Thanksgiving 'cause I didn't ask you."

"I have a lot to be thankful for this year. Finding a new home, a new way of life, new friends, and a lifetime project that will be here long after me with any luck."

"Amen to that. I'd better get going. I can make it to the post office before Arthur's pick up and get these contracts out. Here are the copies for your files."

"Thanks, Josh, and thanks for all you've done to get us this far."

"Aw, it's not all that much." But his expression said how much it meant to him.

Chapter 19

The afternoon of Christmas Eve, Brenda opened the door to a postcard landscape. She filled the bird feeder and swept off the newest sprinkle of snow from the porch before stopping to look over the view in front of the house. Cardinals were bright spots of color among the snow-dotted evergreens, and the fresh snowfall sparkled in the setting sun.

How many times have I looked out in California with glimpses of the ocean? As much as I enjoyed them, none made me feel as much at home as this view does. The phone interrupted her thoughts. She saw Jim's number on the caller id and hurried inside before pulling off her gloves to answer.

"Hey, are you on your way up?"

"I'm leaving now. Dress warm. It gets chilly out caroling."

"Okay. I'm looking forward to it."

She lit the lantern next to the fireplace, turned the flame down low, and checked the effect of the firelight on the tree with its cranberry and popcorn garlands and bright star at the top. Tears stung her eyes when she thought how much her mother would have liked being there to see it, but she shook it off when she heard the crunch of snow as Jim's car came up the drive. She had her coat and hat on before he pulled to a stop and took two shopping bags out to the car. Jim came around to greet her with a hug and open the car door.

"Those twinkle lights around the porch look great! Aren't they a drain on the batteries?"

"Nope. They're solar-powered."

Jim put the bags in the back while Brenda slid into the front seat. "So who's going to be there tonight?"

"Oh, just my sister Mary Beth and her husband Bob and the three kids, my brother Bill and his wife Rita, and their two kids, two aunts and an uncle."

"Will they mind a stranger being there?"

Jim patted her leg. "Don't worry. They'd be glad to see you even if you were a stranger, but you're a member of the community now, and they probably know more about you than you can imagine."

"I guess word gets around in small towns?"

"Oh, yeah. If you haven't already noticed, a lot of socializing goes on in the market. People plan trips into town to go to the post office to pick up the paper, or for club meetings, or to pick up kids from sports. Then they go shopping afterwards. When they run into each other at the market, it gives them the chance to catch up on the latest on who's doing what."

"Have you told your family a lot about me?"

Jim laughed. "A lot? I don't know. My sister started asking questions the night after we went to the American Legion dinner. A lot of people made sure she knew what I was up to. I should hire her as an investigator. She finds out everything, usually sooner than later. But I know they're all going to be happy that I'm there with someone special and not alone as usual."

Brenda flushed with pleasure hearing Jim say she was someone special, but wasn't sure how to respond. She was relieved when the car pulled up in the driveway of a well-kept two-story frame house a couple of blocks past Main Street.

"Here we are." Jim got out and took the bags from the backseat and handed one to her. They walked up to the door which flew open before they reached it. A chorus of "Uncle Jim!" emerged before five children tumbled out to jump up and down around him.

He reached into the large bag and handed smaller ones with gifts to each of the oldest children. "Here, put these under the tree for tomorrow." They cheered and ran to see what the packages looked like.

Brenda grinned and stood back a bit from the tumult.

Mary Beth shooed the kids. "It's cold out! Jim will see you inside. Scoot. Hi, Brenda. Sorry for the noisy reception."

"I can see somebody's popular around here."

"He spoils them rotten."

"I'm just carrying on Mom's tradition."

"You do a fine job of it. Come on in, Brenda. Let me introduce you to Rita while Jim catches up on sports with the guys."

In the kitchen, Brenda unpacked the desserts she'd made—strawberries that looked like little Santas.

"Those are adorable!" Mary Beth handed her a cup of hot spiced cider. "Okay. Now sit down and tell us how you made them." Brenda relaxed and chatted with Mary Beth and Rita. "They're easy. Just slice off the tip at the bottom. That will be the hat. Slice off the stem end and scoop out the white part in the center. Then you use a pastry bag to pipe sweetened cream cheese with some vanilla into the space a little above the top edge and a bit down the front for a beard. Put the cap on, and a dot of cream cheese at the very top. That's it."

Rita picked up one that came apart during the trip and popped it into her mouth. "Well, they are delicious, and I'm glad you made them because I wouldn't have the patience."

Jim stood in the doorway and smiled at Brenda. "Looks like they're taking good care of you. What's that you've got there?" He took one step forward toward the strawberries before his sister stopped him.

"Oh, no you don't. They're for after dinner. How about you round up the kids and get them dressed to go out."

Brenda put her cup in the sink. "I'd better get my things on too."

Mary Beth said, "Dinner will be ready when you get back."

The street lights were festooned in holly, and the houses were decorated with colorful lights. Brenda was almost as excited as the children. "You know, this is the first time I've been out caroling."

One of the girls came over and put her mittened hand in Brenda's. "Oh, Miss Brenda, it's so much fun."

They turned a corner and Jim pointed out a group of people arriving at the town square. "Hey, kids. We're right on time. Now stay together so we don't lose any of you."

The buildings around the square were outlined in lights, and twinkle lights wound around the pillars of the bandstand. A huge tree stood in front, and after the mayor welcomed everyone, one of the town's ministers read the Christmas Story while members of his youth group created a living nativity scene, complete with a cow, a goat, and assorted dogs on leashes. When he finished reading, someone flipped the switch to light the tree.

It took Brenda a few moments to control the surge of emotion at being part of the celebration after spending so many years alone. She joined in on the second line of "Joy to the World." Jim's rich baritone voice pleased her on a visceral level, and when she looked up, it seemed her pleasant alto had the same effect on him.

When the program ended, they started back, with the children still singing. Jim and Brenda walked behind them, arm in arm. *This is like a scene out of a movie. Everything is perfect. The decorated streets and homes, happy kids, and being with Jim.* She was startled to realize they were back at the house.

Mary Beth came out of the kitchen. "So how was it, Brenda?"

"It was a lot of fun. I think the kids enjoyed it too."

"She sings pretty good for a city girl."

"Big brother, what a way with words you have. I have something in the kitchen for you two." When they got to the doorway, she turned and pointed up. There was a bunch of mistletoe tied with a red ribbon hanging there. "Well, now just look at that. Bad luck not to use it."

Jim looked at Brenda. "Do you mind, in front of everyone?"

She shook her head, and he bent down and kissed her lightly on the lips, then changed his mind and kissed her again. Her response left no doubt she enjoyed it as much as he did. She realized everyone was watching and grinning. She fanned her face with her hand and turned to Mary Beth. "I think we could use some of that cider about now."

She laughed and whispered in Brenda's ear. "Thanks for being a good sport. We're really happy you two found each other."

After dinner, Jim got their coats. "Sorry have to leave early, but I've got the early shift tomorrow. Dinner was great. Thank you all."

The others gathered around to say goodbye.

Mary Beth hugged Jim and turned to Brenda. "We're glad you could be here and delighted to get to know you."

"Thank you. I had a wonderful time. I'd love to make dinner for you in the New Year."

"Bob and I will take you up on that."

Jim and Brenda were quiet on the ride up to her home. In the driveway, she asked, "Want to come in for a cup of coffee? I have more of the cookies and strawberries you liked."

"Sounds good. I'd like that."

"I noticed you have your uniform in the back."

"Oh. You did?"

"Yes. So, would you like to spend the night?"

"Can we skip the coffee?"

In the morning, they talked about the evening before over scrambled eggs, sausage and waffles. Jim pushed back from the table. "Wish I could spend the day with you, but work is waiting. I work the holidays to let one or another of the deputies have the day off."

"I packed up some cookies for you to take to the station."

"Thanks." Jim kissed her. "I almost forgot your Christmas present. Let me get it from the car."

Brenda waited for him by the tree and pulled out a package when he came in. "And I have something for you."

They sat on the sofa and tore off the wrappings. Brenda found an elegant black box with a bottle of Shalimar perfume. "Thank you. I've never tried this." Brenda put a bit on her wrist and throat. Her reaction was uncertain. "It is different from those I know."

"My sister said to tell you that it changes after you have it on a little while. So don't judge it by the first sniff."

"Okay, we'll see what it's like later."

"I can check it at dinner at Fanny's."

"That's great. I didn't know you were coming!"

Jim looked sheepish. "I forgot I was planning to surprise you."

"You surprised me now, so that's fine."

He finished opening his gift and pulled out a crocheted scarf in multi-toned grey and white. He wrapped it around his neck. "Did you do this yourself? I didn't know you crocheted."

"I took some lessons from Maggie. I wanted to surprise you."

"You did. Come here and cuddle up for a few minutes before I go." She curled up against him, his arms around her. "I'm going to think of you every time I wear this." He gave her a soft kiss. "There. The perfume has already changed. Do you like it now?"

Brenda sniffed her wrist. "Oh! That is nice. I wasn't sure at first."

Jim stood up and pulled her to her feet. He hugged her and put on his coat. "Well, I'll still want to check it out again tonight."

"Fine by me." She punctuated her words with a hug of her own.

Over the winter, Brenda's garage became the receiving station for deliveries for the chestnut orchard. Stepping over stacks of fiberglass tubing that would become protection for the chestnut seedlings, Brenda called Josh and got his answering machine. "Hi, it's Brenda. Give me a call when you have time please. I'd like your advice on some kind of storage shed for the orchard supplies."

Her initial delight with winter weather had faded by January into a longing for sunshine and warmth. She felt the urge to be working in the garden, but it was still too early to start. She settled for making a loaf of bread and chocolate chip cookies for what she'd come to call Josh's cookie jar.

The phone rang just as she slid the cookie sheet into the oven. Glancing at the caller id first, she greeted Josh with a laugh. "Did you smell the cookies over there?"

"No, but save me some."

"They'll be in your jar."

Brenda negotiated with Josh for four additional men and supplies to build a storage shed. She insisted on including lunch as part of the deal over Josh's mild protest. When the call finished, she checked the pantry. Only a few onions and a half dozen jars of the tomatoes she'd put up last summer were left. The summer windstorm had reduced the harvest by half. Still, the vegetables stretched her budget over the fall and winter farther than she'd imagined possible.

She brought a large mason jar of tomatoes and an onion into the kitchen for the soup before she punched down the bread and covered it again. The landscape still looked winter-bare, but hints of green dotted the land and woods. A second batch of cookies replaced the first in the oven, and Brenda called Fanny, eager to share the news of how well everything was going with the chestnut project. When the cookies were done, Brenda reset the timer for the bread before making a shopping list.

Fuzzy took advantage of the moment and leaped up onto Brenda's lap. She put down the pen and petted him. He purred and rubbed his face against her for a minute before he decided he'd had enough and jumped down to dash into the other room. Brenda checked the time, then called her accountant in California.

"Brenda! How are you? Are you coming back soon?"

"No, actually I'm calling because I won't be back at all."

"Have you found a job there?"

"No, I had an offer, but decided I liked the lifestyle here better, and I'm staying."

"That's a surprise. How are you doing?"

"My cabin's off-the-grid, but modern and I like it. I have a wood stove and solar-powered electricity, all kinds of gardens and trees for fruit and vegetables. I even have a windmill to pump water from the well. Would you believe I've learned to crochet, and I'm going to take quilting lessons."

"Better you than me. I like the excitement of the city. How are you doing for funds. Do you need to liquidate some of your holdings?"

"That's why I'm calling. I need your help to figure the best way to go. I still have some cash from the condo sale that will take care of my expenses for a while. I lost a couple of acres of timber in a windstorm and decided to clean up the area and replant in chestnut trees. I had a few acres of timber cut to sell at the same time to pay for the cleanup and replanting."

"How much property do you have?"

"Altogether, 98 acres. It's not all wooded, but most is."

"Wow. That's a lot of land."

"I'm still getting used to the idea. I haven't even seen all of it yet, but the loggers cleaned up an old road to get to the trees they cut, so I'll be able to drive in from the other side of the hill off the main highway to explore when the weather warms up. So, what documents or other information will you need to do my taxes?"

"Well, let me check the rules on silviculture and casualty losses. My fee's going to be a bit steeper than usual, but it'll include setting up the business for you too. Do you expect to sell more lumber?"

"I can if I need to, but I'd rather keep that to a minimum."

"How about if I work up a few retirement planning options? I'll review your investments and suggest some ways to cover your expenses until you start drawing on your pension fund and social security. Look for an email tomorrow with a list of the paperwork to send. And Brenda, I'm really glad you landed on your feet there."

On Saturday, the shed construction started with the arrival of Josh's pickup followed by a truck loaded with lumber that backed up on the paved area next to the garage. While the men started bustling about unloading the materials, Josh made sure Brenda knew the men would take care of the building, and they'd let her know when it was ready for her to view.

"So you're telling me in a nice way not to get underfoot?" She laughed and turned toward the kitchen corridor. "Okay. I get it. I'll be here when you're all ready to eat."

The sounds of a saw cutting wood and nail guns putting it together soon echoed off the trees. Before noon, Brenda was heating up the soup and making sandwiches. By late afternoon, the roof was done, the supplies moved in, and the men were headed home.

Chestnut Springs was not where Brenda imagined her future, but it was now her life.

By March, Josh had completed fencing the orchard site and constructed gates to the logging road and to Brenda's homestead for maintenance access. A small bridge allowed Josh to drive his pickup over the stream without damaging it.

Josh's whole family turned out for planting day at the end of March, along with friends from the Rescue Squad. The minister from the Christmas Eve tree lighting arrived with the youth group from his church and said a prayer for the success of the project before they began working. With so many willing hands, the planting of 400 seeds and placement of the 2-foot tree guards went quickly. When all the seeds were in and protected, each one was watered with spring water from the stream. Everything was done by mid-afternoon.

Josh and Brenda thanked each person as they left the site and headed into town to the American Legion hall where the Women's Auxiliary from the Rescue Squad had cooked dinner for everyone.

Josh heard his brother call from the path to the driveway. "Hurry up and come on down. We can't start eating until you get there."

"Okay, we'll be right behind you."

Before the last people left, Josh went over to one man and said something. He nodded, and Josh came back to Brenda. "C'mere, Ms. Brenda. Stand here with me."

The man Josh spoke to came over and took a few photographs of Josh and Brenda in front of the open gate with the new orchard behind them. The man handed the camera to Josh and hurried to catch up to the others. Josh closed the gate and walked down the path with Brenda. "We won't know for a while, but maybe we just started something important, and I wanted a picture to remember this day by."

Brenda grinned and nodded, afraid if she spoke, she'd break down in happy tears.

Chapter 20

Two weeks after the chestnut planting, someone knocked at the front door on a bright Sunday morning and startled Brenda awake. Fuzzy growled, his back arched and fur standing up. "What in the world?" She pulled back the edge of the curtain and saw one of Jim's deputies at the door. This time, she heard him call, "Sheriff's deputy."

Heart pounding, she grabbed a robe and pulled it on as she hurried to the door and opened it part way. "What is it? What's wrong?"

"There's been a complaint filed against you, and I need you to come into town with me so we can straighten it out."

Brenda opened the door wider and motioned for him to come in. "What complaint?"

"Sorry, I can't discuss it here, but we'll fill you in when you get there."

"Can I come down later on my own?"

He shrugged. "Sorry, I need to bring you down now to get it cleared up."

"Well, I have to get dressed and feed the cat before I can go. Do you want a cup of coffee while you wait?"

"No, thank you." He looked around the living room. "I've heard about this place, but I've never been in it before. Do you like living up here away from everyone?"

"It's only a few minutes from town, but it is nice to have all this space and great views."

"Mind if I look around while you get ready to go?"

"Not at all. I'll just be a few minutes."

Brenda picked up the cat's food and water bowls and bag of dry food on her way into the bathroom from the hall. She filled the bowls and hurried into the bedroom to pull on a sweater and slacks. She tended the fire and brought the covered pail of ashes into the kitchen with her. "Let me put this into the garage so I can empty it later."

"Could I look at the garage?"

"Sure, come on down." She pointed to the batteries and indicators in the corridor on the way to the garage. "This makes it easy to keep track that everything's working okay with the solar connections."

He looked around at the new lumber scraps stacked in a corner. "Been building something?"

She nodded. "Yes, I had a storage shed built. The supplies for the new project were taking up so much space in here, and I thought it would be good to have a place for all my gardening equipment and supplies if I expand my gardens. I might use the leftover wood to build racks for hydroponic trays to start seedlings indoors and maybe grow a few things over the winter. Have to see if my solar panels can run the lights I'd need first."

"Would you show me the shed?"

"It's nothing fancy, but sure." Brenda opened the door and waited for him to follow as she walked over and opened the shed's double doors. "Once I get some racks and hooks in here, I can move all my garden tools out of the garage. I'm going to extend the driveway around here. That'll make it easy to get things in and out. I might set up a rack for drying herbs too."

"Drying herbs?"

"Yes, I might plant some kitchen herbs and maybe lavender to sell this summer."

"We'd better get going." The deputy closed the doors behind them.

Brenda went back into the house and grabbed her purse from the back of a chair.

The deputy stood at the front door waiting for her. She followed him down the steps, startled when he opened the back of the Sheriff's Department SUV, motioning with his head for her to get in. "It'll be more comfortable for you there."

A skeptical Brenda climbed in, the first twinge of mistrust putting her on edge. "Can't you please tell me what's going on?"

"We'll be at the office in a few minutes."

The ice in his voice made Brenda's stomach flip. She sat back and slipped her phone out of her purse and flipped the switch to silent. She pecked out a text message to Fanny. *Deputy Morris taking me to sta.*

Won't say why. I'm scared. Meet me there. Jim out of town. Leave him msg.

She prayed Fanny had her cell phone on or would look at it soon. She deleted the message and slid the phone back into her purse.

When they reached the station, the deputy opened the door. "Go inside." He stayed a step behind her while she entered. He pointed to a room off to the side and told Brenda, "Wait for me there." Brenda looked around. Fanny wasn't there yet. She entered a room that held only a table with three chairs and turned to face the deputy who had stopped in the doorway.

"Sit down."

Brenda took a step back from him, numb with fright. "What is going on?"

"Just sit there until we're ready to talk to you." He closed the door behind him.

Light grey walls, bare of any decoration, merged with a ceiling of the same color. A recessed fluorescent light illuminated the area over the table, but left the rest of the room in depressing shadows. Brenda set her purse on a chair and laid her coat on top of it. She sat on a wood chair facing the door. The chairs matched, but looked like they'd been handed down from an office of forty years ago. They had nothing in common with the ugly green table. Its heavy metal frame matched the worn inset Formica surface, maybe a work table from the same office the chairs used to inhabit. Brenda glanced at the closed door and slipped her phone out of her purse, checked it and slid it back into an outer pocket of the purse. No reply from Fanny, but it hadn't even been a half hour.

Brenda wished Jim were there. He'd tell her what was happening and not let her sit here, alone and afraid. Or would he? What was the mysterious complaint? Who made it? Why? Thoughts scurried like rats gnawing at what was left of her self-confidence. That must be the point of this ugly room, to make someone lose track of time and be so uncomfortable they'd say anything to get out into the sunshine again.

After a while, she heard several excited voices in the other room, followed by the banging of the front door opening and closing. The deputy opened the door and paused to tell someone, "Label all of it and lock it in the evidence room." Still standing in the doorway, he smiled at Brenda, his face and eyes even colder than before. "April." He called to a middle-aged woman typing at a computer on the other side of the office. "I need you to pat her down for weapons."

The words shocked Brenda like a slap in the face.

As soon as the woman entered, the deputy ordered Brenda to stand up. "Brenda Maxwell, you are under arrest for the cultivation of marijuana and possession with intent to distribute."

Brenda stood while the room swirled around her. She followed instructions as April searched her and glared at her the whole time. When the examination was complete, the woman said, "No weapons."

The deputy pushed Brenda's coat and purse at April and said, "Check these and inventory the contents of her purse." April nodded and left the room.

Brenda's initial shock wore off. "What are you talking about? Why are you doing this?"

"We got information you were cultivating marijuana, and we don't take kindly to activity like that. Maybe it's okay where you come from, but not around here."

"That's ridiculous. I've done no such thing."

"Drying racks for kitchen herbs? Yeah, right. You can tell it to the magistrate. We have a lot of evidence for someone who didn't do anything. Come with me." He steered her to a corner of the office where he photographed her and took her fingerprints. He handed her a wet wipe to clean the ink off her fingers. "Put out your hands."

Brenda blanched at the sight of the handcuffs the deputy took from his belt, but she held out her hands, wincing at the tightness of the cuffs when he fastened them. April draped Brenda's coat over her shoulders. The deputy led her outside and posed next to her while the reporter for the local paper snapped a picture and shouted questions at Brenda. Face flaming with embarrassment, she ignored them and tried to hold her head up as they crossed the street to the courthouse.

Once they were in the courtroom, Deputy Morris unlocked the handcuffs. Brenda rubbed her wrists, the discomfort distracting her while the typical courtroom opening procedures continued around her. She forced herself to focus on the deputy's words to the magistrate.

"These photographs show the plants where we found them on Miss Maxwell's property, and how they were put into these bags. The old stalks and new plants were weighed at the station. There was a total of five pounds of plants. Miss Maxwell recently had an old logging road cleared near where the plants were found. We believe that was to gain easier access. She allowed me to look around her house this morning, and there was no other evidence visible, but there's a new shed where she told me she plans to put drying racks. When we went up the logging road, we saw a fenced in area. Now no one around here puts up fences in their woods. She bought her property and truck for cash last year, and has no visible means of support since arriving from California."

"Well, Fred, sounds like you had more than enough probable cause to justify an arrest. Leave the report with my clerk, and you can have a seat."

"Stand up, Miss Maxwell." The magistrate looked her up and down as if she'd spit in his soup. "Miss Maxwell, you do not need to enter a plea at this time. The complaint is drug possession with intent to distribute. You have the right to retain an attorney or request one if you cannot obtain one. You are not required to make a statement and anything you say may be used against you. You have the right to a preliminary examination. Do you waive your right to a preliminary examination?"

Brenda hesitated. What did that mean? Was it something she should or shouldn't do? Before she could answer, the door to the courtroom flew open. A heavyset man who looked to be in his sixties bustled down the aisle and stood next to Brenda. Your Honor, Jonathan N. Hubbard. I've been retained to represent Ms. Maxwell. She does not waive a preliminary hearing."

"Very well. We'll set the date for ten days from today. According to the arresting officer's report, the defendant is not employed, has no family in the area, and is a recent resident with no substantial ties to the community. He believes she presents a flight risk and requests a high bail be set. I'm inclined to agree."

"Your Honor, Ms. Maxwell has invested in property in this community and chose to make a life here. She has developed close friendships and has been active in the community in the few months she's been here. She's never been arrested and has never had so much as a traffic ticket. She has no surviving family and is supporting herself on savings she put aside from a lifetime of honest work and the sale of her former residence. She is anxious to clear her name of these unfounded charges and has no intention of fleeing this jurisdiction. I ask that she be released on her own recognizance."

"I'm sorry, Jonathan. This is a serious offense, and I cannot ignore the extensive evidence presented in support of the charges. I set bail at $35,000, cash or surety."

Brenda's knees buckled, and Mr. Hubbard put his arm around her to steady her through the closing of the proceedings. After the magistrate left the room, Brenda sank into her chair.

"I'm sorry I couldn't be here sooner. You can call me Jonathan. Mind if I call you Brenda?"

She shook her head, and he continued talking.

"Our friends at the Sheriff's office gave me a run-around about where you were. Fanny's been beside herself trying to find you. She caught up with me at church and practically dragged me to the office to get them to say where they had you."

"Why are they doing this? Who said I was growing marijuana?"

"Shh. Not here. Fanny should be back with the bail bondsman any minute."

Deputy Morris stood in front of Brenda and held the handcuffs out. "All right. That's enough. You can finish your chat in the holding cell. Stand up and put your hands out."

The lawyer stood up. "Come on, Fred. That's not necessary. Are you in a hurry to get to Sunday dinner? Just give us a few minutes so we can complete the bondsman's paperwork."

"Hmph. I didn't know you took care of drug dealers, Jonathan. Thought you were a better man than that."

"Seems I know better than you who is and who isn't one, Fred."

"We got the proof. You can't win this one. No sense tarnishing your name over this drug dealer."

Fanny rushed in, hurrying the bondsman along. The paperwork was soon completed, and the lawyer passed the papers to the magistrate's clerk who scowled and read every word to make sure they were correct before accepting them and signing the release form.

The deputy was no happier than the clerk. "You better show up at the preliminary hearing, or I'll track you down and haul you back."

"You can relax yourself. She'll be there."

The deputy bit back a response and turned and left.

"First of all, sign this agreement that says I'm your attorney of choice. Fanny gave me a dollar for you as a retainer."

"I'll take care of any fees."

He snorted. "That's not a problem. Fanny'd have my hide if I didn't help you, and Janie Allen would fly back here and go after what Fanny left. You haven't been here long, but you've made some good friends. Seems like you found an enemy as well, maybe two."

Brenda took the pen and scrawled her name and added the date.

"Good. Now, anything you say to me is protected."

"So what do we do now?"

"Come by my office tomorrow at 11. I need to see their evidence and talk to a few people first thing in the morning. Find out how this all got started. Oh. One question. Did you call Jim Holt about all this?"

"No, I knew he was out of town at a conference until tomorrow. He's flying back tonight. So I asked Fanny to get in touch."

"That's good. Keeps him clear of this for now. The election's only three weeks away. So there may be some political backlash because he's been seeing you." He grinned at Brenda's surprised reaction. "It's a small town. Going to the tree lighting with him and his nieces and nephews has had tongues wagging since Christmas. A lot of single women are feeling pretty envious about now. Fanny, get her out of here while I start sorting this out."

Brenda put on her coat and turned to the lawyer. "Thank you for helping me."

"It's okay. It's what neighbors do for each other."

Chapter 21

Fanny ushered Brenda out and across the street to reclaim her handbag. April looked over to the deputy and waited for his nod of approval before she retrieved the bag and shoved a form in front of Brenda to sign. As soon as she had, April snatched up the form and the pen and pushed the purse across the counter. Brenda took it and went out the door and turned toward Fanny's. Fanny had to hurry to catch up.

"Slow down, will you. I'm too out of shape to keep up."

"I'm sorry. I just want to get away from that place."

"I don't blame you. This whole thing is unbelievable."

"Did you see the way that woman looked at me?"

"Don't worry. Jonathan will take care of it for you. Now let's get you something to eat before I take you home."

"Thanks, but I'm not hungry."

"Nonsense. You didn't have a chance to eat before Fred Morris dragged you into the office, and it's almost dinnertime now. You have to eat something." Fanny went into the B&B and was on her way to the kitchen as soon as she took off her coat. Brenda followed.

"Sit down while I make tea. Now what will you have?"

"You won't leave me alone until I agree to eat something, will you?"

"Right."

"Toast with apple butter. Okay?"

"Yes. I'll do that and have tea ready in a couple of minutes."

Brenda sat back and ran through the day's events one more time trying to make some sense of it. "Fanny, why was the deputy so ready to believe I did this? It doesn't make sense. Those old stalks had to be a year old at least. I wasn't even here then."

Fanny turned to look at Brenda, shaking her head. "You don't know who Fred Morris is, do you?"

"No. Should I?"

"No reason you should, except it might explain what's going on."

Brenda sat forward. "Why? Tell me."

"Fred is Sallie Ann Miller's brother." Fanny sighed at Brenda's blank look. "Sallie of the evil tongue and dirty looks? She's the only one you've ticked off enough that I can think of. But the other thing you might not know is that Fred filed at the last minute and plans to run in the election for Jim's job."

"Oh no. I've been so wrapped up in the chestnut orchard project, and Jim never let on that there was any real contest. So they plan to use this to discredit him?"

"You got it in one."

Brenda burst into tears. "It's not right. It's just not right."

Fanny shrugged and handed Brenda a box of tissues before she put a plate with a cheese omelette and toast on the table. "Of course it isn't. That's politics and jealousy. A few tears will help clear things up, but don't overdo it. Now blow your nose, and eat this. You need to keep up your strength. I'll get the apple butter."

Brenda ate two bites of the eggs and put her fork down. "So that's what Jonathan meant about political backlash?"

"Yes. Now keep eating, and let's think this through."

The bang of the front door announced the return of Fanny's husband from a men's club program. He rushed into the kitchen. "I'm glad to see you, Brenda. What in heaven's name is going on? Are you okay? I heard some crazy stories."

"Easy, Joe. Let me fill you in while she eats."

After an hour's conversation, Joe and Fanny drove Brenda home. Even though the house was dark inside, it was apparent the front door was ajar.

Joe turned to the women. "You two stay here while I check this out." He took a flashlight from the glove compartment and eased his car door shut. He crept up to the house and took out his pistol before entering. After a few minutes, a lantern's glow shone through the doorway. Joe came to the door and called for the women to come in. He handed Brenda a folded paper. "Search warrant. They made a mess."

"My cat! Fuzzy? Fuzzy?" She lit a lantern in the kitchen and hung it up and lit a second one to take into the bedroom, calling for the cat and looking in every corner on the way. She stepped over the books pulled off the shelves in the kitchen and bedroom and looked in the cat's usual hiding places.

Her bed linens were on the floor and the mattress askew. In tears, Brenda called again, but this time, she heard a plaintive mew in the closet. She hung the lantern on the wall and bent down at the open closet door. "Here, baby. Come here."

Fuzzy took a hesitant step forward, and Brenda reached out and picked him up. She sat in the rocker and talked to him, petting him to soothe him—and herself.

When Fanny slipped in and went right to the fireplace to build up the fire, Brenda noticed how cold the house was. "How could they do this and leave the door open? What if my poor cat had run outside in fright? The deputy knew he was here. I told him I had to feed the cat before I left."

Joe came in and looked around in disgust. "I built up the fire in the stove and put up a kettle for tea. How's the cat?"

"His little feet are so cold, but I think he'll be okay. I don't understand why they did this. Morris came in. He looked all around. He went in the garage and the shed. I didn't try to hide anything. Why did he do this?"

Joe shook his head. "I don't know what he expected to find." He helped Fanny straighten the mattress, and she put on clean linens while Joe picked up the books and put them back up on the shelves.

Fanny bundled up the linens in one of the sheets. "I'll take these down and wash them."

"You don't have to do that."

"But I'm going to." The tea kettle whistled and she hurried to move it off the heat and make tea while Joe stood the kitchen chairs upright and put them at the table.

Brenda tucked Fuzzy under a blanket on the bed and joined Joe and Fanny.

Joe turned to his wife. "Fanny, I want you to stay up here with Brenda tonight. I don't expect any more nonsense, but I'm going to leave my pistol with you, just in case. Just don't use it unless someone is in the house."

Brenda's eyes widened. "It won't come to that, will it?"

"Not likely, but I'll feel better knowing Fanny has it, and she knows how to use it if you're worried about that."

Before Brenda could answer, Fanny's phone rang. She took it out of her pocket, and after a glance at the caller id, she handed it over. "It's Jim. As much as you want to see him, remember what Jonathan said."

Brenda nodded and answered the phone on the way into the bedroom. "Hi, Jim. You in a place where we can talk for a few minutes?"

"Brenda? Why do you have Fanny's phone? What's wrong?"

"She's fine, but I'm in a world of trouble."

Jim listened to Brenda's description of all that had happened before he spoke. "I'm sorry. This is all because of the election. I had no idea Fred would go to such lengths, or I'd have warned you. Not that I could have imagined he'd dream this up."

"It still seems so crazy to me, but he had those dead and live plants. I don't know where they came from."

"I know. Let's not talk any more about it. Okay? I'll call Hubbard tomorrow and see what we can and can't do and say and ask him to tell you the same things. This is going to get worse before it gets better, even if I drop out of the election."

"Don't you dare do that. You can't let him win by this kind of dirty trick. Who needs a sheriff who's willing to do what Fred Morris is doing to get elected?"

"Okay. Okay, I hear you. I want to be with you and hold you and tell you it's all right, but you understand I won't be able to?"

"Joe and Fanny both told me that. My head knows it's what has to be, but it's going to be hard going through this knowing I can't even talk to you."

"I know. I'm glad you have them on your side. That should help with a lot of the people in town too. I need to talk to Joe, but before I do, I have to tell you to remember that no matter what happens, or what you may hear, I care about you. Maybe more than I've ever cared about anyone else. Remember that, okay?"

Brenda choked back tears. "Okay."

"We'll get through this. Now let me talk to Joe."

Brenda went back into the kitchen and handed the phone to Joe. "He wants to speak to you."

Joe took the phone and went into the living room to talk. Brenda sat down and leaned her head on her hands. Fanny reached over and patted her on the shoulder.

"Why don't you go take a shower and get into something warm. I'll find out what Jim had to say to Joe, and tell you when you come out."

Brenda nodded and went to the bedroom to get out her pajamas. When she opened the dresser drawer, she saw that someone had gone through all of her things, unfolding them and stuffing them back in. It was the last straw for her composure, and she fell on the bed sobbing.

Fanny rushed in and saw the open drawer and the tangle of clothes inside. She sat next to Brenda and waited until she'd cried herself out. "Go ahead, and get that shower. We can talk in the morning. I'll set the alarm and see to the house. You just get into bed and get some sleep. I'll borrow one of your nightgowns, if that's okay."

Brenda sat up and nodded, exhaustion etched on her face.

Fanny left the room and closed the door behind her. Joe was waiting at the table.

"She okay?"

"I guess. It's an awful lot to deal with in one day."

"Yeah, it is. I looked to see if Brenda used the same charger to charge up your phone battery, and it was, but it wasn't working. So I checked the house batteries, and when they went through the house today, someone disconnected the lines from the batteries. There was no call to do that. Plain meanness. You make sure you lock up the doors tonight."

"Yeah. I plan to. Were you able to reconnect the wires?"

" I did, but I'll call Josh to come check out the system tomorrow and look around outside to make sure they didn't tamper with anything else."

"Joe, do you think they'd go after Josh too?"

"I doubt it. I don't think Fred would mess with the Barkers or their family. But I've got to get Jim's campaign committee together. We need to decide on a strategy. The sheriff candidates' forum is the day before Brenda's hearing."

In the morning, Brenda dropped Fanny off at the B&B before going to the lawyer's office. She paused outside to look at the spring flowers just beginning to open in the landscaped border along the walk. She wished she were home working on the orchard.

Jonathan Hubbard's secretary showed her into his office as soon as she entered.

Jonathan shook hands with her. "Have a seat and let's get started. We've got a lot to cover. First of all, did you plant or cultivate this stuff in any way, or get someone else to do it?"

"No! Of course I didn't. I have no idea where they got this evidence, or why they think I'm involved." She shook with anger, but looked one blink away from tears.

"Easy, now. I believe you, but I have to know where we stand if I'm going to help you. Fred was right. I don't do criminal work as a rule, and I need more information before I can bring in someone else to help if need be. Did you make any statements?"

"I don't remember exactly what I said before I knew there was a problem. Fred Morris asked all kinds of things about the cabin and the solar power and I answered him. He asked to see the garage and shed, so I showed them to him. When I got to the station, I just said there must be a mistake. That I didn't do what they said."

"West Virginia has very strict rules about prosecuting drug charges. Any amount over 15 grams is considered possession with intent to distribute. Anyone convicted gets mandatory jail time and confiscation of any involved property. They say they collected five pounds of material from your land near the logging road."

"This is crazy. I've never even gone down that logging road, much less had anything to do with what they found."

"Hmm. Wish there were a way to prove that. It would settle the whole thing, but you do own the property and could have gone there."

Brenda turned pale. "Do you think they can make a case?"

"Make one, yes. Win it? Not if I have anything to do with it. Don't jump ahead. Let's just take this one step at a time. I resigned from Jim's campaign committee to avoid any appearance of conflict of interest. One of my friends will take over as legal advisor for the committee to check ads and such. Jim called this morning, and I referred him to my friend. Oh, and no more conversations with him, even on someone else's phone, for both your sakes."

Brenda nodded.

"Joe told me about Fanny's suspicions about Sallie Ann Miller. Wouldn't put it past her to cause mischief like this."

"But how would she know this stuff was there?"

"Interesting question. I don't know, but I want to check into something that might give us an answer." He sat back and frowned.

"Brenda, I'll be honest. I'm worried. They don't have to prove you did anything at this stage, just that it was on your property and you had access."

"Then what can we do? This is a nightmare."

"I know. This morning, I arranged for the sheriff's department to deliver a sample of what they found to the university's botanical lab for testing. Maybe they can give us something from the old stalks to show how long it's been growing to show it was there before you bought the property. I'm going to have Janie Allen come down to testify she never saw it and never took you to that part of the property before you bought it. She's a local gal and her statement might carry some weight."

"Might?"

"Whether this goes forward to trial depends on what the magistrate decides. The state prosecutor is a young guy, and this would be his first high profile case."

Brenda's shocked expression matched her choked out question. "High profile?"

"Guess I could have broken that to you a little better. Sorry, but yes, this is big news for these parts." He shook his head. "Gossip is a big pastime, and this is as juicy as it gets."

"The deck is stacked against me, isn't it?" Brenda slumped back in her chair.

"I'm afraid so. Jim's been fair, but tough, and some people resent it. They prefer Fred's good ol' boy, look the other way for your buddies attitude. So they're happy to see something that could lead to Fred taking over. Add to that you're a recent come-here that only a few people know well. You scored points with some folks by not selling out to the Green Wind people, but you got here and laid out cash for a nice property a lot of them could never afford, especially in this economy, and they're envious. You look a little shaky. Cup of tea?"

Brenda nodded again, afraid to trust her voice.

Jonathan opened his office door and said something to his secretary and sat down again. "It's easy enough for some of them to believe you got the cash illegally than by working hard all your life. And then there's this." He tapped a few keys on his laptop and turned it so Brenda could see the screen. "Tomorrow's front page, above the fold."

Brenda looked in horror at a picture of her in handcuffs with a grim expression on her face next to a grinning deputy on the way to the courthouse. The headline read, "Deputy Arrests Drug Dealer."

"The owner called and told me to open the email he'd just sent me. He asked for a comment. I told him no comment, but I also warned him I'd go after the paper and him once this is dropped if he didn't change that headline."

"What did he say?"

"Not much, but he's changing it to "Deputy Makes Big Arrest" and they'll make sure to say alleged in the story when they talk about the charge."

"I guess that's better, but it's still bad." Brenda wilted further into the chair.

At a tap on the door, Jonathan got up. He thanked the secretary, took a tray from her and pushed the door closed with his shoulder. He slid the tray with two china cups and a teapot across the desk towards Brenda. "Go ahead. Have some tea before I tell you the rest."

Brenda moved like a mannequin, following instructions, holding onto the cup like a magic token that could make everything all right again. Her expression was blank, but her eyes were haunted.

Jonathan watched her over the edge of his cup as he sipped his tea. He put the cup down and leaned forward. "Look, I know this is brutal, but it's better for me to get you up to speed on all of it here in private. Imagine what a field day they'd have if someone sprang that picture at you on the street."

Her shudder said it all.

"Ready for the other shoe?"

"How much more can there be?" Her voice was close to a thin wail.

"Someone at the paper leaked another photo, and it's on Facebook."

Brenda moaned. "Who? Why?"

"Friends of Fred Morris, of course. I can't do anything about that."

"What am I going to do?"

"Nothing for now. Lay low until the hearing and let me do my job. Don't say anything to anyone, except no comment. Lock your doors. Pull the window curtains and wait it out. I talked to Josh this morning and told him to call me if anyone approaches or threatens him in any way, You know that boy thinks the world of you. He never expected someone from the city to care so much about the land or wanting to do something like the chestnut project."

"Can they go after him too?"

"Maybe. I have to decide whether calling him as a witness will help you more than it will endanger him"

"Then don't do it. Keep him out of it."

The lawyer grinned. "That confirms my opinion of you as a good person. Don't worry, he's not at risk. No one's going to go after him because of his in-laws, and they demanded I call them as character witnesses. Like I told you yesterday, no one's fool enough to attack one of the Barker clan. They may be your best hope of getting out of this mess." He glanced at his watch. "Okay, I'm going to send you home now. If you need groceries or anything, don't come into town for them yourself. Call Fanny. I don't want you involved in any ugly scenes. Any questions?"

"When will the tests be back?"

"I'll have them before the hearing. Right now, I have to see if I can find a rabbit to pull out of the hat. Don't look so sad. I just might surprise you."

When Brenda flashed a wan smile, Jonathan said, "That's better. I'll talk to you in a day or two."

Brenda was climbing into her truck when she heard Sallie Ann Miller call out from across the parking lot. "Miss La-Dee-Dah Maxwell don't look so high and mighty now." The three women with her broke into cackles of laughter.

Brenda slammed the door and eased the truck out of the parking lot, ignoring Sallie and the others.

At home, it took her a moment rattling the door knob to realize the door was locked. She fumbled to find the key and locked the door again after she entered. She went into her bedroom and tossed her purse and coat on a chair, kicking off her heels before she changed out of the blue business suit into slacks and a sweatshirt. Still barefoot, she cast about for something to do. Cooking held no interest. Needlework seemed too much of an effort. Instead, she crawled into bed on top of the covers and pulled Fuzzy close. Sleepy as always, he yawned and snuggled up. His purring relaxed her tension as she stared at the bricks above the fireplace. She dozed off until the muffled ring of her phone startled her awake. It took another two rings before she remembered the phone was still in her purse on the chair. She jumped up to snatch it out of her bag and stared at the caller id. The number was vaguely familiar. She answered with a cautious hello.

"Hey, it's Janie Allen."

Brenda's tension drained away in an instant. "Janie! It's good to hear your voice."

"I imagine it is with all that's going on. You certainly managed to get yourself into a hornet's nest of local politics."

"Yeah, and without a bit of effort on my part."

Both women broke into laughter at that.

"You holding up okay?"

"I was pretty shaky today, but I'm feeling better now talking to you. I felt so helpless."

"That's the bitch of it. It's not really about you. It's a pissing match Fred's trying to use to push Jim into reacting and doing or saying something impulsive. If Jim does, Fred gets to be all righteous and point a finger. By the way, I was happy to hear you and Jim are seeing each other. But you could have told me instead of letting Aunt Millie give me the news."

"I'm sorry. I didn't realize everybody knew my business until yesterday."

Janie laughed. "I'll bet there's a lot about living in Chestnut Springs you'll discover over the next couple of years."

"I just hope there won't be any more surprises like getting arrested."

"Hang in there. This'll be sorted out soon enough."

"Jonathan told me today you're coming in for the hearing next week. Thank you."

"It's the least I can do since it's my fault you ended up there."

"I love this place. I never imagined I'd be so happy here. At least I was until all this happened."

"You hold onto the good feelings, and don't let this nonsense get you down. Okay?"

"I'll try."

"Okay. I'll see you next week."

Brenda pulled on her sheepskin slippers and played kitty tag, letting Fuzzy dash after a furry toy dangling from a stick she held out in front of him as she moved around the house. Breathless and in a better mood, she went into the kitchen to make some bread and a batch of cookies for Josh.

The cat stretched out on a throw rug near the stove. Brenda smiled at him. "You know, cat, I really do have some good friends."

Chapter 22

The forum moderator stood up and spoke into his portable microphone. "Well, folks, we've heard from both candidates running for the sheriff's position. Both men have given us their views and answered your questions. Now, they'll each have an opportunity to make a closing statement. Challenger Deputy Fred Morris will speak first, followed by our incumbent, Sheriff Jim Holt."

Fred moved to the podium to applause from about half the audience. "Chestnut Springs is a wonderful place to live. A strong presence in the Sheriff's Department is important to keep it that way. We depend on our out-of-town visitors to support our businesses, but we have to make sure they don't disrupt our community while they're enjoying their vacations." He paused and took note of those in the audience nodding their heads and continued.

"My family's been in this area for generations. My first job was as a clerk in the department, and I moved up to deputy. I've always been here, working for the citizens of Chestnut Springs. The sheriff's done a good job in his time here, but I think I can take it a step further if you'll favor me with your votes. Chestnut Springs has always been the center of my life. I'm still married to the same local girl, unlike my opponent who divorced his wife to travel around the world. And now, he's taken up with a come-here who's awaiting trial on drug charges. Doesn't say much for his personal values or his professional insight. I ask for your vote for me as sheriff, a local man who will always put this community first." He acknowledged the applause with a wave and sat down.

As Jim stepped forward, applause erupted from those who had withheld it from Fred. "Deputy Morris has indeed spent his career as a deputy in the Sheriff's Department, and that's an honorable position. What he missed telling you is I wasn't off backpacking across Europe in my travels, as he calls them, I was serving our country in the Navy for 22 years. Those travels were deployments to fight in wars to protect this country or just to be there in case we were needed. Being in the military can be hard on a marriage. I still have the greatest respect for my former wife, and I will not discuss our personal business in public."

A sprinkle of applause showed approval of his words from some of those listening. Jim waited for quiet and continued. "I worked under two great sheriffs, with eight years as a deputy, four years as chief deputy before you elected me sheriff four years ago. I learned from the sheriffs who came before me that part of being professional means knowing not to discuss pending legal issues in pubic, no matter how much you want to express your opinion. You have to trust the system to come up with the right answers. As sheriff, your part of that means doing a proper investigation and not rushing into actions to further your personal or political goals."

No one in the room missed how Jim turned and threw a sharp look at Fred or how Fred's face flushed with anger before Jim turned back to the audience.

"As sheriff, I've worked to develop programs to keep this town and its citizens safe and help them in times of trouble. Can't say that collecting taxes is the best part of the job, but I've done what needed to be done. I hope you all will vote for me on election day and allow me to continue as your sheriff. Thank you."

Jim's supporters left no doubt about their choice. The moderator tried twice to speak before the crowd settled down. "Thank you, gentlemen, and thank you folks for coming out to our candidates' forum. See you at the polls on election day."

Both candidates came down to the floor, using the stairs on opposite sides of the stage. Well-wishers crowded around each. Fanny and Joe waited until the throng thinned out before approaching Jim.

Joe spoke first. "Hey, Jim. Nice job. Want to come back to our place for a bite to eat?"

"Sure. I'd like that." Jim walked toward the exit with them, shaking hands with people every few steps.

"Fanny, why don't you take our car and head home. I'll follow with Jim when he's done here."

"Good idea. There's someone I need to call before you get there." Joe nodded, and Fanny hurried out to get home and call Brenda before the men got there and let her know how the evening went.

She was just finishing the call when the front door opened. "Okay, they're here, so I need to go. Are you all right?"

"I'm nervous about tomorrow, but I've got to trust Jonathan to handle it for me,"

"He will. Try to get a good night's sleep. We'll be sitting as close behind you as we can. I'm sure Jim will be in the back somewhere. I think this mess is as hard on him as it is on you. He feels responsible for what's happening."

"It's nothing he did, and nothing he could have done differently. We both know who's behind all this and why. Go make sure he eats."

"I'll do that. Sounds like you still remember how to smile when it comes to Jim."

"Yeah. I miss talking to him, but at least I know you're looking out for him."

"Bet you miss a little more than the talking."

"Fanny! You are incorrigible. Good night! See you tomorrow after it's over."

The next morning, the courtroom was packed. Brenda tried to look at ease, but she felt the eyes upon her as a physical pressure. Jonathan leaned close and whispered in her ear with his hand blocking his face so no one could tell what he was saying. "Take a deep breath and let it out. Trust me. This will be over today. Don't say anything. Just relax."

Brenda nodded, reassured by the lawyer's calm voice, and her tension evaporated. The opening statements were a repeat of the arrest evidence presentation until the prosecutor asked Fred Morris about what Brenda said the morning he arrested her.

"Oh, she was bold as brass. Told me all about her plans to rig lights and set up hydroponic trays to grow the stuff in the garage."

The prosecutor grinned. "Thank you, Deputy. That's all I need."

"Jonathan? You got any questions for the deputy?"

"Thank you, I do. Now Deputy Morris, did my client say what she planned to grow in the garage?"

"She said she was going to put in lights to grow plants."

"And you took that to mean marijuana?"

"I sure did."

"Didn't she tell you she wanted to start seedlings for her vegetable garden? Maybe some kitchen herbs to sell?"

Fred hesitated. "Well, maybe, but I figured that was just to cover up what she was really going to do."

"You figured that, did you, hmm? Thank you, that's all."

The magistrate scowled and addressed the state prosecutor. "C'mon, Bill. Let's move this along."

"Of course, Your Honor. To save time, I ask defense counsel to stipulate the facts of the location of the discovery and amount of material the deputy described in his report."

Jonathan stood. "So stipulated." He sat down.

The magistrate looked pleased. "Okay. Keep going."

"Your honor, the state believes there is sufficient cause for the defendant, Brenda Maxwell, to be bound over for trial in state court."

"Thank you, Bill."

"Jonathan, you have anything to say in defense of this woman?"

"I do, indeed. If I may call our first witness, Janie Allen?"

Through careful questioning of Janie first, then Fanny and Joe, Jonathan presented a picture of a smart, cautious purchaser of a property who was not aware of the logging road until she was informed of its existence when she made the decision to log a portion of the property. The local forester confirmed the same fact.

Mr. Barker's answers to Jonathan's questions confirmed the fencing was for the chestnut orchard project, and that Brenda had consulted him about what kind of herbs to grow as a source of income over the coming summer, and that the drying racks were intended for them, not marijuana.

The magistrate was impatient. "That doesn't prove anything. She could have known about the road and not told anyone. Same thing for cultivating the marijuana. No one said the woman was stupid enough to say anything about that. Do you have anything else?"

"Yes, I'd like to call Miss Clara Angel, the County Clerk in Chestnut Springs."

After a ripple of surprise ran through the courtroom, the magistrate banged his gavel. "Settle down, folks. Let's keep this moving."

Jonathan's questioning of the clerk explored the previous owners of the property before Brenda, George Johnston and the estate he bought it from, that of Josiah Adam Morris.

On hearing the Morris name, the prosecutor jumped up. "I object. That the deputy's grandfather once owned the land has nothing to do with this case."

Jonathan countered. "If the Court will permit me to finish my presentation, I can show that it does."

"Get on with it then."

"So Miss Angel, I asked you to do some research on how long the property had been in the possession of the Morris family. Were you able to determine that?"

She twisted a hankie and nodded. "Yes, up to a point."

"And what did you find?"

"It was in the Morris family at least 100 years, probably longer, but our earlier records were lost in a fire."

"Thank you, Miss Angel."

"Bill, you got any questions for Miss Clara?"

"No, your honor."

"Thank you. You can return to your office, Miss Clara."

She nodded and hurried out of the courtroom.

Jonathan waited for the whispers in the courtroom to quiet down. Brenda looked as puzzled as everyone else about the direction of his questions, and Fred Morris had a furious set to his jaw.

"I'd like to call Dr. Howard Sinclair from the state university." After Sinclair was sworn in, Jonathan continued. "Dr. Sinclair, thank you for coming today. Do you have the results of a test on samples delivered to you last week by our Sheriff's Department?"

"Yes sir, I do."

"And what did those results show?"

"The samples I tested were *Cannabis sativa*." The doctor paused while excited reactions echoed through the courtroom again.

Fred Morris's glare changed to a smug grin. The magistrate banged his gavel for order. "I don't want to tell you all again to settle down. And Jonathan, let's get this over with."

Jonathan nodded at the magistrate. "Dr. Sinclair, did your tests show anything else?"

"Yes, the samples were *Cannabis sativa* as I said, but the level of THC was less than 0.3 percent."

"And would you explain why that's important for today's case?"

"Certainly. THC is the psychoactive material in marijuana. The plant material I tested did not have enough THC to have any psychoactive properties. It's not marijuana, it's industrial hemp."

It was Brenda's turn to grin as the courtroom erupted again.

The magistrate seemed at a loss for words while he banged the gavel until quiet returned. Recovering, he leaned toward the witness. "Now, young man. I need you to go over that again for me. You're saying these plants are the same type of plant as marijuana, but not the same? How is that?"

"Hemp was bred to have low levels of THC to use its fiber for various products, like rope or fabric. It's not a drug. No one can use it to alter his mental state. What's more, I can tell you exactly where these plants originated."

Jonathan allowed himself the slightest hint of a smile. "Continue, Dr. Sinclair. How did you determine the origin of these plants?"

"I ran the DNA of the plants, the genetic material that directs what that plant becomes, how it grows, how it looks. And it matched an old university sample."

"What can you tell us about that sample?"

"When we considered setting up a test growing hemp last year, we ran the DNA of material saved from experiments in the 1930's and 40's. The sample I received last week was identical to that used in an experimental plot here in Chestnut Springs, in the 1940's."

"Do you know on whose land that test plot was planted, and what happened to it?"

"Yes, sir. The landowner was Josiah Adam Morris."

The magistrate banged his gavel and glared before the room could respond. He nodded at the witness, "Continue."

"When the university ended its work in that area, the test plots were mowed and plowed under. Apparently, a small patch resprouted and survived here to the present day."

"Thank you, Dr. Sinclair."

The magistrate asked the prosecutor, "Bill, you have anything for this witness?"

"No, I do not."

After the magistrate told the doctor to step down, Jonathan said, "Your Honor, I move that this case be dismissed since we have proven no drug was involved in the plants seized from my client's land."

The prosecutor stood. "I have no objection to the motion."

The magistrate nodded his head. "This case is dismissed. Miss Maxwell, you are free to go." He banged his gavel and left the room looking like he'd bit into a sour lemon.

Jonathan shook Brenda's hand and patted her on the back. "Sorry I couldn't let you in on the report. I didn't want them to have time to dream up a response, not that they'd have had much success."

"Thank you so much. I never imagined it would go this way. I don't know what else to say, but thank you."

"That's fine. You'll get a bill, but I promise, it's not going to be too bad." He was surrounded by people congratulating him before Brenda answered, but her smile was answer enough.

Her friends took turns hugging and congratulating her, until they suddenly stepped back. Brenda looked around to see what was happening, and saw Jim working his way through the crowd to her. He hugged her tight and whispered in her ear.

"I'm so sorry I couldn't be with you through this. It tore me up to have to stand back and not be able to speak out for you. Can you forgive me?"

"There's nothing to forgive. I'm glad you're here now though."

Jim answered by kissing her as the reporter's camera flashed.

Chapter 23

Lights glowed in the twilight from every window downstairs at the bed and breakfast. The polls had closed almost an hour earlier, and townspeople crowded each room, waiting for the election results. A cheer went up when Jim arrived just after 9. He pulled Joe aside after greeting a number of people.

"First returns have Fred up, two to one."

"Don't worry, Jim. It'll come out okay."

Jim shrugged. "Whatever it is, I'll deal with it."

Joe clapped him on the back as well-wishers surrounded them.

Fanny looked around the corner from the kitchen and saw the crowd around Jim. "Brenda, why don't you make up a plate for Jim and set up a place for him here in the kitchen. That man could use a break and a little food. I'll get him in here."

Brenda put together an assortment of the finger foods she and Fanny had made up earlier and another with some desserts and a glass of tea. She looked up to see Fanny shepherding Jim away from the crowd and into the kitchen. "Now you folks let him get a bite to eat. We'll all be here a while tonight."

Jim stepped into the kitchen, and Brenda wrapped her arms around him.

He pulled her close. "I need this a lot more than food right now."

"What's up?"

"Early returns aren't good. Not a lot in yet and scattered all over, but they're heavy in Fred's favor."

"It's so early. You can't go by that."

"I don't know. I might be looking for something else to do tomorrow."

"Sit down for a bit. You've been running from early this morning."

He nodded and sank into a chair. "I keep wondering why Fred chose to do it this way. I might even have stepped down if he'd handled it differently and come to me about it. But to make up that charge against you, what kind of person does that? Maybe I'm not the best person, but the county deserves better than him."

"Eat a little before Fanny comes in and gives me a hard time for not taking care of you." She tilted her head and smiled at him.

"I love that little dimple you get when you smile that way. Okay. Can't have Fanny upset." He picked up a chicken wing and took a bite. "Mmm, that's good. I guess I am hungry after all."

Friends drifted in to exchange a few words with Jim, and Brenda moved into the den where Fanny had a small TV on. She settled into an overstuffed chair.

"Anything new?"

"Numbers are dribbling in. There was some trouble with some of the optical scanners and the ballots had to be run through after the machines were repaired, and it's delayed the returns. How's Jim?"

Brenda took a quick look around to make sure they were out of earshot of the crowd around the big screen TV in the living room and leaned forward. "Your chicken wings did the trick and got him eating, but what's bothering him isn't so easily fixed."

"Fred?"

Brenda nodded. "I don't know if he's more disappointed or angry. Maybe equal measures of both."

"Yeah, I can see that." Fanny pursed her lips. "That Sallie witch is behind all of this. Fred's her younger brother, and from what I've heard, he's always done everything she told him."

The trailer on the bottom of the screen changed with an update flashing the word, "FINAL" Fanny called to Jim "Quick, the final results are coming in now."

Everyone from the other areas of the house rushed into the living room. Jim stood next to Brenda and squeezed her hand. They all watched the various races scrolling past, and at last were rewarded with, "Holt over Morris by 119 Votes."

Cheers and shouts greeted the news. Joe poured drinks for everyone and led a toast. "To Jim Holt, our sheriff and the best man for the job!"

The party broke up and folks headed home after another round of congratulations, backslaps and handshakes. Fanny, Joe, Brenda and Jim made quick work of putting away the leftover food.

Joe turned off the TV. The silence hung loud in the room after the night's excitement. "Jim, you working tomorrow?"

"Nope. I worked today, so you know who is on duty."

"Couldn't happen to a nicer guy. Why don't you spend the night? We got the blue room all ready just in case. We'll have a big breakfast in the morning, and you can go about your day from there."

Fanny piped up. "Joe, close the shades and curtains please. Jim, Brenda's staying, so you two can sit up a while if you want. Joe and I need to get some sleep. You two know where everything's kept."

Jim started to say something, and Joe interrupted. "See you in the morning for breakfast."

Chapter 24

The Monday after the election, Mr. Barker knocked on the doorframe of Jim's open office door. "Hi, Jim. Got a minute?"

Jim closed the computer file he was working on. "Sure. Come on in. What brings you here?"

"I'm here on official business."

"What's wrong?"

Mr. Barker sighed. "Nothing, really. As a member of the Board of Canvassers, I have to deliver this notice to you." He handed Jim a sealed envelope and waited while he opened it and read the page inside.

Jim refolded the notice and slid it back into the envelope. "So Fred wants a recount of our local precincts. That explains why he's been avoiding me."

"Yep. He filed a written request and posted the bond the minute we declared the vote official today."

"So when will you do the recount?"

"We can't do it until at least three days after we notify you, so we wanted to get that done right away. We plan to start early Friday morning. You can attend, and it's open to the public too if you want members of your committee there."

"Thanks, I'll let Joe figure out who should be there."

"Well, I'll head back to the store now. See you on Friday."

After Mr. Barker left, Jim shut his door and phoned Joe to read him the notice and relay what Mr. Barker had said. "You think Fred really expects this will change anything?"

"It's just a formality, Jim. Don't let it bother you. Nothing's going to change."

"Yeah. I don't expect it will. I'll give you a call tomorrow. I've got to get back to work."

Jim went out into the main office. "April, where's Fred?"

"He went out to deliver a bunch of notices from the courthouse."

Jim's eyebrows went up.

"Yeah, surprised me too. He always manages to put that on one of the other guys."

"Bart's due in at noon today, right?"

April flipped through the duty roster. "Yep."

"Okay, send him in when he gets here please."

Jim went back to his office to go back to the file he'd been reading when Mr. Barker arrived. The budget cuts to his department for the next fiscal year were worse than Jim feared. As some coal companies shut down and the production of others dropped, tax revenues plummeted. With more than half the state's workers out of work, every other area of state income was down too.

Bart's arrival interrupted Jim's review of the dismal economic facts.

"You wanted me to come by?"

"Yes. Shut the door and have a seat."

The chief deputy frowned and ran his hand through his thinning hair. "You've been shutting your door an awful lot the past few days. People are noticing."

"Probably as good a way as any to let them know I've been wrestling with some serious stuff. I just got the final budget."

"Man, it's that bad?"

"Worse. We've got to lay off five guys."

Bart swallowed hard. "You know who yet?"

"Not you. I've got to train someone to follow me in four years, and if you're interested, you're my choice."

"Yeah, I'm interested—and relieved. With two kids in college, the last thing I need is to get laid off."

"Part of being in this chair is having to make tough decisions, but I need some help on this one. Have any of the older guys talked about retiring lately?"

"Chet. Maybe Phil."

"They're both eligible. So thanks, I'll talk to them first and see what they say. If they do take retirement now, I'll only have to drop three others."

"Maybe only two."

"How's that?"

"Let's just say you need to talk to Fred too. More than that, you'll need to find out from him."

"Okay, I appreciate that." Jim picked up a file the size of a small phonebook and held it out to Bart. "Why don't you do a little homework and look this budget over. See if you can spot any other places we can tighten up or cut out. I've marked a few places, but maybe you'll catch something else."

Bart nodded and stood up. "Jim, one other thing. Do this sooner than later. Everyone knows it's coming, but not knowing who, or how many, is getting the guys down."

"Thanks. I will. And Bart, leave the door open."

Bart grinned. "Sure thing."

The next morning, Jim spoke to the two men who were eligible for retirement, one after the other. They both admitted they'd considered putting in their papers, and after a few minutes of discussion, decided to complete the process.

Jim turned back to the list of deputies he'd been going over since the night before. He muttered to himself. "Well, I started with the two oldest, might as well go to the two youngest."

The first man said he'd been looking into going back to school for an advanced degree because of the budget reports in the newspaper.

"I'd be eligible for a scholarship and loan program, and it would give me more options in the future. Would you be willing to write a letter of recommendation for me?"

"Of course. Give me the name and address and an idea of what would stand you in good stead with them. You haven't been here long, but you've showed a lot of promise. I'll help any way I can."

With three successes, Jim wasn't expecting the angry outburst he got from the fourth man.

"Do what you want. Just don't expect me to make it easy for you." He slammed the door on his way out.

A few minutes later, the door opened after a quick knock. Bart came in balancing two cups of coffee and kicked the door closed behind him.

"I think you could use this about now."

"Yeah. Thanks. I understand his anger. There are no jobs around here."

"Which means his choices are to go into the military, work on the farm with his father, or look in another area where there are jobs."

"Sounds simple to spell it out that way, but none of those are going to sound good to him."

"No, but that's life. Look at what your lady friend did to cope."

Jim smiled. "She's a special person. It took a lot of courage to strike out to a new place the way she did."

"Don't worry about the kid. I mentioned the budget troubles to his father, and he'll help him sort it out. Let me grab the budget. I did find a few things we can think about to cut costs."

On Jim's way out at the end of the day, April handed him a note before she hurried out ahead of him. It was a request from Fred for personal time off through Friday afternoon.

On Friday, Jim went to the office as usual and left the recount to Joe and another of his election committee members. He spent the morning taking care of the usual details. After he handed the next week's schedule to April, he settled in to write up his monthly report for the Town Council meeting. A half hour later, he looked up and saw Joe standing in the doorway.

"Mind if I come in?"

"Hey. C'mon in." Jim waited until Joe settled into a chair. "Well, what happened?"

"Much ado about nothing. There was one change. A ballot that had been disqualified as too hard to read was judged valid and added to the count." Joe laughed. "It was for you, so your official tally puts you at 120 votes ahead of Fred and confirms you as the winner."

"Man, I'm glad that's over."

"Why? You weren't worried, were you?"

"Not about the election, but I need to know what Fred's planning to do. He's stayed away from me all week until this was settled."

"Chet was over last night and told us about the layoffs. Are you going to let Fred go?"

"To be honest, I'd like to at this point, but it would be seen as retaliation, so I really can't. Now if he decides to leave on his own, that's another story, but I haven't a clue what he's going to do."

"I'm going to head home then and leave the chair available." He stood and shook hands with Jim. "Congrats on your win."

"Thanks, buddy. Maybe I'll drop by over the weekend."

"Hope you do. Take it easy in the meantime."

Jim nodded and watched Joe leave the station, leaning on the doorframe of the office.

One of the deputies called over to him. "So boss, is it official?"

Jim grinned. "Yeah. You're stuck with me for the next four years."

The man came over and shook Jim's hand and clapped him on the back. "Glad to hear it."

A moment later, Fred came in the front door. "Jim, got a minute?"

"Yeah, sure. Come in." He waited for Fred to enter his office and closed the door behind him.

"Congratulations."

"Thank you." Jim sat down and waited for Fred to speak.

Fred stared at the floor for a minute, then looked up. "I think it's best if I move on. I heard from the Charleston Police Department today. I applied last week. They offered me a job and I took it."

"I wish you the best, Fred."

"I'm sorry for some of the things I said during the campaign. It wasn't right."

"It's okay, but thank you."

Fred nodded and stood up. "I'm going to clean out my desk and locker and say goodbye to folks. I have a week's vacation coming. So how about if I resign after that?"

"That'll be fine." Jim shook Fred's hand. "Good luck."

Fred just nodded and left, closing the door behind him.

Jim sat down again and leaned back, relieved his staff reduction wouldn't put another person out of work, but feeling bad for Fred in spite of his behavior during the campaign. He shook off the mood and went back to work on completing the monthly report muttering to himself. "At least I can tell them we handled their cutbacks."

Chapter 25

On Saturday, Jim drove up to surprise Brenda at lunchtime. He'd stopped at the diner to get ham and cheese sandwiches with lettuce, tomato and mustard on rye bread—one of Brenda's favorites. He got two more of her favorite dishes, the diner's cucumber and onion salad and peach cobbler with vanilla ice cream.

He dashed up the porch steps and knocked before he walked in.

"Brenda, I brought lunch."

The only answer was Fuzzy rubbing against Jim's leg.

"It's nice to see you too, cat. But where's your mama?"

Jim unpacked the food containers in the kitchen and put the ice cream in the tiny freezer compartment in the refrigerator, then went out the back door to look for Brenda. She wasn't in the vegetable garden, so Jim turned toward the shed. A quick look inside, and he returned to the path behind the house. He spotted Brenda up the hill, standing at the orchard's fence line. "Up with her chestnuts, where else?" Jim grinned and trotted up the path to her.

As he approached, she heard his footsteps and turned. They each ran a few steps toward each other, and he picked her up and swung her around, her arms around his neck. Both of them laughed until they were breathless, and he put her down. They walked up to the fence, her arm around his waist, his across her shoulders. They looked out over the new orchard with offset rows of tubes to protect the young chestnuts from gnawing critters. A wide tuft of glossy green leaves rose above each tube.

"Think you can leave them to grow on their own for a while and come have lunch with me?"

Brenda playfully poked him in the ribs. "I had to come up and check if the ones at the edge needed some water, but they were all fine. So yeah, I stopped to watch them and think about what they'll be like in a few years."

"I guess you're going to expect me to help harvest them then."

"I think I'm going to have a lot of volunteers to help. Did you know the youth group is testing the soil on the hill next to the church to see if it would be suitable for a demonstration plot? The kids have asked Josh if they can help up here to learn how to take care of theirs if it works out. And some of them are talking to the biology teacher at the high school to do the same thing there."

"If you get them into this, I know a few of the parents have land that's a lot like yours."

"Josh is convinced we can bring back chestnuts all over the county. I think it's going to take more than my lifetime to do it, but he's still young."

Jim gave her a squeeze. "It's a fine idea." They turned and started down to the house, and Jim said, "I don't know if you're aware we can only serve for two terms as sheriff here."

"No, I didn't know that. Have you thought about what you'll do after this term?"

"To be honest, I hadn't planned that far ahead. I haven't had to support anyone else, so I've put some money away. What I'm thinking now is I'd like to go to some places just because they're there. There's a few I never want to see again, but others, I'd like to go as a civilian—and take you with me, if they're places you'd like to see." Before Brenda could speak, Jim continued. "You've been through a lot the past couple of years, so I'm not asking for any promises now. I want you to know there's a place for you in my future, if you want to be there, but more than anything, I want you to be happy."

Brenda stopped and turned to face him, then stood on tiptoes to kiss him on the lips. "Sounds like a good plan to me." She grinned and started running toward the house, stopping long enough to call back, "First one to the house gets to decide what we do after lunch!"

Jim burst out laughing and took off down the hill after her.

Acknowledgements

Caroline Leavitt: I wouldn't have started down this road if it weren't for your class. Thank you.

A grateful thank you to the members of the Chesapeake Bay Writers chapter of the Virginia Writers Club and two affiliated critique groups who gave me invaluable advice and support as Chestnut Springs evolved.

I thank Roger Gosden, who led the Williamsburg Critique group, for his insightful comments and information about West Virginia.

Thank you, Janet Fast, for facilitating the Rappatomac Writers group, always offering good advice, and supporting writers through *Chesapeake Style* magazine.

My gratitude to:

Jackie Guidry, Cindy Howland, and Jerry Peill for their support, encouragement, and helpful suggestions.

Lynne Pryde, for her friendship and late night phone support.

Carolyn Carpenter for her eager interest and encouragement.

The many residents of Mathews, Virginia, who welcomed a come-here and showed her the warmth and community of rural life. A special thank you to Al Carpenter, Davie Cottrell, Jamie Davis, Ellen Farrell, Sharon Frye, Cheryle Hugo, Ruth Litschewski, Marie McDonough, G.C. Morrow, JoAnn & Ray Mulvany, Marilyn Rainville, Sue & Bob

Sherrill, and Elena Siddall. And to Betsy Ripley, Joanna Mullis Nix, and Janice Phillips, thank you for sharing your extended family and celebrations with me.

Special thanks to Dr. Brian Perkins, Glenville State College, Glenville, West Virginia, who provided links to information about establishing a chestnut orchard in West Virginia.

The American Chestnut Foundation is committed to restoring the American chestnut tree to eastern woodlands. Four billion trees once flourished in the eastern U.S. until most were killed by a blight fungus between 1904 and 1950. Please learn more about their work at https://www.acf.org/ and support their efforts.

About the Author

Carol J. Bova spent thirty-five years in business and nonprofit administration in New York and California before she found a new lifestyle as a writer in Mathews, Virginia, a rural Chesapeake Bay peninsula. Carol is a novelist, non-fiction author, columnist for *Chesapeake Style* magazine, and blogger. Her debut novel, *Chestnut Springs*, is set in West Virginia, where her father's parents emigrated from Italy before later moving to Philadelphia where she was born.

Her 2014 non-fiction book, *Drowning a County: When Urban Myths Destroy Rural Drainage*, addressed the impact of failed Virginia Department of Transportation maintenance, a subject she's worked on since being on the Steering Committee of Virginia's water quality improvement plan for the Piankatank River and fifteen creeks.

She was President of the Chesapeake Bay Writers chapter of the Virginia Writers Club from 2014-2018. When not writing, Carol enjoys photography, genealogy and creating silver jewelry.

Nonfiction By Carol J. Bova

Drowning a County: When Urban Myths Destroy Rural Drainage links myths created by the Virginia Department of Transportation with Mathews County highway drainage failures. The flooding of private property and timber crops has lowered values. Roads are being damaged, and the health of residents and of the Chesapeake Bay are endangered. Budget constraints decades ago reduced ditch maintenance, and VDOT-created myths reduced it further. Working from an urban stormwater management perspective, VDOT officials act without an understanding of the rural watersheds inside the Chesapeake Bay Impact Crater, ignoring their own maintenance manuals.

Drowning a County reveals the origin of the VDOT-myths and offers facts about drainage, sea level rise and elevation in the county. It counters incorrect planning district reports with details from the Virginia Institute of Marine Science, the U.S. Geological Survey, the National Oceanic and Atmospheric Administration, and other reliable sources. *Drowning a County* shows how flooded ditches increase the risk of mosquito-borne disease and toxic cyanobacteria, and includes still-valid recommendations from a 1960 U.S. Army Corps of Engineers report and a County-sponsored 1980 drainage study.

Mathews County, a rural Chesapeake Bay peninsula with the same population as in 1910, has preserved much of its pre-development hydrology. Its open network of grass-lined roadside ditches used to offer an efficient system of biofiltration and transport of fresh rainfall. This source of adequate sediment through outfall ditches sustained the County's extensive tidal marshes and brought oxygenated water to the county's creeks, rivers and bays. Restoring the ditches of Mathews County can help heal the Chesapeake Bay, and *Drowning a County* shows what's needed.

Now Available at Major Online Retailers

Made in the USA
Middletown, DE
18 March 2022